Holy crap! Dusty had taken off his shirt.

And he'd most definitely worked up a sweat, which darkened his blond hair and glistened on his chest in full-out beefcake calendar mode. He sure could swing an ax and get results. He was a machine when it came to turning big pieces of wood into little ones.

Amy came to a standstill, and her mouth dropped open. She might have drooled a little. Muffin barked.

And Dusty stopped swinging his ax. "What?" he asked.

He reminded her of the Michelangelo statues Daddy had insisted she see during that trip to Italy they'd taken after Mom died. She hadn't been all that blown away by the marble, but in the flesh, Dusty sure did impress.

Last Chance Knit & Stitch

Last Chance Book Club

Last Chance Christmas

"Amazing...This story spoke to me on so many levels about faith, strength, courage, and choices. If you're looking for a good Christmas story with a few angels, then *Last Chance Christmas* is a must-read."
—**TheSeasonforRomance.com**

"Visiting Last Chance is always a joy, but Hope Ramsay has outdone herself this time. She took a difficult hero, a wounded heroine, familiar characters, added a little Christmas magic, and—voilà!—gave us a story sure to touch the Scroogiest of hearts."
—**RubySlipperedSisterhood.com**

Last Chance Beauty Queen

"4½ stars! Enchantingly funny and heartwarmingly charming."
—*RT Book Reviews*

"A little Bridget Jones meets *Sweet Home Alabama*."
—**GrafWV.com**

Home at Last Chance

"An enjoyable ride that will capture interest and hold it to the very end."
—**RomRevToday.blogspot.com**

"Full of small-town charm and Southern hospitality...You will want to grab a copy."
—**TopRomanceNovels.com**

Welcome to Last Chance

"Ramsay's delicious contemporary debut introduces the town of Last Chance, SC, and its warmhearted inhabitants...[she] strikes an excellent balance between tension and humor as she spins a fine yarn."
— *Publishers Weekly* **(starred review)**

"[A] charming series, featuring quirky characters you won't soon forget."
— **Barbara Freethy,** *New York Times* **bestselling author of** *At Hidden Falls*

A
SMALL-TOWN
BRIDE

A
SMALL-TOWN
BRIDE

HOPE RAMSAY

FOREVER

NEW YORK BOSTON

Forever
Hachette Book Group
1290 Avenue of the Americas, New York, NY 10104
forever-romance.com
twitter.com/foreverromance

First Edition: March 2017

Forever is an imprint of Grand Central Publishing. The Forever name and logo are trademarks of Hachette Book Group, Inc.

The publisher is not responsible for websites (or their content) that are not owned by the publisher.

The Hachette Speakers Bureau provides a wide range of authors for speaking events. To find out more, go to www.hachettespeakersbureau.com or call (866) 376-6591.

ISBNs: 978-1-4555-6484-2 (Mass Market); 978-1-4555-6485-9 (ebook)

Printed in the United States of America

OPM

10 9 8 7 6 5 4 3 2 1

*For Aunt Annie, who taught me
the joy of gardening.*

Acknowledgments

Writing is a solitary occupation but no writer ever finishes a book without a lot of help. Once again I'd like to thank my friends and critique partners, Carol Hayes and J. Keely Thrall, for their invaluable help in plotting this book. I'd also like to thank my editor, Alex Logan, for helping me cut out all the boring parts. I'd also like to humbly thank the wonderful art department at Forever Romance for the beautiful cover art, which truly captures the heart and soul of this story. And finally, many thanks to all my readers. Y'all make my characters come alive every time you read one of my stories, and that fills my heart with joy.

A SMALL-TOWN BRIDE

Chapter One ————————

Amy Lyndon's first clue that her life was about to change came at eleven forty-five on a sunny Friday, the last day of March, when Daddy stormed into her room without knocking. Luckily, Amy, who had just gotten out of bed, was wearing her bathrobe or there might have been an embarrassing father-daughter moment.

"I've had it up to here with you," Daddy said, gesturing wildly, his face as red as a glass of Bella Vista Vineyards Pinot Noir.

"What's the matter?" Amy kept her voice low and calm. She'd learned this trick from Mom, who had been an expert at handling Daddy's sudden, but infrequent, rages.

"What's the—" His words came to a sputtering stop as a vein popped from his forehead. Uh-oh. The vein thing was a bad sign. And his complexion had turned almost purple, closer to the color of Malbec than Pinot Noir.

"Daddy, calm down. You'll give yourself a stroke or something."

He spoke again in a voice that rattled Amy's bedroom windows. "Get dressed. Then get out."

"What?"

"You heard me. I want you out of this house by..." He checked his Rolex. "Noon. That gives you fifteen minutes. And if you're smart, you'll run straight to Grady Carson. I understand he's proposed. Congratulations."

"How did you know that?"

"Everyone knows it. You've been dating him for a year and a half, and he's everything you need in a husband."

Amy said nothing because Grady Carson was most definitely not everything she needed. Who knew he was planning to pop the question at Tammy's wedding? Like from out of nowhere. She'd turned him down in no uncertain terms and kept her mouth shut about the whole thing. If Daddy knew about Grady's proposal, then Grady must have told him.

Damn him. Damn both of them.

"Daddy, I don't plan to—"

"Don't tell me you don't want to get married. Because, to be honest, Amy, I'm tired of you living off my goodwill. It's time you go live off someone else's." Daddy waved a piece of paper in front of Amy's nose, then pulled his reading glasses down from their resting place above his bushy eyebrows. The paper appeared to be an American Express bill. "You spent twelve hundred dollars on shoes last month? Really?"

"They were Jimmy Choos, and I—"

"I don't give a rat's ass who made them. Amy, your credit card bill last month was more than ten thousand dollars."

"Oh? That much, huh?" She was bad with money, like Mom had been. Most of Daddy's rages were precipitated by the arrival of credit card statements. This was a known fact.

"You're twenty-eight, still unemployed, and living at home. This can't go on any longer. Either accept Grady's proposal or move out. Today." He marched out of her bedroom.

She followed him out into the hallway. "You can't make me go," Amy said to his retreating back. "And you can't force me to marry someone either."

He turned, one eyebrow arched in that classic angry-daddy look. "Wanna bet? Now, get your things out of here before noon."

"But the Z4 won't hold all my stuff." The sports car held two people, barely.

"Oh...that's too bad. When you come back engaged to Grady, I'll let you get your stuff. Until then, it's *my* stuff. God knows I paid for it all, including the sports car."

They stood with gazes locked for a moment. "I'm not marrying Grady. He's an idiot."

"No, he's not. He's made a fortune as a hedge fund manager, and that takes brains. Honestly, if you were more like your brothers or cousins we wouldn't be having this discussion." Daddy stopped yelling at her and strode down the hallway.

Amy didn't argue any further; she'd heard Daddy's complaints many times over the years. She just didn't measure up like her brothers and her cousins, most of whom were super smart, had gone to Ivy League colleges, and completed law school. Amy was just...ordinary.

She returned to her room and stared at the clothes in her

ginormous walk-in closet. She'd give Daddy a couple of hours to calm down about the credit card bill. That's how Mom had always handled him. Tomorrow he would be his normal, happy self.

In the meantime, she needed to get out of the house.

She threw on a plain white tank top, a pair of Rag and Bone boyfriend jeans, her new Isabel Marant sneakers, and the black Burberry biker jacket that had most definitely contributed to the size of her Amex bill this month. Daddy needed to get over it. She only went shopping in New York twice a year. And besides, she'd had to go shopping— Tammy, one of her sorority sisters, needed someone to help her pull together her honeymoon wardrobe, and Amy had a killer eye for fashion.

Thoughts of Tammy and Evan off together on a three-week honeymoon tour of Paris, Rome, and Athens unleashed a wave of envy. She could have a honeymoon like that, but marrying Grady would be too high a price.

She headed out to the circular drive and fired up the BMW Z4. Fifteen minutes later, she took a seat at the Red Fern Inn, a two-hundred-year-old taproom and restaurant in downtown Shenandoah Falls. She waited a long time before Bryce Summerville, the inn's owner, came over to the table, wringing his hands.

"Miss Lyndon," he said in a deferential tone. "I'm sorry to ask this, but how do you intend to pay for your lunch today?"

"What?"

"Um, this is sort of embarrassing, but your father called not five minutes ago and told me not to accept your credit card."

"He did what?"

"He called me—"

"I heard you. I'm just having a hard time believing you. How did he know I was getting lunch here?"

"You get lunch here quite frequently."

That was true.

"He told me he's canceled your card."

Heat climbed up Amy's face. "I'll pay with cash, and I'd like the eggs Benedict." Her appetite had disappeared, but she couldn't get up and walk out now. Not with Viola Ingram and Faye Appleby, card-carrying members of the Shenandoah Falls gossip association, sitting at the adjacent table listening in.

Amy waved at Viola. "Hey, Ms. Ingram. How're you doing today?"

"Just fine and dandy," the senior citizen said in a bright voice. "I heard that you and Grady Carson are about to make a big announcement."

Oh, great. Everyone in town must know about Grady's proposal. "No, Ms. Ingram, no big announcements are pending," she said. She was going to kick Grady's ass the next time she saw him.

When her lunch finally arrived, Amy could only choke down two or three bites. She sat there steaming about Grady and Daddy for a long time and then paid her check with the last of the cash in her wallet.

She strolled down Liberty Avenue to the Bank of America branch, where she visited the ATM only to discover that the machine wouldn't give her any money. The bank said she was overdrawn, but Daddy had deposited her allowance last week. Daddy was a joint signer on the account, which made it easier for him to transfer funds. And that's when it struck her, literally like a hammer to the head, that what Daddy could transfer in, he could just as easily transfer out.

How dare he?

She drove back to the four-thousand-square-foot California contemporary that she shared with her father. The house sat up on the ridge not far from Bella Vista Vineyard, the winery Daddy had started thirty-five years ago, before Virginia wines had become all the rage.

She stormed up the front walk and discovered a locked front door. That was surprising since Daddy's office was located in the house, and even if he'd gone up to the vineyard, Lucy, the housekeeper, was always around.

She dug out her house key, but it wouldn't work the lock. What the hell? When had she started hallucinating? She pinched herself.

Ouch.

In desperate need for reassurance, she reached for her iPhone, but it might as well have been a brick. She had no bars of service.

That's when the panic set in. She ran the short distance up the drive to the Bella Vista Vineyard's headquarters, and by the time she arrived, gasping for air, her panic had morphed into a dark sinking hole in the middle of her stomach.

Ozzie Cassano, Daddy's chief winemaker, greeted her in the courtyard right by the entrance to the tasting room. It was almost as if he'd been waiting for her.

"Where's Daddy and Lucy?" she asked without preamble.

"Lucy's on vacation."

"Since when?"

"Since this morning. And your father isn't here either."

Ozzie's soft Italian accent failed to calm her. "What do

you mean? Daddy's always here unless he's at home or at Charlotte's Grove."

"I'm sorry. He told me to tell you he's taking a vacation too."

OMG! She hadn't seen this one coming. "Not with Lucy, I hope."

"I don't know, miss."

"Look, Ozzie, can I borrow your keys to the house? Lucy and Daddy locked it when they left, and my key doesn't work."

Ozzie stared down at his dusty boots and shrugged his shoulders. "I'm very sorry, Miss Lyndon," he said. "Your father, he told me you were not to be let into the house under any circumstances. He also told me you were getting married soon." Ozzie finally looked up and flashed his gold fillings. "Congratulations."

If there'd been a pay phone anywhere in Shenandoah Falls, Virginia, Amy could have called Grady and demanded that he rescue her. But pay phones were like dinosaurs, totally extinct.

And if she'd had the forethought to fill up the Z4's tank last night, she could have driven herself to DC and rescued herself. But she hadn't filled the tank because she'd planned to do it this morning.

Proving that procrastination could be a mean bitch. Or maybe procrastination had saved her from making a bad decision.

She parked in the town lot and spent the afternoon thinking things through.

Daddy assumed she would find an easy way out of this predicament. At the very least, he would expect her to run up to Charlotte's Grove and throw herself on Aunt Pam's mercy, which would be about the same as calling Grady and telling him she'd changed her mind about marrying him. Or maybe Daddy expected her to call her brothers, Andrew and Edward, but Grady was their friend and landlord. So asking her brothers for help—assuming she could beg a telephone for that purpose—was out too.

She was not going to take the easy way. She'd show Daddy. She would sleep in her car.

This decision proved more challenging than it sounded. The Z4 had two bucket seats with a console between them, and neither of the seats reclined enough to make sleeping easy. Plus the sunny March day turned into a bitterly cold March night. Could a person die from exposure in forty-degree weather? She would have asked Siri if her iPhone had been working.

By the time the sky began to turn pink, she felt as if she'd won a moral victory even though it was hard to feel morally victorious when you were starving, had to pee, and didn't have a bathroom handy.

Lucky for her, Gracie's Diner was located a block away from the garage, opened early, and had a bathroom.

Amy had never set foot in the diner before eleven in the morning, so it surprised her when she opened the door and discovered no other customers. Damn. Her plan depended on Gracie being too busy to notice Amy slinking in to use the bathroom.

Instead, Gracie was on her the moment Amy stepped through the door. "'Morning, Amy. You're here early today. You want the usual?"

So awkward. How could Amy use the diner's bathroom and not purchase anything? But what other choice did she have? She was in danger of wetting her pants. "Uh, I'm on my way out of town," she lied, "but I needed the restroom."

Gracie cocked her head and gave Amy a once-over. Oh my God, she probably looked like a mess after trying to sleep in a Z4. Not knowing what else to do, and needing to pee really bad, Amy turned her back on Gracie and walked to the ladies' room with her shoulders straight.

She was a Lyndon, a prominent, wealthy, and influential family. She did not need to beg for the chance to pee in a toilet instead of somewhere outside. The thought of peeing in the woods left her trembling. How did a girl do that, anyway? And what about toilet paper? Since she'd never been a Girl Scout, she didn't know the answers to these suddenly existential questions.

The diner's bathroom was basic but clean. She did her business, washed her hands and face, and gave her hair a quick comb. She felt much better.

Hungry, but better. She lingered for a while, hoping other customers might show up, and trying to figure out how to leave the diner without humiliating herself. She'd just started running various scenarios in her head when the truth descended like an atom bomb.

She was homeless. And penniless (almost—she had fifty cents in her purse).

How did a person do poor, hungry, and homeless? Amy had never wanted for anything in her life. Maybe she should say sayonara to her hard-won moral victory. She could always borrow Gracie's phone and call Grady.

A knock sounded on the door, followed by Gracie's

voice. "Hon, are you all right? You've been in there a while, and I..."

Amy opened the door. "I'm fine." Her voice wobbled. She would not ask to borrow the phone. There had to be another way.

"No, I don't think so," Gracie said. "You come out and have your eggs and bacon."

Oh crap. What was she supposed to do now?

"I...I...don't. I mean I can't..." She let go of a long, trembling breath. "Daddy locked me out of the house yesterday and told me I had to marry Grady Carson. Then he took all the money out of my checking account. And I probably should call Grady, but I have to borrow your phone." The words came out in a terrible, hoarse whisper.

She expected Gracie to yell at her for using the bathroom without having any intention of buying food. Or, worse yet, to take her into the back room and hand her a phone. But instead Gracie draped her arm over Amy's shoulder. "Come get your breakfast. You can pay me for it later, after you sort things out with your father. And no woman should ever marry someone she has second thoughts about. Shame on your daddy."

The tense muscles in Amy's neck and shoulders relaxed as Gracie led her to the counter, where a plate of eggs and bacon awaited. "Eat your breakfast. You'll feel better."

Amy did as she was told, downing the eggs and bacon like a starving person. She had no idea where her next meal would come from, so she allowed Gracie to refill her coffee cup several times while the diner filled up with the usual Saturday crowd.

Pippa Custis, the owner of Ewe and Me, the yarn shop in town, came in for a bowl of oatmeal.

Walter Braden came in holding hands with his new wife, the former Poppy Marchand. For a couple of old people, they were sweet. They ordered two big breakfasts and spent the entire time gazing into each other's eyes.

Alicia Mulloy, the hygienist at Dr. Dinnen's office, ordered three different kinds of donuts. Amy wondered if Dr. Dinnen knew about Alicia's sugar habit.

And then Dusty McNeil strolled through the door and turned Saturday into Man Candy Monday. Wow. He was like some unholy combination of Thor and Captain America all rolled into one gorgeous example of maleness.

Gracie swooped down on him with a cup of coffee and a plate of eggs and bacon, as if she'd been expecting his arrival. He gave Gracie a smile full of laugh lines and dimples and white teeth. And then he turned toward Amy.

Unlike the other customers, he didn't pretend she was invisible. Oh no. He gave her a long, assessing gaze that made Amy's pulse jump. Dusty McNeil had a badass reputation as a player who preferred the showgirls and cocktail waitresses who worked up at the casinos in Charles Town, West Virginia.

So why was he ogling her?

She had no idea, but she returned the favor. Who wouldn't enjoy gazing at that chiseled face or those bright baby blues or all that golden blond hair?

And that's when a crazy idea popped into her desperate head. Maybe she could invite herself over to his place for some Netflix and chill. Spending a night with him wouldn't be much of a sacrifice. And it would probably be way more fun (and warmer) than sleeping in the Z4.

Or sleeping with Grady for that matter.

But no. Initiating a booty call would not be the right

next step. She'd chosen to sleep in her car instead of falling back on a man. She'd taken a principled position. So she pushed the ridiculous idea of sleeping with Dusty McNeil out of her mind and concentrated on her coffee mug while she tried to figure out what her next step ought to be.

She came up with exactly nothing.

"Y'all seem to be busy up at Eagle Hill Manor these days," Gracie said to Dusty. And since Amy didn't have anything better to do, she eavesdropped.

"Yep. Ever since that article in *Brides*. Willow's hiring another event planner. Know anyone who might be interested?"

Gracie shook her head. "No, but I'll keep my eye out."

A job.

Why hadn't Amy thought of that before?

A job would solve all her problems. And becoming an event planner sounded like the perfect fit except for the fact that she had zero real work experience. But she had been her sorority's social secretary and had planned all kinds of themed parties and charitable events. She'd even had a hand in helping several of her sorority sisters with their wedding plans.

This was perfect. She'd get a job instead of a husband. And wouldn't that blow Daddy's mind?

Chapter Two

Eagle Hill Manor had been built in the late 1800s in the style of an antebellum mansion, with a massive portico held up by a dozen classical columns. David's wife, Willow, had recently refurbished and enlarged the place, adding a gazebo and a swimming pool on the west lawn, converting an old carriage house into a sizable reception hall, and restoring the manor's many outbuildings to create guest cottages with quaint porches and window boxes.

The December issue of *Brides* magazine had done a seven-page feature article on the manor house, with photos of the inn's sweeping half-circle staircase and guest rooms decorated for the holidays and images of the nearby Laurel Chapel all blinged out for a Christmas wedding. The magazine had also praised the inn's food and beverage operations, as well as its daily breakfast service.

That famous breakfast was still being served when Amy dashed up the steps onto the front portico and through the double doors into the lobby. She got as far as the dining room and stopped. Willow was there, making the rounds of the tables and chatting up her patrons.

Even though Willow had only married into the Lyndon family, she still managed to convey the air of power and authority that every Lyndon was supposed to have. She had a master's degree from Wharton and had single-handedly exposed a huge case of Medicare fraud, winning a million-dollar settlement from Restero Corporation. A lot of that money had gone into the inn's restoration, although Willow also had a silent partner in her business—Jeff Talbert, a bona fide billionaire and another one of Amy's exceptional first cousins.

David, yet another one of Amy's brilliant first cousins, had walked away from a career in politics in order to marry Willow.

Amy couldn't imagine any man giving up anything for her. Unlike Willow, she was an ordinary person. Not brilliant and not particularly stunning. She stood barely five feet tall with absolutely no breasts to speak of and standard-issue brown hair that went limp whenever it rained. She had a degree in English from a small, liberal arts college that catered to rich students with less-than-stellar SAT scores. She did not speak in full sentences or have an Ivy League education like Willow. She was, in a word, unremarkable.

In a family composed of smart, beautiful, well-educated people, Amy was a poser.

The moment Willow spied her lurking in the doorway, she concluded her conversation and proceeded across the dining room, surprise all over her face. "Wow, Amy, you're up early. Have you come to talk about the wedding?"

Damn. Damn. Damn. Had Grady posted lies about her

on Facebook? With her phone out of commission, Amy had no way of finding out. She would kill him if he had. She met Willow's probing stare. "No. I'm here to apply for the job. And for the record, I'm *not* engaged."

Willow's eyes widened a moment as she gave Amy's outfit the once-over. Right. Bad move. Showing up for a job interview wearing sneakers probably ranked right up there on the things-not-to-do-during-a-job-interview list at Gen Y Girl.

"Which job are you talking about?" Willow asked.

"The event planner job. I don't have a lot of work experience, but I was the social secretary of my college sorority. And I've been a maid of honor seven times. I know a lot about weddings, believe me."

Willow's green eyes softened. "Oh, Amy, I'm sorry. I had no idea you were interested in a job. I filled the event planner job yesterday. Honestly, I thought you were—"

"No, I'm not marrying Grady." She balled her hands into fists. "Everyone needs to get that in their heads, okay?"

Willow took a step forward. "Are you all right?"

"Uh, yeah, I'm good. But I need a job," she said on a shaky sigh as a tear escaped from her right eye. She turned her back on Willow, forcing herself to walk slowly toward the door breathing normally even though her pulse had taken off like a runaway jet engine.

"I have another job opening, if you're interested. It's seasonal, and it only pays minimum wage," Willow said to her back.

Amy stopped. Did she want a minimum-wage job? No. But what other choice did she have? In the let's-face-reality department, she had no skills and no real experience, and with a résumé like that, she should probably expect to start at the absolute bottom.

She turned. "I'll take it," she said.

Willow cocked her head. "Don't you even want to know what the job is?"

"Whatever it is, I'll do it."

"It's on the grounds crew. We need extra hands in the summertime to keep up with the gardening chores and set-ups for weddings and other events. It's a lot of physical labor. You up for that?"

Amy nodded. Physical labor didn't sound like much fun, especially since it had been months since she'd visited the gym. But, on the other hand, becoming a laborer was exactly the kind of thing that would annoy the crap out of Daddy. And that thought warmed her through and through. He'd be so sorry he'd locked her out of the house, drained her bank account, and left her with only enough money to buy eggs Benedict at the Red Fern.

"Okay," Willow said with a nod. "The job is yours. You'll be reporting to the Eagle Hill facilities director, Dusty McNeil."

Dusty loved his little office with the big picture window and the view of the Blue Ridge Mountains. It occupied space in the new outbuilding everyone called "the barn," because it had replaced the old one that had been there for a century. This building was much more than a barn, however. It served as the state-of-the-art headquarters for Eagle Hill Manor's facility-management team. It had Internet, a workshop, garage space for a fleet of golf carts and utility vehicles, and storage for all manner of folding chairs, tables, trellises, tents, columns, pedestals, and fountains.

It also had a kennel for Sven, Natalie Lyndon's gigantic labradoodle, a doggie obedience school dropout three times over. Right now the dog was being a good boy, sitting at Dusty's feet while Dusty enjoyed his second cup of coffee. In Dusty's opinion, Sven needed a firmer hand and a little more attention—something ten-year-old Natalie didn't quite get and her busy parents had no time for. That was Dusty's fault in some ways, because he'd been the one to give the dog to Natalie in the first place, the Christmas before last.

He gave Sven's head a little scratch as he reviewed the upcoming schedule for the day. The Chapman-Cuddy wedding would be taking place at one o'clock in the Laurel Chapel with a small reception under a tent on the terrace to follow. The Ganis-McQuade two-hundred-guest wedding reception was scheduled to begin at six o'clock in the Carriage House.

Dusty was jotting down notes for the day's activities when Sven suddenly sprang to his feet and started barking. "Hush," he directed, just as Willow knocked on the doorframe of his always-open office door.

"Got a minute?" she asked as Sven jumped up on her, earning him a scolding. "Why is he here?" she asked.

"Because he gets lonely when Natalie's at school. He keeps me company in the mornings, and I return the favor."

Willow gave him the evil eye. "Maybe you should have kept him instead of giving him to Natalie."

Yeah, maybe he should have, but he didn't have room for Sven in his tiny house or his single life. "What's up?" he asked, ignoring the gibe.

Willow strolled into the office without answering his question, and that's when Dusty noticed Amy Lyndon hovering in the doorway, eyeing Sven like he was one of those dire wolves from *Game of Thrones*. Why was Amy here? And why had she been having breakfast at oh dark thirty at Gracie's?

She looked like a windblown juvenile delinquent in those ragged jeans and that biker-girl jacket. 'Course that only proved that he knew nothing about fashion. If Amy Lyndon was wearing it, then it cost the moon. Dusty would never understand why rich folks spent good money for jeans with holes in them.

"Good news," Willow said in a falsely bright voice. "I've found you the helper you needed." Willow gestured toward Amy. "Come on in, Amy. Dusty doesn't bite."

"Does the dog?" Amy continued to eye the pooch as if Sven might attack at any moment.

"Sit," Dusty commanded, and Sven actually complied.

"How'd you get him to do that?" Willow asked.

"I don't have any trouble with him." He cast his glance from Willow to Amy and back again. This had April Fools' prank written all over it. Willow was notorious for her April Fools' pranks. Last year she'd wrapped his entire office in Bubble Wrap. This year he'd retaliated with toilet paper. Had she visited her office yet this morning? Was this her weird way of getting him back?

"Ha-ha. Funny. But the Bubble Wrap last year was better," he said.

Willow's cheeks pinked. "Um, Dusty, this isn't an April Fools' prank. I'm not joking. I've hired Amy to be your summer intern."

Amy took a cautious step into the office and shoved her hands into her back pockets. "Yeah. Like she said, I'm not a joke."

"What?"

"You heard me," Willow said, giving him a serious stare. "I'm sure Amy has a lot to learn from you."

"But—"

Willow turned her back on him and headed toward the exit like a coward running from a fight.

"Wait, Willow," he said to her retreating back, but she didn't stop.

"You, stay right there," Dusty said, pointing at Amy and Sven at the same time. He turned and scooted after Willow, catching up to her on the gravel walk that led to the manor house.

"I need a hand, not an...itty-bitty, spoiled rich girl who's scared of dogs."

Willow lifted her chin. "Dusty, you know better than to judge her that way."

Yes, he did. But it was hard not to. "Come on, Willow. She's not strong enough to haul stuff or dig holes. She probably doesn't even weigh a hundred pounds."

"I know, but here's the deal. I never in a million years expected Amy to ever even *think* about getting a job, much less a minimum-wage job. I don't know what's gotten into her, but I think her wanting a job—any job—is a good thing. And, to be honest, getting her hands dirty will be good for her. I can't think of anyone better than you to teach her what she needs to learn."

He held Willow's gaze. "So, just to be clear," he said, "you aren't expecting me to treat her with kid gloves?"

"Did I say I wanted you to do that? She's been hired to be a seasonal helper on the maintenance crew. Do I need to e-mail you the job description?"

"She won't last a day."

"So?"

"C'mon, Willow, you can't be serious."

"I am serious. And now I've gotta go. Courtney and Brianna, the new wedding planner, need help managing today's bridezillas and their equally scary mothers."

Dusty stood on the path for a solid minute watching his oldest friend rush back to the manor house. Well, didn't this beat all?

He was scratching his head as he returned to the office and found Amy backed up against the wall with Sven sitting right in front of her. The dog wasn't doing anything but giving her his adorable cocked-head puppy-dog appraisal.

Boy, she was a tiny thing. She'd be useless in the garden. And she was clearly scared of her own shadow. How the hell was he supposed to manage her?

"The dog isn't going to hurt you. He might jump up on you from time to time, but that's only because he's friendly," he said.

She jumped as if he'd hit her with a Taser. "Uh, sorry," she said, although he couldn't figure out what she was sorry about. Then she simpered a little, which annoyed the hell out of him. He wasn't going to fall for that poor-little-rich-girl routine.

"So Willow says you need this job, huh?"

She pressed her lips together and nodded, even though her chocolate-drop eyes watered up a bit. Crying was not allowed on his crew, so he steeled his heart against the adorable, sad puppy-dog look on her face. It was a toss-up as to which of them, Amy or Sven, had the poor-pitiful-me look mastered.

"So what do you want me to do, Dusty?" she asked.

Her high-handed and familiar tone seemed at odds with that sad look on her face. It chapped his butt. "First of all, you will call me Mr. McNeil."

Did she roll her eyes? Yup, she did. He folded his arms and glared at her while the silence unreeled.

She finally cleared her throat. "May I ask a question, *Mister McNeil*?"

"Sure."

"When do I get paid?"

"Paid? You gotta work first. Payday is every other Friday." He glanced at the whiteboard calendar on the wall. "So I guess you'll get paid in a week."

She paled but said nothing.

"As for stuff you need to do, first thing is you need to go home and change clothes."

"What?"

He waved at her outfit. "I've got a golf shirt for you, and you'll need to get a pair of khaki pants and some work boots. Everyone on the grounds crew wears a uniform. We supply the shirts. You supply the rest." He walked into the back storage room and rummaged through the boxes of golf shirts until he found a men's small. It would be too large for her, but he didn't have any women's shirts. Amy was the first female on his crew.

He tossed the blue shirt at her, and she managed to catch it. "It's a busy day. We've got a one o'clock wedding at the chapel with a small reception afterward and a two-hundred-guest reception here starting at 6:00 p.m. The set-ups are mostly done for the early wedding, but we've got boatloads of work for the evening reception." He checked his watch. "Be back in an hour, dressed for work."

Chapter Three

Amy's jaw hurt from grinding her teeth. Dusty McNeil was the most irritating, high-handed, infuriating man ever. He wanted her to fail. A pair of work boots and khaki pants? For real? Where did a person buy clothes like that with only an hour's notice? Not to mention the fact that she had no money to buy anything.

She drove back into town, tears stinging her eyes. She didn't want that stupid job anyway. She'd let her pride get in the way of her good sense. Maybe the time had come for her to give up this fight and throw herself on Aunt Pam's mercy.

She let that thought blossom in her mind with all its permutations and complications. Pam would side with Daddy. Even worse, Aunt Pam would start planning the wedding of the century for her. There would be fights and drama. Not to mention a groom that Amy didn't love. It would be dumb to let that happen.

So ten minutes later she walked into the Haggle Shop, the consignment store on Liberty Avenue. She had never in her life set foot in this store, but if she needed cheap clothes, this was the place to go.

The store must have been a furniture showroom or something, because all the interior walls had been torn out, leaving a concrete floor and cinder-block walls and rack after rack of used clothing. No fancy wallpaper or carpet here. No gilt-edged dressing rooms. And every piece of used clothing hung on a wire hanger. Amy shivered. She hated wire hangers.

She found a rack of women's pants but couldn't find a single pair of khakis in any size. Either the less-well-off were wearing khakis this year and the store had sold out of them or the well-off were not donating their used khakis anymore.

Come to think of it, Amy had never owned a pair of khakis in her life. They were...beige. And Amy liked black and red and royal blue.

So she turned toward the men's department, where she found khakis in abundance, including a pair in a smallish size that would stay up if belted around her waist. She would have to roll up the legs until she had enough money to get them altered. She also found a pair of size six-and-a-half hiking shoes, which almost fit her size six feet. The shoes weren't exactly work boots, but what choice did she have? She wasn't going to garden in her six-hundred-dollar sneakers.

The total price for the boots and pants was fifteen dollars. It might as well have been a million.

Amy stepped up to the counter, where a tall woman with a boyish haircut was sorting a box of baby clothes. She had a sharp blue gaze that widened in recognition the moment it landed on Amy.

"Ms. Lyndon, welcome to the Haggle Shop. I'm Cornelia, the owner. It's nice to meet you." She held out a bony hand. Amy shook it. The woman had a super-strong grip.

Cornelia glanced down at the pile of ugly clothes and then back at Amy, a question in her eyes.

"I'm doing some painting and odd jobs, you know, so I needed some grungy clothes," Amy explained.

Cornelia blinked a couple of times and then gave her a fake smile, probably because Cornelia found the idea of Amy painting or doing odd jobs around the house laughable. Yesterday Amy would have agreed with her.

"Let me see what you've got," Cornelia said as she checked the price tags. "These are all pretty worn. Why don't we call it ten bucks for the whole lot?"

Wow. Amy wasn't used to getting immediate discounts on merchandise. But even at ten dollars, the clothes were beyond her means. She needed to bargain the price down further—another thing she had never done in her life.

"These clothes are literally ready for the landfill," she said. "I feel as if you should give them to me in return for word-of-mouth advertising."

Cornelia stared with her mouth slightly ajar. "Um, I'm sorry, but I can't give away my merchandise, especially to a person who can afford the price. Ten dollars is a bargain. If you want a handout, go to the Goodwill in Winchester. Although, to be honest, they only give clothes to the homeless."

Was that a snarky tone? Yes, definitely. And she could even understand Cornelia's attitude. But Amy couldn't tell this woman she was homeless. That would be a lie. Amy had choices and options that real poor people didn't have. Amy's situation was a result of her refusal to exercise those options.

She cleared her throat. "I'll make a deal with you. I'll trade you my sneakers for these shoes and pants."

Cornelia appraised her sneakers. "Those aren't Nikes or New Balance, are they?"

"No. They're Isabel Marants."

"Is that a brand name? I never heard of it. People want brand names, Ms. Lyndon."

And Isabel Marant wasn't a brand name? What planet did this woman live on? Well, forget it. She loved her Isabel Marant sneakers anyway. "How about this?" Amy opened the edge of her jacket to expose the signature Burberry plaid.

Cornelia's eyes lit up. "I guess you wouldn't be wearing a knockoff, huh?"

"No, I wouldn't." Amy couldn't even believe Cornelia had questioned the authenticity of her brand-name jacket.

"So why would you trade a Burberry coat for that pile of rags? Is this some kind of April Fools' joke?" Cornelia asked.

"No, it's not a joke."

"Okay. I'll take the jacket for the clothes."

Cornelia's response came at Amy so fast that she immediately realized her mistake. If she'd given a little thought to this, she could have gotten a whole wardrobe of hand-me-downs for the jacket.

Cornelia wiggled her fingers, as if she couldn't wait to get her hands on the jacket. Amy suddenly didn't want to give it up—another cold night in the car without a jacket would be miserable. Dangerous even.

She glanced at a rack of clothes to the left of the check-out. "Okay, you can have the Burberry in trade for the pants and the boots and that jacket right over there." She pointed to an ugly camouflage coat with a bright orange fleece lining. The coat would undoubtedly swallow Amy whole, but its gigantic size would make it perfect as a combination coat/blanket.

Cornelia glanced at the camo coat and then back at Amy. No doubt about it, Cornelia had put two and two together and come up with a nice, round, desperate number.

Thank God Cornelia didn't ask any more embarrassing questions. She merely held out her hand and said, "All right, it's a deal. Hand over the Burberry."

Dusty had hoped that Amy Lyndon would get the message and not come back. But she returned an hour later wearing her oversized golf shirt, baggy pants with turned-up cuffs, and a pair of worn-out hiking shoes. What the hell? Had she gone Dumpster diving to find her uniform?

She was a hot mess. And he would have sent her home again, but he needed her help because Mario Hernandez, his chief porter, had come down with some kind of stomach flu, but only after he'd hauled the chairs for this evening's wedding reception from the barn and neatly stacked them at the side of the room awaiting their placement at the tables, which meant he'd touched every single one of them.

Eagle Hill Manor didn't need a member of the crew giving the wedding guests a rotavirus. So he'd sent Mario home, and now he had the perfect job for little ol' Amy—

setting up the folding chairs and wiping every single one of them down with a sanitizing cleaner.

A kid without a brain could do this job.

He pointed to the white resin folding chairs. "I need you to haul those chairs into position, ten to a table round. And then you need to wipe them down with this cleaner." He gestured toward the cleaning supplies. "You got gloves?"

She shook her head.

Crap. He'd forgotten to tell her to get gloves. "Look, Amy, you have tomorrow off, so do us all a favor and get yourself some pants that fit and some good-quality work gloves. You'll need them."

Her big brown eyes widened, but she nodded, her ponytail dancing. Damn, but she was a little-bitty thing.

"All right, go put on those gloves." He pointed to the rubber gloves that had been left with the cleaning supplies. "They'll protect you from any germs Mario might have left behind before he started hurling."

She grabbed the gloves, but like the rest of her outfit, they were too large.

"We're behind on the setup for this reception, so this job has to be finished in no more than an hour. Courtney needs to make the place look pretty. Carry the chairs two at a time, under your arms. They're stacked in rows so you can get them distributed quickly. Got it?"

She bobbed her head again, and the ponytail continued to swing back and forth.

"All right, let's see you do it."

The itty-bitty woman took off toward the line of chairs, grabbed one, and tucked it under her arm. Unfortunately, it didn't quite fit because she was very short, and her over-sized gloves made it hard for her to hold on. As she reached for a second chair, the first one slipped from her fingers and got caught in the rolled-up hem of her pants. When she tried to catch the wayward chair, it decided to unfold itself and knocked her sideways, causing the second chair to trip her forward, right into the neatly stacked rows of folding chairs.

She fell on her face, and the stacked chairs toppled like dominoes, leaving Amy sprawled on the floor with a dozen chairs on top of her.

"Dusty, what the hell is going on?" Courtney Wallace, the head of special events, yelled as she rushed into the room carrying a lopsided flower arrangement that looked as if it had had an unfortunate run-in with the Tasmanian Devil. She took one look at the heap of overturned chairs and started cussing like a sailor.

When Courtney started using four-letter words, Dusty stayed the hell away from her and tried his very best to remain calm and carry on. Courtney had a stressful job dealing with temperamental brides and their mothers. Small snafus could escalate into gigantic drama, and judging by the broken stems in the centerpiece she carried, today's flower problems were anything but a small snafu.

"No worries. We've got everything under control," he lied. Right now, he needed someone competent to take care of the chairs. He had issues up at the chapel and on the terrace for the early wedding that required his immediate attention. He had no time to babysit his summer intern.

He started pulling chairs off Amy, praying that she hadn't seriously hurt herself. "Are you okay?" he asked when he finally uncovered her.

Amy looked up at him out of her adorable puppy-dog eyes and ignited a warm, lusty flame right in his core.

Whoa. His gonads needed to get back in line. She was his employee, at least for the moment. Not that he expected the charmingly cute, accident-prone debutante to last more than a couple of hours.

"I'm okay," she said. "I may have bruised my hip, but I'll live."

Dusty extended a helping hand as she started to get up. She rejected it with enough of a flourish that he reestimated her staying power. Maybe she'd make it through a day before she quit.

He gave her his best drill-instructor look. "Those pants are a danger to you and everyone else who works here. On Monday you need to be wearing pants that fit."

"I'm sorry. But these were the only pants I could get on short notice. You told me I only had an hour." Her chin firmed, and a defiant spark fired up in her deep, dark eyes.

"How long does it take to get a pair of khakis? It ain't like shopping for clothes at Bloomingdale's."

She put her hands on her tiny hips. "And where would you expect me to find khakis in a size four petite with an hour's notice?"

"She's got a point," Courtney said in her I'm-really-ticked-off voice.

Dusty turned toward the director of special events, who'd just brought in another centerpiece with a bunch of broken yellow roses. "What the hell happened to that?"

"The florist's delivery van was T-boned by a truck. No one got hurt, much, except the centerpieces. Half of them ended up broken like this. Honestly, I'm starting to think this wedding is cursed." Courtney put the flowers down on one of the tables and retreated into the workroom at the back of the Carriage House.

Dusty turned back toward Amy. "As you can see, Courtney's got a disaster on her hands. And the bride has already had about three dozen hissy fits this morning. We all need you to step up, okay? If you want to keep this job, you'll get your ass in gear and get these chairs around these tables and then sanitize every single one of them."

A muscle pulsed in Amy's jaw. "Yes, sir, *Mister McNeil.*"

Amy got to work hauling chairs, but she didn't try to carry them two at a time. She worked fast, carrying and wiping them down with disinfectant. All the while, Courtney fussed and fretted over the centerpieces, removing the broken roses. By the time Amy had placed and cleaned all the chairs, dozens of roses littered the floor, and Courtney had gone into bitchy wedding planner mode, screaming at some poor florist on her cell phone. From the one-sided conversation, Amy surmised that there wasn't a yellow rose to be found in all of Northern Virginia.

The poor bride. She'd probably spent months planning her big day down to the smallest detail, and a fender bender had messed it up. Life could be so random sometimes.

Courtney ended her phone call and assessed the room. Amy braced herself for another volley of profanity and prepared to be bawled out. But instead, Courtney gave her a little smile and said, "Wow, you did that fast. Thanks. You can go get lunch now."

Lunch would have been nice if Amy had any money to buy it. But since she didn't, she escaped to the gazebo on the western lawn, where she stretched out on one of the benches. The bright April sunshine slanted through the building's latticework, creating a warm, cozy spot to relax...and doze off.

Her nap didn't last that long because Dusty—Mr. McNeil—discovered her and awakened her with a jab to the shoulder. Her eyes flew open just as he said, "I can see you're doing your best to impress me by sleeping on the job."

Damn. What did she have to do to get him to lose that tone of voice? She shaded her eyes and looked up at him. The sunshine turned his blond hair golden. "No, I'm enjoying my lunch break."

"Lunch break ended fifteen minutes ago. Where were you?"

"I was right here."

His hands met his hips in an annoyed-male stance. "Lunch for staff is served in the dining room. It's the only perk that comes with the job."

Damn. She could have had a free meal? Her stomach rumbled as if it were also bawling her out.

"I need you to weed the flower bed around the pool house," Mr. McNeil said. "I've brought down a wheelbarrow with some garden tools." He pointed over his shoulder to the footpath by the gazebo, where a heavy-looking wheelbarrow sat loaded with rakes, hoes, clippers, and other assorted tools.

Amy stood up, her sore muscles screaming. She would not let *Mister* Dusty McNeil show her up. You didn't have to be a brainiac to garden, although she was beginning to realize just how out of shape she'd become in the last few months.

"You need to pull out the dandelions and chickweed,"

Mr. McNeil said. "You know what a dandelion is, don't you?"

She nodded. "Of course I do."

"Yeah. And chickweed?"

She nodded again, even though she had no clue. But figuring out chickweed couldn't be that hard. It would be ugly because it was a weed. Besides, she didn't want to admit her ignorance and have to listen to him smugly explain things to her. His whole approach to chair-carrying hadn't exactly worked for her, had it?

"Good. I'm glad you know something," he snarled. "Get to work." He left her and headed off toward the barn with a cocky stride. Amy paused a moment to admire his tight, well-formed butt. He was a looker for sure. But not a very nice man, all things considered.

She stretched her aching muscles and dragged herself off to the wheelbarrow, which was exactly as heavy and unwieldy as it appeared. It took her almost five minutes to push it to the pool house.

When she finally reached her destination, she was out of breath and took a moment to inspect the bed. There were, like, three dandelions growing along the edge near the footpath, but otherwise, the flower bed seemed pretty weed-free to Amy. What the hell? Had Mr. McNeil made her push the wheelbarrow just to exhaust her?

What a douche.

She ripped out the dandelions and stood back to admire her work. The flower beds were thick with blooming daffodils in front and flowering shrubs with long arching stems in the back. Some kind of ground cover with tiny white blooms wove its way through the dandelions. In all, it was super pretty.

And yellow. Even the shrubs in the back had delicate four-petal yellow blossoms that contrasted nicely against the dark brown of their woody stems.

A wonderful idea sprang to life.

She could cut the daffodils and a few branches of the yellow shrub, tuck the flowers into the ruined center-pieces, and save the day for Courtney and the bride. No one would notice anything wrong with the flower bed because the white ground cover would hide the missing flowers.

She went to work, cutting the daffodils and shrubs and loading them into the wheelbarrow. Then, leaving all the tools behind except for the garden shears, she hurried back to the Carriage House.

She hoped Courtney would still be there, but the room was abandoned. Someone had put white tablecloths on the tables, but the ruined centerpieces still sat on the counters in the back workroom.

Time was of the essence, so Amy didn't ask permission before she went to work, tucking the daffodils into the arrangements where the yellow roses had once been and filling some of the voids with branches from the yellow shrub, whose name she didn't know. She also redistributed the unbroken roses so that every centerpiece there were twenty of them—had at least a few.

It took her the better part of an hour, and all the while she anticipated Courtney's return. Amy was positive she'd improved the flowers, making each centerpiece more dra-matic and memorable, and she hoped that fixing this prob-lem might help to convince Courtney that she had some skills as a wedding planner.

Unfortunately, Courtney never returned. Instead, Mr.

McNeil strolled into the Carriage House from the terrace and said, "Where the hell have you been?"

"I've been fixing the flowers," she said, stepping away from the centerpieces as if she were unveiling a masterpiece. She expected him to be overjoyed with her quick thinking.

But clearly, she had miscalculated.

"What have you done?" His blue eyes almost bugged out of his face.

"I told you. I fixed the—"

"Did you cut those daffodils from the flower bed by the pool house?"

"Well, yeah, but it's okay, because I left the white stuff and I only took a little bit of the yellow shrub."

"The yellow shrub is called forsythia."

"Oh, okay. I think it looks great in the centerpieces, don't you?"

"You weren't hired to do centerpieces. You were hired to weed the bed."

"There weren't many weeds."

"What are you talking about? The bed's a mess; it's got chickweed growing everywhere. Leave that. Follow me."

It was a command, so she followed, disappointed that she wouldn't be able to show Courtney what she'd improvised.

Mr. McNeil marched across the terrace and off to the pool house on his long legs. When he walked fast like that, Amy had to jog in order to keep up. And since she hadn't been to the gym in, like, forever, she was wheezing by the time they arrived.

"Oh, shit. I can't believe it. You cut the daffodils and left the chickweed?"

"Chickweed?"

He pointed to the ground cover with the delicate white blossoms. "That stuff. It's a weed. Obviously you lied when you said you could recognize chickweed. And also, did it ever occur to you that we planted the daffodils so they would look pretty this time of year? Those flowers will bloom for the better part of two weeks out here in the garden if it doesn't get too warm too fast. Back there in the centerpieces, they'll wilt before the party is over."

Crap. When would she learn? She had never been good at anything in her life. No matter what anyone asked her to do, she managed to screw it up.

Chapter Four—————————

Dusty swallowed back the profanity that wanted to explode out of him. Dammit to hell and back. The crew who'd planted those bulbs last fall had busted their asses, and now the bed would go naked unless he filled it in with some pansies that would have to be removed before the summer's heat.

Willow had given him the authority to fire her ass, and messing up the flower bed seemed like a good enough reason to do it. But Amy was a member of Willow's family—by marriage. So he needed to tread carefully.

Besides, he should have kept an eye on her. Rich debutantes didn't know squat about gardening because they lived in big houses with paid help to do all the dirty work. On the other hand, this particular debutante had some talent for flower arranging. Not that Dusty would ever forgive her for cutting his daffodils.

When he turned around, the tears in Amy's eyes actually

looked legit, like maybe she wasn't trying to manipulate him. Like maybe she regretted what she'd done. A pang of pity settled in his gut. Okay, so he wouldn't fire her, but he needed to teach her a lesson about asking questions—even stupid ones.

"Come with me," he snarled.

He pivoted and headed across the lawn toward the barn. She followed him, jogging to keep up.

"Wait here," he directed when they reached the barn. He headed into the warehouse and rummaged around until he found what he needed: an empty plastic bag that had once held bird seed, a flashlight, a pinecone, and the leftover jar of peanut butter he'd used a couple of months back to trap a raccoon that had been raiding the garbage.

He returned to find Amy still winded from her jog across the lawn. He stopped to assess her. Underneath those gigantic clothes, Amy was an attractive woman. A little part of him argued that he should send her home for the day and start fresh on Monday.

But a much larger part of him argued back that this was a teaching moment. And hadn't Willow told him to teach the girl? Yes, she had.

"I've got an important job for you," he said in a chipper voice. "It's an after-hours job, so you'll get time and a half. You interested?"

"Time and a half?"

Her stunning lack of knowledge surprised the hell out of him, but then again, she was a little rich girl who had grown up in a giant bubble. She knew nothing about the real world, and it was his job to teach her how things really worked. "Never heard of time and a half?" he asked.

She shook her head.

"It means you get fifty percent more each hour than you do during normal working hours. But I figure a rich girl like you doesn't really care about money, do you?"

"What makes you say that? Everyone cares about money." She tilted her chin up, and he had to hand it to her; she'd come back with a really good answer. He also remembered her asking him about payday. Why would a woman like Amy take a job like this? And why would she be so interested in payday? Those questions were like giant red flags that he chose to ignore.

"I guess you're right about money," he said. "So you're interested in this job?"

She nodded.

"Okay, here's the deal. We have a small snipe problem up at the chapel," he said with his utterly straight face. "You know what a snipe is, don't you?" he asked, just to be sure. If she asked him to explain, he would let her off the hook.

But instead she rose right to the bait. She nodded vigorously, like she'd been snipe hunting dozens of times, thereby proving beyond a doubt that she was a rube ready to be pranked.

"All right, here's what I need you to do. There's this snipe about yea long"—he measured twenty inches between his fingers—"that's been digging holes under the foundation of the old church. I need to get rid of that critter. But unfortunately, snipe only come out at night."

"Uh-huh." She nodded, and he struggled to keep from smirking.

"So you know how to catch a snipe?"

Amy shook her head. The hook was set.

"All right, here's what you do." He opened up the bag

and pulled out the pinecone and jar of peanut butter. "You take this peanut butter, and you put it on the pinecone, and then you put the pinecone in the bag and you wait. When the snipe comes along and takes the bait, you grab the bag. I put a flashlight in the bag for you too." He gave her a reassuring smile, and in response, she gazed up at him like a trusting puppy.

Maybe he shouldn't send her off on a snipe hunt.

Nah. She needed to learn her lesson, so he doubled down. "The snipe don't come out until at least nine o'clock. You know how to get to the old chapel?"

"It's down that path." She pointed.

"Yeah. Set your trap right at the edge of the woods, before you get to the meadow."

"Okay."

"But not before nine. Now, you go on back to the pool house and pull up all the chickweed. And tomorrow morning you bring me back that snipe, you hear? I'll meet you right here at nine o'clock."

She bit her lip as if it had only now occurred to her that she might not actually catch the snipe. Which was exactly what would happen, since snipe didn't exist and he'd just sent her on the proverbial wild-goose chase.

The sounds of the wedding reception drifted across the lawn all the way to the corner of the parking lot where Amy had parked the Beemer. How she wished she were one of the wedding guests, drinking champagne, dancing the night away.

Instead she huddled in a big, ugly camo coat, watching

the dashboard clock click down the minutes to 9:00 p.m. and trying to talk herself out of the snipe hunt. She could be extremely inventive when it came to excuses for not doing stuff she had promised to do. In fact, finding excuses was her biggest gift besides covering up her mistakes.

But she'd done the math. If she spent four hours hunting that snipe, it would mean fifty dollars in her pocket. A few days ago, she wouldn't have thought twice about spending fifty dollars on a bottle of crappy wine at a DC restaurant.

Today fifty dollars represented a large enough sum to have her seriously contemplating the idea of going wild-animal hunting—an activity that was so far out of her comfort zone that thinking about it made her stomach tie itself into knots and her hands go cold and clammy. She was not an animal person. Not even dogs or cats. Not even fish.

She didn't want to go out there into the woods at night. It scared her way down deep where all those kid fears lurked—the ones that grab you when you're young and you never get over. Yeah, she wanted to come face-to-face with a snipe about as much as she wanted to sleep in her car.

But the alternative came with too many hidden price tags.

So when nine o'clock finally arrived, she locked the car and headed toward the chapel footpath. But as she approached, her fear got the best of her, and she took a sharp detour, drawn by the sound of dance music and laughter.

The camo jacket hid her in the night shadows as she slipped through the bushes planted around the Carriage House and peeked into the French doors. Golden light washed the room and sparked in the crystals sewn into the bride's bodice, refracting like tiny jewels as she danced with her groom. She literally sparkled. And the flowers were so beautiful and dramatic and...*not* wilted.

Mr. McNeil was wrong.

Amy clenched her fist, raised it high above her head, and gave it a couple of pumps, as if she'd just won a gold-medal race or something. *Yes!* Her quick thinking had saved the day for the bride. But the pool house flower bed looked a lot like scorched earth now that she'd pulled up all the chickweed.

Who decided what was a weed and what was a flower, anyway? And was it better to have saved the centerpieces and made today's bride happy or kept the daffodils in their flower bed for future brides to enjoy?

Life was like this—one complicated trade-off after another. This ability to see both sides of every question explained Amy's difficulty making choices. She always got lost in the pros and cons, dithered around, and then took the easy way out.

She turned away from the light and took the footpath into the woods that stood as a buffer between the manor house and the chapel. Maybe the flower centerpieces were like a sign or something. Maybe she needed to stop dithering.

Out here, beyond the party lights, the night and the woods loomed as dark as her deepest nightmares and cold enough to seep through the heavy coat. She huddled deeper into its gigantic confines, her heart thudding in her chest. She'd won a couple of tiny victories today: getting a job, fixing the centerpieces. She could handle this snipe hunt too.

She snapped on the flashlight and headed into the woods, stopping right before the path reached the meadow where the old chapel stood. It was time to lay her snipe trap, which might prove slightly problematic because she'd eaten the bait. She hadn't meant to eat all of the peanut butter, but she'd been ravenous. Now only a tiny bit clung to the sides and bottom of the jar—not enough to smear on a pinecone.

She didn't think the pinecone was essential. After all, the peanut butter would lure the snipe no matter what, right? So she improvised and put the whole jar in the bag.

She set up the bag, moved about five feet away, and turned off the flashlight. She didn't know anything about hunting, but it stood to reason that no wild animal would approach if she kept the flashlight burning.

She would have preferred to move a whole lot farther away from the bag and keep the light on, but the scarcity of peanut butter and moonlight made her worry that any snipe that ventured into the bag might escape if she didn't stay close.

She settled in, her body tense with fear. Who knew the woods could be so noisy at night, what with the whisper of wind through the branches and lots of tiny sounds that emanated from the leaf litter on either side of the footpath? Her imagination magnified every tiny snap, crackle, or pop into giant spiders, centipedes, and poisonous reptiles.

She was already twitching with unease when a new, much louder rustling sound reached her. Footsteps. In the woods. Coming toward her. And then a shadow emerged from the undergrowth and moved toward the bag.

Her stomach clenched with sudden nausea, and she wished with all her heart that she hadn't eaten the peanut butter. What now? She didn't know. She wasn't cut out to be a snipe hunter. Or a gardener. Or anything else of any use to anyone. What had made her think she could catch a snipe?

She crawled down the footpath away from the bag, thinking of nothing but escape. But to her horror, instead of going after the peanut butter jar, the snipe turned and headed toward her, snuffling and panting as it approached, as if it liked her scent.

Crap. She must smell more peanut buttery than the jar in the bag. This was what came of eating peanut butter with her fingers because she didn't have a knife or any crackers or anything.

She strained to see in the dark and then wished she hadn't when the animal's shadow moved again. Holy crap. It was a lot bigger than twenty inches. It would never fit in the bag Mr. McNeil had given her.

Oh, God. Where the hell had she put the flashlight? She groped around on the ground and finally found it. But before she snapped it on, she remembered something she'd seen on Animal Planet about bear attacks. She was supposed to stay still and not move. Or do anything dumb like shine a light into a wild animal's eyes.

Easy to say but hard to do when facing down a snuffling beast in the woods at night. A beast heading in her direction. Maybe she should have asked a few more questions about snipe. Were they vicious? Did they have sharp teeth? Could they give her rabies? Or fleas? She was an idiot to have put her life in danger for fifty bucks.

She would not panic despite her racing pulse. She would get through this. She squinted in the darkness, trying to measure the size of the animal. It wasn't a bear. Maybe more like a groundhog. How big was a groundhog? She didn't know.

The internal debate raged on as the creature approached,

getting close enough to sniff her feet. She let out a terrified squeak, and the animal growled. Old fears of spiders, cats, dogs, and worms returned with a vengeance. How sharp were a snipe's teeth? Did they bite? Did this snipe think she was a nice, tasty morsel?

She drew in her legs, slowly, and the animal kept coming, sniffling and snuffling, crunching the footpath's gravel as it advanced. Screw Animal Planet. She needed to know what she faced, but her hands shook so badly she couldn't manage to switch on the flashlight. Another panicked whimper escaped her. The animal stopped its forward progress. Was it getting ready to pounce?

Now was a good time to run. She scrambled up from the ground and bolted in no particular direction, right into the underbrush. Twigs smacked her face and pulled at her hair. She got all turned around in the dark, her panic mounting until she stumbled from the woods right into the old cemetery adjacent to Laurel Chapel.

If she didn't know better, she might have thought she'd fallen into one of those horror movies where the sweet, naive girl goes out at night and gets gobbled up by the monster living in the cemetery. Dammit.

Did that make her too stupid to live?

No. She was better than that.

She found the flashlight's switch, snapped it on, and aimed it at the woods. The creature stopped, its retinas eerily reflecting light in the narrow beam. What was that thing? A wolf? A coyote? She backed up, tripping over gravestones until she found the footpath again. Then she turned tail and ran all the way past the reception in the Carriage House to her Z4, which was parked in the back corner of the inn's lot.

She climbed into the driver's seat and locked herself in for the night.

Traveling with Mia Paquet and the cast and crew of *Vegas Girls* was a gigantic pain in the ass, but Daniel Lyndon endured it for the sake of Scarlett, his eighteen-month-old baby. Danny might be old-fashioned, but he believed a man should marry the mother of his child. He also wanted Scarlett to be acknowledged as a full-fledged member of the Lyndon family.

For two years he'd been begging Mia to marry him, and she'd finally said yes on the condition that they make their wedding a story line in Mia's reality TV show. He'd quickly agreed to that quid pro quo before he realized that the producers wanted more than just a televised wedding. They wanted him to bring the showgirl back home to meet his family...without giving his family any warning.

In short, they wanted him to ambush Uncle Mark, the senior senator for the Commonwealth of Virginia. Unfortunately, the show's producers were so frugal that they booked the cheapest multistop plane tickets from Vegas possible, so they missed their connection in Chicago and were now running five hours behind schedule.

It was after 9:00 p.m. when the two vans carrying the *Vegas Girls* stars, their wardrobe, and the camera crew turned into the long driveway leading to Charlotte's Grove.

"The light sucks," Antonella Mastriani, the show's executive producer, snarled.

Daniel suppressed a smile. Maybe the ambush homecoming would end up on the cutting-room floor. It would serve the producers right. Coming here to Charlotte's Grove made no sense in the real world. Danny's parents lived down the road about half a mile, and it seemed to him that the prodigal son should go all the way home instead of stopping off here.

But the producers disagreed with that logic because his folks were too ordinary for the story line. Mom was a housewife, Dad was a country lawyer, and his parents lived in a 1960s split-level tract house. His folks had plenty of money; they just never had lived very sumptuously.

In contrast, his uncle Mark was a senator and lived in a three-hundred-year-old registered landmark. The producers were practically orgasmic about Charlotte's Grove because it resembled the governor's mansion in Williamsburg. The house would be prominently featured in exterior shots because it underscored the narrative of the showgirl marrying an American prince. Not that Danny regarded himself as a prince, but since when was reality television ever about the real world?

"Holy shit," Mia said, as the mansion came into view. "You weren't kidding. It's, like, I don't know, the set for frigging *Downton Abbey*."

Daniel refrained from pointing out that Charlotte's Grove didn't look a thing like the castle in *Downton Abbey*. Built in 1730, the house provided a classic example of ruthlessly symmetrical Georgian architecture. Its unrelenting brick facade was practically austere. Tonight the exterior lights were ablaze, and a number of cars were parked in the driveway, suggesting that Aunt Pam and Uncle Mark were entertaining.

Oh joy.

Antonella's assistant, George, brought the van to a stop,

and everyone piled out, leaving David to unbuckle Scarlett from her car seat. His daughter drooled a little out of her sleepy mouth as he pulled her into his arms. Her head hit his shoulder like a deadweight, and he rested his mouth against her downy head as a rush of unconditional love coursed through him.

It was unquestionably wrong to surprise Mark and Pam this way, but he hoped they would be happy to meet their new niece. Scarlett belonged to the Lyndon family and, by God, Daniel would do anything to make sure she got his last name.

"All right," Antonella said. "Everyone ready?"

"As I'll ever be," Ivory snarked. One of the three Vegas girls that the show revolved around, Ivory had been pissy about the entire wedding extravaganza from the beginning because it meant Mia would get more camera time than she would. Like any Hollywood wannabe, Ivory yearned to be the center of attention at all times. But she'd had her chance last season during her brief but fiery affair with Demont Robinson, the forward for the Los Angeles Stars. Unfortunately for Ivory, Demont had taken his millions and moved on. So had the show.

Pearl, the other principal cast member, made no snotty comments, although Danny was certain she resented being here as much as everyone else. Beneath that quiet, composed surface, Pearl harbored a cynical and dark view of the world and acted on those beliefs whenever it advanced her personal agenda.

Who could blame any of them? All three of the Vegas girls had come up the hard way. Daniel admired them for their tenacity, even as he wished that his daughter had not been born into their particular world.

"Okay, Daniel, you're on. I think carrying Scarlett is the right approach." Antonella stage directed everyone before Daniel finally got the go-ahead to ring the doorbell.

Daniel didn't know what Antonella expected to happen, but he wasn't at all surprised when Pam's longtime housekeeper, Lydia, came to the door wearing her black uniform with a white apron—a uniform that definitely conveyed an old-fashioned picture of wealth and privilege. Lydia also had a working-class English accent that would have been right at home on the back stairs of Downton Abbey.

"Oh my goodness," she said, her blue eyes lighting up. "Danny boy, is it you? Oh, and look, you've brought the baby."

She flew through the door and cooed all over Scarlett as if she were his mother. It took a moment before she realized that a group of six people were standing behind him, several with video cameras bearing telescopic lenses.

"Oh. My." She paused a moment, confusion on her face as the cameras zoomed in.

"I'm home to get married, Lydia," he said. "Mia and I want to tie the knot at Charlotte's Grove."

"Oh. Dear. I should go get your mum. She and your dad and Mr. Kopp are here. We've been talking about Brandon's wedding."

And with that, she disappeared, leaving Daniel on the doorstep with his baby and his bride-to-be and a half dozen other hangers-on.

"Who's Brandon?" Mia whispered. "I don't want to compete with one of your cousins."

"Brandon's the son of August Kopp, the managing partner of Dad's law firm. Dad, Uncle Mark, and August are fishing buddies and good friends. And I had no idea Brandon was getting married."

An instant later, Mom came running through the formal parlor, dressed as always like a fashion plate from *Town & Country*. Dad followed in his gray worsted and red power tie. Behind them came Aunt Pam and Uncle Mark, followed by August Kopp and his two children, Brandon and Roxanne, flanked by a blond woman Daniel assumed must be Brandon's fiancée.

He did a double take the moment Roxanne came into view. Wow, she'd grown up. As a kid, she'd been tall and awkward—all elbows and knees. But no longer. Take her out of the conservative black dress and put her in some spangles, and she'd give any one of the Vegas girls a run for the money.

"Danny. Oh my goodness. Danny," Mom said, pulling his attention away from August Kopp's daughter. Mom gave him a hug that took him back to his carefree childhood. A deep, hollow longing filled him.

He'd been away from home for too long. He couldn't even remember what had made him so angry that night he'd stormed off and vowed never to come back. Where had that angry boy gone?

Mom pulled back, cocked her head, and melted with her first up-close look at her granddaughter. Scarlett slept on, oblivious to the noise and craziness going on around her. But then, the baby had had lots of practice, living in the middle of a three-ring circus.

"Oh, Danny, she's the spitting image of you at that age." Mom moved in, took the baby from his arms, and kissed the top of her head. "I've waited so long to do this," she said, her eyes filling with tears. "Look, Charles." She turned so Dad could see his granddaughter. "Isn't she beautiful? Just like Danny at the same age."

By the besotted look in Dad's eyes, Daniel knew his father had lost his heart to the little girl. Scarlett could be charming even when she snoozed.

"Daniel, what's all this?" Roxy asked. While everyone else had focused on Scarlett, Roxy had noticed the cameras, and a big frown now rumpled her forehead. She gave him that brown-eyed stare that he remembered from childhood.

Roxy had despised him once, and he hardly blamed her. He'd been a total jerk around her when they were kids. He'd pulled her pigtails, called her names, and even put a frog down her shirt one time. By the frown on her face, she hadn't forgotten or forgiven.

Roxy poked Aunt Pam's shoulder and nodded toward the cameras. Danny's aunt followed Roxy's gaze, and her posture visibly hardened.

"Danny, this is such a surprise," Pam said in her unmistakable Voice of Disapproval.

And right then Danny felt the camera crew's excitement. Up until this moment, his family ambush hadn't produced any conflict, just joy, but a show like *Vegas Girls* needed conflict—any kind of conflict, even the manufactured kind—to make the show interesting. So Pam's disapproval fed right into the story line.

It was time for Danny to provide the punch line.

"I know everyone is surprised," he said, plastering a big, phony smile on his face. "But I have great news. Mia and I are here to get married at Charlotte's Grove. We're going to put the entire thing on television. Won't that be fun?"

Chapter Five ─────────

Amy slept surprisingly well considering how badly the beast in the woods had scared her. It had to be exhaustion, because she drifted off to sleep before the wedding reception ended and didn't wake up until nature called just as the sun peeped over the horizon. The Z4's clock said she had three hours to kill before she needed to report in to Mr. McNeil.

She would have to come up with a good excuse that didn't expose her as a wimp. But before that, she desperately needed a bathroom.

And a shower.

Good thing she'd already worked out a solution to both of those problems yesterday, while weeding the pool house flower bed. The pool house might be shut down for the season, but it wasn't locked. She'd thoroughly investigated the building during one of her breaks and discovered its bathrooms and showers. Even better, they'd stored folded beach towels in some big plastic bags in the storage room.

Having a rock-solid plan that didn't involve peeing in the woods emboldened her. She bundled up her Rag and Bone jeans and the tank top she'd put on two days ago and sneaked off to the pool house. Luckily, it was crazy early in the morning, so no one saw her as she slipped into the building.

After availing herself of the toilet and stealing a beach towel, she headed into the women's shower, where, miracle of miracles, she found soap in the shower dispensers. She shucked out of her filthy clothes, hopped into the shower, and turned on the water.

What the hell?

She'd been prepared for a cold shower, but what she got was no water at all. Damn. The water had probably been turned off for the winter, which explained why the toilet hadn't flushed properly.

At home, the shutoff valve for the pool was located in the utility room along with the pumps and filters and other stuff that kept the pool clean. There had to be a utility room for the inn's pool too.

She wrapped a towel around herself and went exploring, but she couldn't find a door to any utility rooms. She ventured outside for a perimeter search, and out back she found a six-foot privacy fence with a gate secured with a gigantic padlock.

She peered through the fence's latticework and spied a door on the other side labeled "utilities." She'd have to decide—either climb the fence or live without a shower. It didn't take long to make up her mind. She tucked the end of the towel more firmly around her chest and started to climb.

It wasn't easy. The holes in the trellis provided small,

sharp toe holds, and her towel kept slipping down. She tried to squeeze her arms tight to her body to keep the towel in place, but that made climbing almost impossible.

The worst happened when she reached for a handhold near the top of the fence. The towel fell off, fluttering to the ground like a wounded butterfly. Another life choice presented itself: Go back for the towel or keep climbing. Another no-brainer. She forged on and discovered that climbing was easier unencumbered by terry cloth.

She topped the fence and slipped down the other side, then streaked to the door, where God must have been on her side because, unlike the gate, the utility room door was unlocked. She quickly found the well-labeled water shut-off valve right beside a tankless water heater. This was her lucky day. She might get a hot shower after all.

She headed outside, feeling accomplished, and scampered up the fence. She had just thrown her leg over the top when a deep, masculine voice said, "Have you ever considered gymnastics? You've got a real talent there."

Dusty McNeil leaned against the fence, his baby blues doing a slow, thorough circuit of her body. The smirk on his lips torched a fire in Amy's belly. He had bedroom eyes—the kind that reeked of hot, sweaty sex. And she was already naked.

No, squash that thought. Mr. McNeil was her *boss*. Embarrassment swept the momentary lust away, sending a full-body flush right through her that had nothing to do with hot, sweaty sex.

Mr. McNeil's smile deepened to reveal rugged laugh lines at the corners of his eyes. "Did you lose this?"

Dusty tried not to grin like a fool, but little ol' Amy Lyndon had a nice body on her. So he looked while he wondered why she'd been climbing the fence to the pool utility room at seven in the morning. Her nudity was almost a minor detail. A pretty nice detail, but secondary, all things considered.

She blushed cute though. From the tip of her toes to the tip of her breasts. Yes, sir, that color is what people called rosy.

He reluctantly handed her the towel, and she wrapped it twice around her slender body. He could see how climbing a fence wearing a towel that big could prove challenging.

"I guess you want an explanation, huh?" she said, not meeting his eyes.

"Yup."

She turned her back, and he amused himself by watching the rise and fall of her delicate shoulders. The sunlight glistened on her skin, giving it the luster of alabaster. He caught his breath. She was beautiful.

She finally turned to face him. "Look, I'll tell you the truth, but you have to promise not to tell anyone, especially not Willow or David. And not my aunt Pam either."

"I'm not exactly on speaking terms with your aunt."

"Good. This wouldn't be a time to develop a bosom friendship, okay?"

He nodded.

"It's like this. My father threw me out of the house yesterday. He changed the locks, took all the money out of my checking account, canceled my credit cards, and then told me I had to marry someone I don't want to marry."

Dusty blinked. "Really?"

"Yeah. He thinks we're living in the Middle Ages."

Dusty said nothing in response. What could he say? He had never understood the lifestyle of the Lyndon family. Except for David, whom he understood completely because David was a simple guy who loved his daughter and his wife and fishing in that order of priority. The rest of them weren't like David at all.

"So you see," Amy said, "I didn't have a place to take a shower. And I only have, like, fifty cents in cash. And about my work clothes...they were the best I could find at the Haggle Shop."

"And the fence?" he asked, glancing at the fence and then back at Amy.

"I had to break into the pool utility room to turn on the water."

Impressive. Never in a million years would he have guessed that little ol' Amy Lyndon would have a clue about water shutoff valves.

"And about the snipe," she continued, her voice wavering.

"Oh, well, I'm—"

"I couldn't catch it. It was way too big for the bag you gave me. And to be honest, I ate most of the peanut butter, and the snipe decided it wanted to eat me and I got scared and ran all the way back to my car, which is parked in the lot. I slept there last night."

A tear escaped one of her big, chocolate-drop eyes, and guilt assailed Dusty. What an idiot he'd been for sending her off into the woods. It had never occurred to him that she might meet up with a critter. A raccoon could be downright terrifying to the uninitiated. And pranking someone who didn't get the prank wasn't any fun at all.

"I guess I don't get my overtime pay, huh?"

"At least you tried. How many hours were you out there snipe hunting?" His lips definitely twitched when he said this. Good thing she was looking down at her cute little naked feet.

"I'm not sure. A couple of hours, I guess," she said without making eye contact.

Shoot. He needed to do something about this situation, especially since he might have put her in danger. If anyone in her family ever found out about this, they would make his life a living hell. He didn't need any more trouble with those people. He'd have to pay her off or something.

"Why don't you go take a shower and meet me up at the barn in about half an hour? I'll pay you for your work last night."

Her head came up, her face a study in gumption. "I'll go out snipe hunting tonight if you want. I'm sure I can catch it for you, now that I'm fully prepared. The truth is, I could use the money."

Damn. What now? "Uh, no, I don't think so. The animal you just described sounds more like a galawackus. They are known to hunt snipe."

"They must like peanut butter too."

"Yep. They're what you call omnivores. Like bears. It wasn't a bear you saw, was it?" He would be roasted alive if anyone discovered he'd sent her out into the woods only to meet up with a bear. Black bear sightings weren't all that uncommon in these parts.

"I don't think so. I thought it might be a wolf or a coyote."

Wow. It might well have been a coyote for all he knew. The coyote population had been exploding in the mid-Atlantic for some time. He didn't want to alarm her, although he mentally kicked himself for all kinds of stupid for sending her out into the woods alone. His joke had backfired.

"It was probably a galawackus," he said in a light tone. "They usually move on once they get their snipe."

Despite the serious nature of the situation, a laugh wanted to bubble up out of him the minute Amy nodded her head like the most gullible of rubes. He forced the laugh back down since this had ceased to be a laughing matter.

"I'm sorry I couldn't catch it," Amy said.

Why the hell was *she* sorry? Her words were a big red flag. It struck him right then that he'd never heard a Lyndon apologize for anything. And in this case, Amy had nothing to apologize for. Even her boneheaded move with the daffodils had turned up roses, so to speak. Last night's bride had gushed over the centerpieces.

"It's okay," he said. "Just remember to ask questions if you don't understand something I've asked you to do. Okay? There's no such thing as a stupid question." Or a galawackus. Or a snipe, for that matter.

She nodded and then turned and scampered away toward the pool house entrance like a tiny pixie or wood nymph, all slender and pale, with hair the color of sweet birch bark in winter.

❦

Amy's humiliation was complete. Mr. McNeil had seen her naked. Even worse, he now understood her desperation.

So, naturally, she wanted to slink away and hide, but she needed the money if she intended to continue to defy her father. That made her both desperate and determined, so after her shower she pulled her wet hair back into a ponytail, put on her boyfriend jeans, less-than-clean tank top, and oversized camo jacket, and headed up to the barn to endure a face-to-face meeting with Mr. McNeil she would rather have avoided.

A fresh morning breeze chilled her wet head, but the sunlight cresting the mountains promised a beautiful day ahead. Birdsong trilled on the air, which carried a scent of something Amy had always associated with the turning of the seasons from the frozen cold of winter to the early days of spring. This morning, as she walked up to the barn, she had a name for that smell—dirt.

Who knew that the ground smelled like anything? And yet knowing this, having learned it yesterday weeding the bed by the pool house and breaking every one of her fingernails in the process, seemed like a victory over *Mister McNeil* and his sultry and judgmental stares.

She found Dusty in his office, wearing a beige fishing shirt and looking like a model for the L. L. Bean catalog. He hunched over a fly-tying vise with a pair of thick magnifying glasses perched on his nose.

She'd watched her father tie flies for years but had never paid much attention to it. Now suddenly her attention was riveted to Dusty's broad, long-fingered hands as he delicately wrapped a thread around a tiny fishing fly. His hands were competent, skillful, and even elegant. She stood silent for a long time, oddly drawn to the deep quiet that emanated from him.

The moment lasted until Dusty looked up, giving her a googly-eyed stare from behind his magnifying glasses. Amy giggled, and some of the tension eased from her neck.

He snatched the magnifying glasses from his face and assumed his *Mister McNeil* expression, all frowny and stiff-jawed and judgmental.

Here it came—a lecture on her failure as a snipe hunter. How she didn't deserve to have this job. How she had failed at everything he'd asked her to do. And all of that was made even worse by the fact that he'd seen her naked and knew exactly how desperate she'd become. She braced herself.

"Hungry?" he asked, surprising the crap out of her. "How 'bout breakfast at Gracie's? I've got time before David gets back from church. He and I are going fishing on the lower Shenandoah this afternoon."

Wait, what? Why was he asking her to breakfast? Because he'd seen her nude or what? She didn't want to have breakfast with him at Gracie's. She wanted to crawl into a hole somewhere and not come out until Daddy changed his mind and let her come home without any strings attached.

On the other hand, if Dusty McNeil planned to *pay for* her breakfast, maybe she ought to take him up on the offer so long as there weren't any strings attached to *that* invitation. But of course there were strings, because he'd seen her naked.

What should she do? The offer of a free meal was worth a lot. But was it worth her integrity?

"Aren't you hungry?" he asked.

"I came up here to see if you'd pay me for the work I did last night. I don't want any handouts. And I don't want you to get the wrong idea about me. I know I didn't catch the snipe, but—"

He stood up and held out his hand in the universal stop gesture. "Amy, it's okay." Then he pulled his wallet from one of the many pockets on his fishing pants. "I'm going to pay you off the books for the snipe hunt. And I would be obliged if you didn't tell anyone about this. Just like I have no intention of telling anyone you're sleeping in your car. Okay?"

She nodded. But she wasn't sure why he wanted to keep stuff secret.

"You see," he said, "if I put your time on the books, then Willow has to take out withholding and social security and a whole lot of other stuff, and by the time that happens, well, it wouldn't be much money. So I'll pay you time and a half for three hours' work. That comes to about thirty-five dollars."

He pulled a twenty, a ten, and a five out of his wallet and handed them over.

Thirty-five dollars wouldn't buy all that much at the places Amy usually shopped, but for some reason, those bills in her hand meant freedom from being hungry for a few days. Maybe it would be okay. Maybe he didn't expect something from her that she didn't want to give.

"Thanks," she said, and started to turn.

"I'd still like to buy you breakfast. Call it payment for the scratches you got on your face. And I'm hungry. I'm sure you are too. Snipe hunting is pretty hard work."

But his tone told her that she had the freedom to walk away from him if she chose. On the other hand, the hollow places in her stomach and her wallet reminded her that she also had the freedom to accept a meal from him. In fact, given her situation, how could she refuse a free meal?

"Okay," she said in a tiny, strangled voice. For some odd reason, she resented the fact that her present circumstances required her to take this handout. She'd never been too proud to spend Daddy's money, so why did it bend her out of shape to accept charity from Dusty McNeil?

🐾

In Dusty's experience, poor folks were often too proud to take handouts, but rich folks regularly gathered around the public trough and called it good citizenship.

Take Pam Lyndon as an example. That woman was hell-bent on beautifying downtown Shenandoah Falls. After an attempt to bully the building owners along Liberty Avenue into making renovations had failed, she'd gone off to Richmond and bullied the state for the money to get the job done.

Now that Liberty Avenue had been "beautified" at the taxpayers' expense, Pam Lyndon and her friends at the Jefferson County Historical Society had set their sights on turning Dusty's land into a new park for the county. To Dusty, Pam's wholesale hunt for the public money needed to force him off his land only proved that rich folks felt entitled to every handout they could finagle.

But Amy's hesitation to his breakfast invitation seemed different somehow. Amy had options. She didn't have to sleep in her car or shower in the pool house. She could always haul her butt up to Charlotte's Grove for a warm bed and a good meal. Her aunt and uncle would take her in. Amy also didn't need a minimum-wage job. She didn't need to buy castoffs at the Haggle Shop. She didn't need to go snipe hunting to earn a few extra dollars. But she'd done every one of those things with a square set to her shoulders and a defiant set to her chin.

And, of course, Dusty had sent her into a dangerous situation last night. And now that he knew she was sleeping in her car, a small part of him wanted her to make use of those other options. A woman shouldn't be left alone to fend for herself like that. He knew how hard fending for yourself could be.

He was worried about her, and he owed her because of his own stupidity. Buying her breakfast seemed a small enough price to pay for what he'd unknowingly put her through yesterday.

But the instant he and Amy strolled into Gracie's Diner, Dusty realized he'd made a terrible mistake bringing her here for breakfast. The place was busy with the usual Sunday crowd, and every single one of those customers looked up from their meals and stared at them as if he and Amy were doing the Sunday-morning walk of shame.

Even Gracie seemed surprised as they settled in one of the window booths. She arrived bearing coffee and glanced from Dusty to Amy and back again with her eyebrow arched the way Dusty's third-grade teacher's used to do when she was about to kick his butt for some not-so-minor transgression.

He needed to nip the conclusion Gracie had jumped to right in the bud. "Hey, Gracie. Amy's a new member of my grounds crew. We're here to discuss work." Oh boy, that sounded stiff, rehearsed, and lame.

Gracie turned toward Amy and gave her the patented X-ray stare. "Is that right, Amy?" The note of skepticism in her voice rang like bells on Christmas Eve.

Amy nodded. "I heard you and Dusty talking about the event planner job yesterday at breakfast, but by the time I got up to the inn, Willow had already hired someone. So she gave me a job on Mr. McNeil's crew."

"Mr. McNeil, huh?" She gave Dusty the stink eye.

"That's what everyone on my crew calls me."

"Uh-huh."

"So anyway," Amy said, clearly oblivious to the subtext of Dusty's conversation with Gracie, "I'll pay for yesterday's breakfast. I've got a few dollars now. So if you can bring the check, that would be great." She folded her hands on the table and dropped her gaze.

Damn. Why did he have the sudden urge to protect Amy? He didn't like the idea of her sleeping in her car, but he knew she wouldn't go up to Charlotte's Grove for help. It was up to him, but he couldn't very well invite her to sleep on his Murphy bed, not after seeing her naked. Besides, what would folks think if she were actually sleeping at his house?

Nope. That couldn't happen, for both their sakes.

"Honey, have you already been paid for your work?"

Amy met Gracie's probing stare. "I did a little overtime last night," she said, and Dusty almost groaned. Why had he brought her here?

Gracie turned and glared at him for a long, uncomfortable moment before she turned back toward Amy and spoke in a motherly tone. "Honey, it's okay. Yesterday's breakfast was on the house. I don't want you to feel like you have to do things your daddy won't approve of just to get a square meal."

And with that Gracie turned her back on them and hurried away to attend to other customers. Amy, oblivious to the shit storm she'd just unleashed, cupped her coffee mug with both hands and inhaled deeply. "I love the smell of coffee in the morning. Don't you?" She closed her eyes and took a sip, her expression orgasmic.

Gracie glared at him from across the room.

"Uh, hey, open your eyes," he said.

She blinked them open and gave him one of her big, brown-eyed stares. Oh boy, a guy could get totally lost in those eyes. But he would resist that urge.

"I need a favor," he said. "After breakfast, would you mind talking to—"

"Gregory Dustin McNeil Junior, you two-timing, low-down, rotten bastard."

Oh crap. Could this morning get any worse?

Dusty turned in time to see Zoe advance across the room on a pair of black stiletto heels that displayed her long legs. Her black leather miniskirt and spandex halter hugged every curve of her body. And what a body it was. Luscious and yet athletic. Tight and yet flexible. Accommodating always.

"Where were you last night?" she demanded

"Uh, baby, let's not talk about it here. Let's—"

"No. I'm not going to let you go ghost on me, Dusty. You haven't texted or e-mailed or called in two weeks. Where have you been? I expected you to come by the casino for a drink last night."

"Did I say I was planning to come by?"

She growled at him, showing perfect teeth. "Baby, you always come by late on Saturday night."

"Doesn't mean I come by every Saturday. I got busy talking to my attorney about my eminent domain case."

"Eminent domain my ass." Her gaze bounced from Amy to Dusty and back again. "Honestly, this is what you cheat on me with?"

"Now, sweetie, I wasn't—"

She raised her hand, palm outward. "Stop. I'm done

with your excuses. For almost a year, I've been your fall-back girl, Dusty, and I'm damn tired of it. Are you ever going to get off your ass and pop the question?" Her hand went down and came to rest on her hip.

"What question?"

"The marriage question, Dusty. Good Lord, you work at a marriage factory. You'd think you'd be able to pull off something romantic."

"Uh, what? Marriage? Are you crazy? I never said—"

"Fine. That lets me know exactly where I stand." Zoe turned her back on him and spoke to Amy. "Honey, you take it from me. Don't be fooled by that whole strong, silent routine of his. He may be killer in the sack, but he won't ever commit. To anything. Not to you or to that stupid idea he has of starting a fishing resort or whatever. Do yourself a favor and walk away. Now."

And with that Zoe turned on her high heels and strutted from the room with that loose-hipped walk that had once made him burn. But not anymore. The high-heel strut had gotten old, and now he found himself wondering if Zoe could walk like a regular person without all that hip action.

She'd become a royal pain the last few months.

But as the diner's front door closed behind her beautifully shaped ass, Dusty realized he had a major problem on his hands. Everyone in the restaurant stared at him as if he'd thrown over his steady girlfriend for a member of the Lyndon family.

Chapter Six————————————————

Well, that had been awkward...and surprising. How could a gorgeous woman like Zoe think Dusty would sleep with an ordinary person like her? Unfortunately, Amy knew the answer. Daddy's money. And thinking about Daddy's money made her second-guess herself.

Especially when Mr. McNeil dropped her off at the Eagle Hill Manor parking lot and proceeded to drool over her Z4. He ran his hands over the beautifully painted and waxed surfaces like he might caress a woman. It almost turned her on until she remembered that every other guy she'd ever met had thirsted after that car.

"So does she have the 2.0 liter or the 3.0 liter?" Dusty asked.

"Um..."

"You don't even know, do you?"

She shrugged. "It goes fast."

"Yeah, I bet it does. But I'm thinking it's a bitch to live in."

The humiliation she'd been wrestling with all morning morphed into a resentment that purred along her sinews and made her hands close into fists. She raised her chin. "Don't judge me," she said in a voice that almost sounded kick-ass—a term she had never applied to herself. "I'm doing the best I can."

Dusty surprised the crap out of her by nodding his head. "Yeah, I reckon you are."

A little of her swagger melted away. Was he putting her down or affirming her? She wanted affirmation, especially from Mr. McNeil. Still, praise from him wouldn't buy her a burger at McDonald's. But doing her job to his satisfaction would.

"You need me for anything else today?" she asked, trying to imagine him without his clothes. Unfortunately, the image of Dusty McNeil naked did nothing to cut the man down to size.

"Nope. I'm done with you for today." He paused for a moment, his gaze sweeping over her and the Beemer. "But there is one thing I have to insist on. If you're living in the car, you can't keep it parked here overnight."

"Why not?"

"For two reasons. First, the guests are likely to figure it out. And second, Willow *will* figure it out. And if Willow figures it out, she'll tell David, and David will tell his momma, and then you'll have Pam Lyndon on you worse than stink on a skunk. I figure you don't want your aunt interfering with your life right at the moment; otherwise you'd have gone up the hill to Charlotte's Grove a long time ago."

Wow. Warmth spilled through her. Dusty understood her problems better than she realized. Maybe she'd judged him, too, because of his mountain accent and his blue-collar profession. "So what do you suggest?" she asked.

"If it were me, I'd park the car in the chapel's parking lot. It's down Morgan Avenue, right where—"

"I know where it is."

He nodded. "You can park your car there at night. No one will notice. And if you get here before dawn, no one will notice that you're using the showers in the pool house."

He moved off in the direction of the barn, stopping again when he'd gotten halfway across the parking lot to look over his shoulder. "Don't pilfer all the towels. Use just one, and launder it yourself."

She nodded.

He tilted his head and regarded her for a long, uncomfortable moment. "Lock yourself in at night, you hear?"

❧

Amy spent the rest of Sunday getting her life in some semblance of order. She figured she had three priorities for the thirty-five bucks she'd earned: gas for the car, clean laundry, and food.

She spent five dollars on gas and then scoped out the Wash 'n' Go coin laundry on South Second Street, where her small stash of cash was reduced by another four dollars and fifty cents. She needed to find dinner—cheap.

So she drove down to the McDonald's at the highway interchange. She had eaten there only a few times in her life and hadn't paid too much attention to the cost of meals.

But holy crap. McDonald's rocked when it came to cheap food. Amy selected a delicious double cheeseburger and a filling side of fries from the dollar menu, and the meal literally cost only two dollars.

She also found a discarded copy of the Sunday edition of the *Winchester Daily* and passed the late afternoon drinking free water and reading the paper from cover to cover. For the first time in her life, she understood why Daddy liked to read the paper every day.

She dived into the employment classifieds first, looking for a better job. But most of the job listings, both white- and blue-collar, required special training or education or experience. The unskilled jobs were all pretty much on par with the job she already had.

When she'd finished reading every single want ad, she turned to the front page of the paper, which featured an article written by a reporter named Sally Hawkes about the park Jefferson County wanted to build in downtown Shenandoah Falls. The plan called for tearing down the abandoned Liberty Furnace building, a redbrick monstrosity that had been empty for decades. Then the county planned to restore a historic blacksmith's forge located directly behind the old building in order to turn it into a living history site, where wrought iron would be made once again. The rest of the land—almost forty acres, according to the article—would be turned into a river walk down by the run, with picnic tables, hiking trails that connected to the Appalachian Trail, and public fishing access.

Amy was vaguely aware of the park plan because it was Aunt Pam's pet project, and she knew that the owner of the property was fighting against the plan in court and had hired her cousin David to represent him—causing a huge family rift.

But Amy was really bad about details, and she didn't fully connect all the dots until she read the article. Dusty owned the property in dispute.

Up until that moment, Amy had been mystified by David's decision to fight his own mother in court, but maybe David had chosen the right side. Taking away someone's property didn't seem right, even to build a park. She didn't blame Dusty for fighting the county. And it seemed to her that his decision to stand fast didn't make him a loser the way the article suggested.

Sally Hawkes kept talking about how Dusty's family hadn't done anything to develop the land since the old Liberty Furnace Company, once owned by Dusty's ancestors, had gone out of business in 1910. The article even made a point of Dusty's occupation, calling him a gardener, instead of his true position as the head of facilities for one of the bigger businesses in town.

After reading the article, Amy decided two things: First, she would never let Aunt Pam or Daddy push her around again. She admired Dusty and her cousin David for standing up to them. And second, she would become the best gardener possible, because Sally Hawkes had used that word as a slur.

Amy stayed at the McDonald's until almost sunset, then drove the Z4 to the small gravel parking lot at the Old Laurel Chapel. Dusk had fallen, but a crescent moon already hung low in the sky and cast a silvery glow over the chapel's stonework and the old grave markers in the cemetery.

She'd seen plenty of horror movies that involved old

graveyards at night. Last night the cemetery had scared her silly, but tonight in the moonlight, it looked almost enchanted. She wrapped herself in the big camo jacket, reclined the seat, and fell asleep stargazing through her moonroof.

She awoke five hours later to a night without moonlight. The clock on her dashboard said 3:00 a.m., and unfortunately her bladder was making an urgent call.

Damn.

Sleeping in a car was so inconvenient. She grabbed the penlight she kept in the Z4's glove box and set off down the path through the woods to the pool house. The night seemed quiet and peaceful except for the whisper of a breeze through the trees, and the woods smelled of pine needles and something darker, earthier, but still pleasant. Despite the lack of a moon, Amy felt a sense of competence as she walked down the path. She'd conquered some of her fears.

She made it to the pool house and was returning down the path to the chapel when a slight rustling on the left side of the trail froze her midstep. She gripped her flashlight tighter as the hairs on the back of her neck stood up. Not again. She'd done so well in the last fifteen minutes that she'd forgotten how terrifying the sound of that animal had been last night.

She didn't want to come face-to-face with a coyote, or a snipe, or worse yet, the snipe-eater she'd encountered last night. What had Dusty called that animal? A galawacus or something.

She took a step backward, reluctant to move forward as her heart jumped up into her throat. The combination of wind and her racing pulse made it difficult to pick up any other night sounds. But just above the pounding of her own heart, she heard the rustle of the creature's footsteps in the underbrush beside the path.

She stiffened and tried not to scream. And then the creature made another sound, not a growl or a roar, but a whiny squeak.

Was she freaking out over a mouse? Or a rat? Did rats squeak?

Or was it the snipe after all? In which case Amy should have come armed with a bag and peanut butter. Maybe if she trapped it, Dusty would give her a bonus.

Just then, a four-legged animal of some kind padded onto the footpath a few yards in front of her. The animal stopped and dropped to the ground, blocking her way back to the Beemer.

What now? All her bravado about snipe hunting disappeared.

"Shoo," she said in a totally wimped-out voice.

The animal didn't move. Instead it made another almost pitiful sound, a whiny wail that was so lonely it knifed its way into her heart. Was the creature hurt?

She took one step forward before raising her feeble penlight. Through the flashlight's weak beam, she confirmed that the animal wasn't a bear or a raccoon. It had dirty gray fur, and it appeared to be shivering. Was it cold? Or frightened? She found it affirming to think that the creature might be scared of her.

She took a few more steps forward until her flashlight fully revealed the animal, and as she approached, it raised its head and stared back at her out of a pair of dark eyes that spoke of abandonment and hopelessness.

This wasn't a wild animal intent on eating Amy alive.

Her scary snipe killer turned out to be a dog. And a small one at that.

"Sally Hawkes made me sound like a douche bag in that article," Dusty railed as he paced the length of David Lyndon's tiny eat-in kitchen, located in the caretaker's cottage behind Eagle Hill Manor. Dusty paced across the room in two strides, then turned around for a return trip. Sven the labradoodle watched him like a spectator at a Ping-Pong match, while David tucked into his breakfast of French toast and bacon, sent from the inn's kitchen a short walk away.

"What the hell am I going to do?" Dusty asked on his next circuit of the room. "I've been working all my life to get the folks in Jefferson County to realize I'm not my father's son." His voice wavered with more emotion than he wanted.

David said nothing.

No surprise there. David never talked too much, but he listened about as well as anyone on the planet. A surprising trait in someone from the Lyndon family.

"I get that the *Winchester Daily* has to write about the park proposal," Dusty continued. "But that article wasn't fair or objective. The whole bit where she talked about my family, that was low." He turned and paced the length of the room again, feeling like an angry caged tiger.

Sven got bored of watching and moved to sit down by David with a please-feed-me-a-piece-of-your-bacon look, which immediately scored him a piece. David, Willow, and Natalie were too easy on that dog.

"You want some bacon too?" David asked.

Dusty shook his head. "No. I'm fine. I'm not hungry. I'm mad is all."

"Okay, but we knew going into this fight more than a year ago that everyone was going to be against you for holding out on this park plan," David said.

Dusty stopped his pacing long enough to glare at his friend and attorney. "It's my land and I have plans for it. Besides, my ancestors built that forge."

"I know. But the county has competing plans and a lot more power."

"We need to meet with the reporter and—"

"No. That would be a mistake. Sit down, Dusty." David gestured toward a second stool at the breakfast bar. "I've got more bacon here than I can eat."

Dusty slumped into the chair and snagged a piece. Sven immediately moved toward his side and tried the poor-starving-dog routine again, but Dusty knew all of Sven's tricks.

"Listen to me," David said, pointing his bacon slice at Dusty. "Right now the county doesn't have the money for this park. They've held three public hearings, but they haven't approved anything. That being the case, your best defense is a good offense. You need to come up with a competing plan for that land that will add something to the tax base. You do that and you'll start peeling off votes."

Dusty took a bite of his bacon, the salty maple flavor bursting on his tongue. He crunched the meat for a long moment before he let out a deep, frustrated sigh. "I could come up with plans out the wazoo, but I can't get financing for anything with this thing hanging over me."

"Oh, I don't know. Jeff is investing in all sorts of projects," David said mildly, and then took a long sip of coffee. Jeff Talbert was David's cousin—the only other person in the Lyndon family who had crossed Pam and lived to tell the tale. Jeff was also the sole heir to the Talbert billions.

"You think Jeff would invest in a fishing camp for high-end anglers?"

David planted his elbows on the counter and leaned toward Dusty. "He might. But here's the thing: In order to peel away votes from the park proposal, you'll have to brand your plans accordingly. You'll have to convince the county that your development will create more jobs and more tax revenue. So instead of calling it a camp, maybe you should use the word 'resort.' I'm just saying that if your plan is to put up a cabin and invite a few well-heeled fishermen in for private fishing, that's not enough. But if you want to build a resort, that's different."

"And if I built a resort on Liberty Run, I'll have a bunch of environmentalists and angler associations all over my ass. That's not what I have in mind. I want a guide service and a first-class lodge for people to stay when they come out here to fish on the Potomac watershed."

"Okay, but where's your plan? The one written down on paper. The one you need if you're going to try to get financing instead of assuming that you won't get it."

Dusty scrubbed his face. "I don't know squat about business plans."

"But I happen to be married to someone with an MBA from Wharton. Willow is happy to help."

Dusty hated the idea of Willow helping him. He also

hated the idea that his two best friends talked about him when he wasn't around. "This whole business plan idea was hers, wasn't it?" he asked.

David nodded.

"So I guess that means I'm now the subject of pillow talk, huh?"

"When we have time to talk," David said with a straight face.

Dusty refrained from rolling his eyes. David and Willow had known each other for years before they finally tied the knot last Christmas. Both of them were brilliant, well-educated professionals. But when they were together, sometimes they acted like a couple of goofy teenagers.

"The fact is we can't beat something with nothing," David said in a more serious tone. "If the county was offered a choice between projects, you'd have a better chance of success or even compromise. But if you ask people to give up something they—"

"David, are you in there with Dusty McNeil?" The perpetually unlocked kitchen door banged open, and Pam Lyndon came through it dressed in blue and battle-ready.

David hopped up from his stool and intercepted his mother at the same time Sven approached seeking attention. Sven tried to jump up on her, but David edged the dog aside and bestowed the deferential kiss Pam expected. He also said, "Good morning, Mother. What a surprise."

She batted her son away with almost the same motion that David had used on the dog. "I'm not here in the capacity of your mother. I'm here because I'm furious."

Seemed like the same thing to Dusty, but he refrained from saying that out loud.

David, ever the diplomat, gave his mother an amiable smile and said, "I have an antidote for anger right here." He pivoted and picked up the plate of bacon and shoved it in his mother's face. "Bet you can't eat a slice and stay furious."

Sven watched the bacon plate with longing in his dark puppy eyes.

Meanwhile, Pam glared at her son and pushed the plate away. "If Willow was any kind of wife, she wouldn't let you eat that stuff."

David picked up another slice and made a great show of savoring it while the old biddy got red in the face. When he'd finished the bacon he said, "Mother, if you don't want to have breakfast, I'll have to ask you to leave because I'm having a conversation with my client and—"

"Did you know Willow hired Amy to work for that man?" She pointed at Dusty as if he were something a flea-ridden cat had just dragged in from the wild.

"Uh . . ." David stuttered.

"He took advantage of Amy."

David frowned and turned toward Dusty. "Did you take advantage of my cousin?"

Uh-oh, Gracie Teague or one of her Sunday customers must have run their mouths. This could be bad. "I did not. Although I confess that I sent her out snipe hunting on Saturday. And she—"

"You sent her snipe hunting?" David's voice rose along with his eyebrows.

"Oh my God, what does that mean?" Pam asked in a frantic voice, as if snipe hunting were code for something straight out of a porn movie.

David's eye roll conveyed his incredulity. "It's a prank,

Mother. You send someone out into the woods to catch a snipe, and they end up waiting all night for something that doesn't exist."

Pam frowned. "Why would Amy go hunting? In the dark? For anything? She's afraid of the woods, and most animals I can think of."

"That's kind of the point, Mother," David explained, then turned toward Dusty. "Does Willow know you sent Amy snipe hunting?"

"Well, I—"

The sound of a dog barking out on the west lawn saved Dusty from having to make a full confession. Sven snapped to attention and started his own chorus of woofs. And trilling above the canine serenade came a human voice screaming, "Wait, come back. I haven't dried you yet."

In the next instant, a tiny, wet, painfully thin dog appeared in the open kitchen door. Unlike Sven, this mutt had not perfected her food-begging skills. In short, she took matters into her own paws and made a beeline for the plate of bacon in David's hand at the same moment that Sven made a beeline for her. In the process, Sven knocked over Pam and the new dog tripped up David.

Pam careened in Dusty's direction, and even though he disliked the woman, he caught her mid-sprawl, just as the plate of bacon shattered on the kitchen floor with a crash. David managed to catch himself but not before the two dogs pounced on the breakfast food like they hadn't been fed in days.

"Unhand me, you ..." Pam said, scrambling out of Dusty's grasp.

Just then, Amy appeared at the kitchen door, wearing

her oversized golf shirt and baggy pants and carrying a filthy pool-house beach towel. "Muffin," she said, stamping her clunky hiking boot, "stop that right now. You need to come back and let me dry your hair and make you beautiful before you eat breakfast."

Chapter Seven

Muffin trembled when Amy wrapped her in the towel and took her outside. Despite the morning shower, the dog's fur still hung in dirty, tangled dreadlocks and would have to be cut off as soon as Amy could scrounge up the money for a groomer.

But the dog's unsavory looks and behavior didn't matter at all. She rested her head on Amy's shoulder and gave her a bunch of sloppy kisses. Was it possible to go from hating and fearing dogs to loving them in a few hours? It had taken a lot of courage for Amy to approach the dog last night in the dark—courage that had already been rewarded. She squeezed the dog a little closer to her chest. No doubt about it, Muffin was the best thing that had happened to her in a long, long time.

"Amy Jessica Lyndon, you're a mess. Put that filthy animal down before it gives you fleas."

Leave it to Aunt Pam to destroy the moment. Amy kept

her back to her aunt and whispered soothing words to the dog, who continued to tremble in her arms. She wrapped the towel even tighter around Muffin, and that seemed to help a little.

"Did you hear me, Amy?" Pam bellowed from behind, setting off a new wave of Muffin shivers.

"I heard you," Amy said, turning around and meeting her aunt's furious stare. Pam may not have been born a Lyndon, but she had appointed herself the matriarch of the Lyndon family when Grandmother died fifteen years ago. She now saw her job as ensuring that the younger Lyndon generation took their rightful places in politics, business, and society. Aunt Pam expected every Lyndon woman to stand tall, walk with grace, dress like a fashion plate, speak like a well-bred lady, and marry someone important, powerful, and rich.

Amy had failed on every front even though she'd spent a lifetime trying to please the woman. So why try anymore? For Muffin's sake, Amy needed to stand her ground and not simply give in because Pam insisted upon it. "I am not putting Muffin down. She's scared. And hungry. She's been living all by herself out in the woods." Amy turned toward Dusty, who, like David, had followed Pam out onto the cottage's tiny patio. "Mr. McNeil, I don't think it was a snipe digging those holes near the chapel. I'm pretty sure it was Muffin. She's very sorry about that."

Cousin David met this speech with laughter. So typical. All her cousins, with the possible exception of Daniel, thought she was a joke.

"What?" she asked him, her tone defiant. Judging by the smirk on his face, he still didn't take her seriously. "Fine, laugh at me," she said. "But I'm serious." Amy's voice cracked, and her throat cramped up. She hugged Muffin even tighter as she stomped away in the direction of the barn. Thank God neither David nor Pam followed her.

But Dusty McNeil did. "Wait," he shouted at her back. She stopped because Mr. McNeil hadn't laughed at her, which struck her as a minor victory given how he'd judged her the last two days.

"What are you going to do about the dog?" he asked as he caught up to her.

Amy raised her chin. "No one thinks I can do anything. But I'm going to keep this dog."

She expected him to argue, but instead he gave the dog a good scratch under her chin with his broad, work-roughened hands. Her mind flashed on the elegance and skill she'd seen in those hands yesterday when he'd been tying flies. His hands were strong with close-trimmed nails. Calloused, but gentle. Muffin's shivers stilled the moment he touched her.

"What kind of dog do you reckon this is?" he asked.

Amy shook her head. "I don't know. To be honest, I know nothing about dogs. But I'm going to learn. I'm going to let her sleep in the car for a little while and then—"

"You can't keep a dog in the car. It's not fair to the dog."

She closed her eyes, and a tear leaked out. Would she have to choose between her job and the dog?

"I've got an idea," Dusty said, pulling her from the angst that threatened to overwhelm her.

She opened her eyes. "I'm listening."

Dusty glanced at the guest house, checking to make sure neither David nor Aunt Pam were listening before he spoke again. "Let me tell Willow that you've been sleeping in your car. I'm sure she'd be willing to—"

"No. I don't want her to know. She'll tell David. And he'll tell everyone. I need to teach Daddy a lesson."

Dusty's face grew solemn. "Amy, I understand why you feel that way. I even admire you for wanting to make a stand. But I don't like the idea of you sleeping in your car. I was worried about you last night. I even drove by the chapel a couple of times to check on you."

"You did?" A warm flutter trembled in her chest like butterfly kisses. Never in a million years would she have expected a man like Dusty McNeil to care.

"Let me see if I can find you and Muffin a place to live, okay?" he said.

"What, like a flophouse for the homeless? They won't let me keep Muffin."

He shook his head. "No. I think I can do better than a homeless shelter for you or a dog shelter for Muffin. In the meantime, I have a flat of pansies down by the pool house flower bed. Come on, I'll introduce you to pansies and show you how they should be planted. And Muffin can stay in the kennel with Sven while you work. We'll give her a big bowl of Sven's kibble."

They started toward the kennel, but Aunt Pam intercepted them. "Amy, I'm not happy with you right now. I can't believe you took a job working as a gardener. But more important, I cannot condone the fact that you made the entire family the subject of unsavory gossip yesterday morning at Gracie's Diner." Pam finished her little tirade and gave Dusty the Laser Look of Lyndon Disapproval.

To Amy's joy and amusement, the look bounced off Dusty as if he were the proverbial Man of Steel. Made bold by that fact, Amy squared her shoulders and addressed Pam as an equal. "I didn't subject the family to gossip yesterday. I had breakfast at Gracie's with my boss, Mr. McNeil. If people want to make something nasty out of that, then that's their problem. But in my opinion, the people in this town have dirty minds."

"Amy," Pam said on a long-suffering sigh, "I need you to stop with this behavior. We have a family crisis on our hands. And I need your help."

Aunt Pam needed her help? That was a new one. "For what?"

"Danny's come home with the entire cast and crew of *Vegas Girls* in tow. The show wanted us to host the wedding at Charlotte's Grove. I said absolutely not. Which is why I'm here. I hate to say it, but if there has to be a big wedding, we'll have to have it here."

"Danny's marrying Mia? For real? That's good, isn't it?"

Pam glanced heavenward as if to say that Amy was too dense to understand the problem. "Do you want to be put on national television as part of a reality TV show?" Pam asked.

"Uh, no, I guess not." Pam had a point.

"So we need to convince Danny and Mia to get married privately. Maybe with a justice of the peace. Anyway, you do understand that the last thing the family needs is a televised, Vegas-style wedding?"

"Of course I do."

"Then you need to talk him out of it. You're the only member of the family Danny is likely to listen to. You have always had a special relationship with him."

Amy's chest swelled at the unexpected praise. When had Pam ever needed her for something important? Like never. This was a big deal.

"So where's Danny now?" Amy asked.

"He, Mia, and the baby are staying at Charlotte's Grove. The rest of the cast checked in to the inn last night. We're having a family dinner tonight so everyone can meet Mia and the baby, and I want you there to talk Danny out of this foolish idea. And remember, the dinner tonight is going to be taped for the television show, so you'll need to get your hair highlighted."

Disappointment surged through Amy. Nothing much had changed even though she'd made a stand, slept in her car, and refused to marry Grady. For once, she let her annoyance show. "Well, Aunt Pam, if I have to get my hair professionally styled before I attend dinner, I'll have to pass on the invitation. Sorry."

"What are you talking about? Of course you'll show up appropriately turned out." Pam wasn't used to taking crap from Amy.

"No, afraid not. I have to work today, and that means I don't have time to get my hair highlighted. I also have nothing to wear."

"Amy, you have a gigantic walk-in closet filled with—"

"Yeah, but Daddy locked me out of the house."

"What?"

"He changed the locks, took all the money from my checking account, and told me to get out. He gave me, like, fifteen minutes, so I didn't have time to pack."

"Well, just tell him to take you back. This is a family emergency."

"I can't. According to Ozzie, he's on vacation. Apparently Lucy's on vacation too."

"Good God." Pam seemed momentarily at a loss for words.

"I know. It's a bad mental image."

Pam recovered quickly. "Oh my God. You poor thing. No wonder you took this ridiculous job. Shame on Willow for making you work at such a low occupation. Well, we can just tell her you've quit. I'll get Ozzie to open the house for you."

"That might be hard. Daddy told him not to let me back in."

"I don't care what your father told him. Ozzie will damn well do what I tell him to do." Pam's tone had changed to cool fury. She paused a moment, clearly gathering her composure before she continued. "I need you tonight. So I'll transfer some money to your account. How much do you need? Would a thousand tide you over?"

A thousand dollars hadn't seemed like a lot of money in the past, but right at this minute, it seemed like a minor fortune. Having access to a thousand dollars would open up so many more choices—like finding a permanent home for Amy and a dog groomer for Muffin.

But if she gave in now, she'd prove nothing. To herself. To Daddy. To Aunt Pam and the rest of the family. So she made another gutsy, emotional choice. "Thank you, but please don't transfer any money. I don't want to go back home. I don't want to be bailed out. I need to prove something to Daddy. In fact, I'm determined to do well at this job, which means I don't have time to go to the hairdresser."

"Don't be ridiculous. Grady likes your hair highlighted. You need to—"

"Oh, I forgot to mention that part. I'm not marrying Grady either."

"What? Of course you are. Grady is—"

"An idiot." And not very exciting in bed either, but Amy chose not to share that information.

"He is not an idiot. He's a hedge fund manager who's made millions."

"Okay, he's not an idiot. But I resent the fact that Daddy expected me to go running to Grady when he locked me out."

"But...Wait a second. If your father locked you out, where are you staying?"

Something snapped inside Amy. She didn't like David laughing at her or Pam trying to change her or Dusty trying to protect her. She was so done with all of that.

She lifted her chin and met Aunt Pam's stare. "I'm living in the Z4. I take my showers in the pool house when no one is looking, and I have exactly twenty-one dollars and seventy-three cents that will have to last for the next four days until I'm paid. But you know, that money is the first money I ever earned for myself, and it's like gold to me."

"But...Honey, are you crazy?"

"Is it crazy to be independent?"

"You call having twenty-odd dollars independence? Because, darling, that sounds like poverty to me."

Pam had a point. "Okay, so I'm impoverished, but at least I have a job. There are lots of people who don't have even that."

"Amy, stop being ridiculous," Pam said. "You have better things to do. Besides, right now we have to solve this reality TV show problem. So I need you to stop being a brat and get with the program. You are the only one in the family who could ever talk sense into Danny."

With that pronouncement, Aunt Pam whipped out her

cell phone and connected with Bella Vista Vineyard. It took her less than thirty seconds, once Ozzie came on the line, to have every single one of Daddy's orders countermanded.

So that was it. Amy could give up her job and go back home. But she didn't want to.

"Ozzie will have keys waiting for you," Pam said as she tucked the phone into her Kate Spade purse. "Lose the dog, take a shower, go to the hairdresser, and be at Charlotte's Grove for cocktails at six thirty on the dot."

Willow stared at Dusty as she sat behind the fancy mahogany desk in her office on the third floor of the manor house. With its antique, hand-carved scrollwork, the desk gave her an aura of wealth and power at the same time as it reeked femininity. Willow, a former tomboy who now dressed in girlie-colored business suits and dresses, fit the space perfectly. She had certainly grown up to become a woman in control of herself and her life and everything that happened at Eagle Hill Manor.

Right now Willow's brow was wrinkled up like a crumpled piece of paper, and her green eyes were focused on Dusty in an uncomfortably narrow gaze. "Why on earth didn't you tell me Amy was sleeping in her car?" she demanded.

He tried not to squirm in the straight-backed chair that sat in front of Willow's desk. "She asked me not to. I promised."

"Some promises are meant to be broken. How could you let her do that?"

"I checked up on her last night. She was fine."

"If you thought it wise to check on her, then she wasn't fine. Dammit."

"I know. That's why I'm here. Got any ideas?"

"She can go home. Pam's interceded."

"But she doesn't want to go home. It's a matter of pride now."

Willow leaned back in her chair, steepling her fingers. "Why are you so hot to take her side?"

He didn't quite know the answer to that question. "She's got grit."

"Amy? I don't think so."

"Well, you're wrong about that. I told her I'd find her a place to stay. A place where she can keep the dog."

"She has a place to stay. She can go home or she can go to Charlotte's Grove."

"There are two reasons that ain't gonna work. First of all, she won't go. Pam and her daddy are determined to marry her off to some guy named Grady. I don't hardly blame her. Grady is a wussy name for a guy."

Willow leaned forward. "Grady Carson is a hedge fund manager worth millions. She's been dating him for more than a year. She could do a whole lot worse."

"And you think it's okay to marry for money?"

"Point taken," Willow said, her shoulders sagging a little. "What's your second reason?"

"If Amy goes home, she'll probably give up her job."

"So?"

"I think this job is important to her. I think she wants to succeed at it."

"I find that hard to believe. Neither one of us expected her to last more than a day."

"I know. But she's a surprisingly hard worker. She's a little crazy, but she means well. And even though she ripped up the daffodils and forsythia, it was for a good cause, right?"

Willow's frown disappeared. "Amy saved the day for the Ganis-McQuade wedding? Really? I thought you had come up with the brilliant idea of using the pool house daffodils."

"I plant flowers, Willow. I don't cut and arrange them."

Willow's lips twitched. "Okay, Dusty, maybe I could talk Mom into letting her stay at Serenity Farm for a while. Mom has a sweet spot for homeless people, but—"

"I have a better idea," Dusty interrupted. "What about Jeff's fishing cabin?"

"I don't know. I can't see Princess Amy staying up there. It's remote and rustic."

"It's a whole lot better than a car, and it's precisely the right kind of place for Amy to learn all those things you told me three days ago that she needed to learn."

"What things? Did I say anything about her learning from you? I must have been out of my mind at the time. Dusty, I emphatically don't want you messing around with David's little cousin. You hear me?"

An image of Amy all pink and naked came immediately to mind. "I am not messing with Amy," he said, shaking the image of her naked bod out of his brain. "I'm teaching her stuff."

Willow lowered her chin and gave him her evil eye. "What kind of stuff?"

"You'd be surprised," he said in a dry tone.

"David told me you sent her snipe hunting."

"Let's not talk about that, okay? She hasn't even figured out the joke yet, which makes it no fun at all."

Willow cocked her head. "You like her, don't you?"

Her words prickled along his skin. Did he like Amy Lyndon? Yeah, he kind of did. She was just so adorable and accident prone. "So, you'll call Jeff about the cabin?"

Willow gave him a long, sober look before she nodded. "Okay." Then she leaned forward. "But, Dusty, you keep your distance from her, okay? I don't want to have to explain to Jamie Lyndon how I let my best and oldest friend break his daughter's heart. She's not like the show girls you pick up in Charles Town. Speaking of which, it's all over town that Zoe dumped you."

He shrugged. "It was inevitable."

"Yes, it was. But it didn't have to be that way. I liked Zoe."

"I liked her too. But I didn't want to marry her."

"Dusty, I will always have your back, but when it comes to your love life, you keep disappointing me."

He rubbed the stubble on his chin. "I'm sorry, but I'm just not cut out to be a family man, Willow."

Uncle Thomas's fishing cabin sat high up on the Blue Ridge with a sweeping view of the Shenandoah River Valley. Built in the 1930s by Amy's great-grandfather, it had two tiny rooms, a wood-burning stove, and not a single closet, walk-in or otherwise.

Amy needed a closet because she'd taken advantage of the fact that Aunt Pam had bullied Ozzie into opening up the house. She'd gone home and packed up a few suitcases, thankful that her days of living with just one pair of underwear were over. With additional bras and panties, she wouldn't have to run to the coin wash every day.

Now her crap sat in a heap in the middle of the cabin's front room—the living room, dining room, and kitchen combined, and not in a modern "open concept" way either. The place mostly had a rustic-country, *Little House on the Prairie* vibe, right down to the threadbare quilts on the iron bed in the back room. Thank God Granddad had added a bathroom forty years ago with actual running water.

She checked the old Mickey Mouse watch that she had to wear because of her nonfunctioning smartphone. She had several hours before Aunt Pam's mandatory dinner at Charlotte's Grove—plenty of time to take a shower and do her makeup and tackle Muffin's beauty problems.

The dog was having the worst hair day ever. Dreadlocks did not become her, and besides, she smelled. Bad.

Just as soon as Amy could sell some of her designer clothes at the consignment shop, she'd schedule Muffin for an appointment with the doggie hairdresser. But that would take days to accomplish, and right now the dog needed a real bath because the quick shower this morning hadn't done the job.

She had just dumped the dog into the deep farm sink in the kitchen and was working her own Shorea and palm-oil shampoo with built-in silicone detangler into the dog's matted fur when someone came thumping up onto the porch.

Visitors already? Who had Pam sent to check up on her? "Who is it?" she called.

"It's me," a deep male voice said.

Amy turned just as Dusty opened the front screen door. "Amy, this cabin is way off the beaten track, so you should keep your doors locked at all times. No telling who or what might come wandering around. In fact, I'm starting to regret that I suggested this place."

Amy resisted the urge to challenge his logic. It seemed to her that the potential for break-ins and serial killers was much greater in a city, where there were people all around, not out here in the wilderness.

"I opened all the doors and windows because it was stuffy when I got here," she said, turning back to Muffin, who decided right then to give herself a body-long shake, flinging soapy water right into Amy's eyes.

"Ow." She stepped back from the sink, her eyes burning. "Ow, ow." The shampoo had momentarily blinded her, and with her hands all soapy, she didn't dare wipe it away.

Dusty came to the rescue with one of the towels Amy had purloined from her bathroom at home. "Here, let me see," he said in that deep, soft mountain accent of his. He tilted her head up with one of his fingers, his touch light and warm and erotic as hell.

The lust rushing through her made her dizzy. Wait, what was up with that... besides curiosity? No. Hooking up with her *boss* was on the do-not-ever-contemplate list for young, upwardly mobile millennials like herself.

But hey, the guy sure had a gentle touch as he wiped away the tears and soap with those long, elegant fingers that didn't quite belong to his broad hands. She blinked her eyes open and lost her breath at the sight of him, so tall and so close that she could catch the faint scent of something profoundly male coming from his direction.

With all that tanned skin, sun-kissed hair, and craggy goodness, Dusty McNeil had missed his calling. He should have been a male model.

She expected him to pull away, but instead he stood

there hovering as the moment unfolded, giving Amy time to contemplate the shadow of ginger stubble on his cleft chin. She wanted to trace the angle of his jaw and stroke the texture of his skin. She might have succumbed to the curiosity and heat percolating through her, but Muffin issued several yips followed by a little, sad whimper.

"Oh my God, she's probably freezing." Amy turned away from the eye candy to discover that her soapy dog was, in fact, shivering. She picked up the hand sprayer and finished rinsing with warm water.

Dusty assisted, standing at Amy's elbow. When the dog was de-soaped, he swooped in and lifted Muffin out of the sink, wrapping her in a towel. "Hey, girl," he said in a low, sweet voice. "I think you're a cockapoo."

"What?"

"A mix between a cocker spaniel and a poodle. She's got floppy spaniel ears and curly poodle fur. She's not some stray mutt, Amy. Someone docked her tail, which means she was probably bred special. She probably belonged to someone, but judging by the matted fur, she's been on her own for a while."

"Oh." Amy's heart wrenched. Did Muffin have an owner looking for her? Or had she been abandoned, like Amy herself? "Poor doggie. I'm sorry you've been alone for so long. But you're with me now." She looked up at Dusty. "I've got a comb and scissors. If you put her on the kitchen table, I can cut off some of the matted fur and get her dry."

"You need more than scissors for this," he said. "Wait right there. I've got a few things out in the truck." He put the dog on the table, and Amy took over the job of giving her a good rubdown with the towel.

Dusty returned a minute later with a cardboard box in hand, which he set down in the middle of the floor, next to her suitcases. "I stopped by the Food Lion and got Muffin some dog food, and then I went to the hardware store, where I found food bowls and a leash and collar. I also got this." He held up a plastic blister pack containing a small appliance.

"What is that?"

"It's an electric dog clipper." Dusty grinned like a schoolboy who's just discovered the joy of handing out valentines to the girls in the class. Not only did the corners of his eyes crinkle up, but a little dimple showed in his left cheek. A wave of affection squeezed Amy's heart and filled up a hollow place inside that she hadn't even realized was there.

He was kind. He did things for people. And that made him so different from the usual self-involved stockbrokers, lawyers, and politicos her family approved of. His kindness made it harder to stand her ground, but she knew she couldn't accept gifts from him. Not if she wanted to hold fast to her principled position. Not if she wanted to prove that she could make it on her own.

"Thanks so much, Mr. McNeil," she said, "but I can't afford to pay—"

"You can pay me back, a little at a time. I bought these things for Muffin, not for you. The dog needs these things right now, and I know you're not yet on your feet. Please let me help."

She nodded, justifying her decision to accept the gifts because of the dog. But she also found herself wondering what Grady might have done in this situation. No doubt he would have insisted that she send the dog to the pound and come home to his apartment in DC. Grady was allergic. To everything.

"Here, put the leash and collar on her so you can hold her still." Dusty passed over an adorably pink collar and leash. The guy got points for going with the girlie color. She could just imagine the studly Dusty McNeil standing in the checkout line at the hardware store with a pink leash and collar in his hand. Wow. She could get into a guy like that.

Chapter Eight ————————————————

The rain set in about five o'clock that afternoon, just as Dusty was leaving Amy's cabin. It spoiled his plans to fish Liberty Run for a few hours. Instead, he ended up at home tying flies, sitting by the woodstove that was enough to heat his small A-frame house.

He was working on a few wooly buggers, trying to imagine how they would glide across the water as he tugged on the line, but his thoughts kept wandering back to that moment when he'd wiped the soap from Amy Lyndon's eyes.

He shouldn't have done it. Nor should he have bought the dog food or the leash or any of that stuff. He had no business taking care of Amy, or even having thoughts about her, unless they were strictly related to the work they both performed at Eagle Hill Manor.

But instead of concentrating on his fishing flies, Dusty worried about Amy living way up there on the ridge. He hoped to hell she figured out how to start a fire in the wood-burning stove. She had enough wood for tonight's fire. He'd made sure of that. But someone would have to split some logs for her. He didn't think Amy knew how to use a hatchet or an ax.

Who would do that for her if he didn't? And since he'd been the one to suggest the fishing cabin, he felt responsible for her somehow. Tomorrow he'd run up there and split enough wood for a week. And maybe by then she and her father would figure things out and she'd go back to living in the lap of luxury in that stone mansion up near the vineyard. Her daddy had probably paid more than a million bucks for that house, which had more square footage than any two people would ever need.

She would never understand the beauty of his small, hand-built house. He pulled the magnifying glasses from his face. Damn. He needed to quit thinking about her. Maybe he should run up to Charles Town and grovel for Zoe's forgiveness.

He jettisoned the idea almost as soon as it crossed his mind. He didn't want Zoe. She'd been nothing more than a diversion on those nights when even a tiny house got lonely. Going up there wouldn't be fair to the woman.

He got up and restlessly stared out the floor-to-ceiling picture window. A tiny vibration hummed inside him, and he imagined that a maple might feel the same restlessness in the springtime when it awakens after a long winter. His tiny house felt like a cage tonight.

Just then headlights cut through the rain, announcing a visitor. Dusty rarely had company out here, and never unannounced. He flicked on the front floodlights to reveal a beat-up Ford pickup coming to a stop in his drive. He didn't recognize the truck, but he sure recognized the man who got out of it and dashed through the downpour to the roof overhang by the front door.

Damn it to hell and back again. He yanked the door open. "You aren't welcome here," he said, staring into his father's face.

Daddy had sure gone downhill in the last eight years. Rheumy, bloodshot eyes squinted at Dusty from out of a waxy, gray face, and a jack-o'-lantern grin exposed wide, gaping holes where teeth had once been. The scent of booze and cigarettes clung to his dirty clothes, the familiar reek unleashing a shit ton of bad memories for Dusty.

"What'd you do with my house, boy?" Daddy said in his broken-down voice.

"Tore it down. Now, get going. I don't want you here."

"Got nowhere to get to." Daddy leaned into the doorframe, his body language as evil as ever. "You know Sally Hawkes over at the *Winchester Daily?*" he asked.

"Yeah, I know her." The question tweaked Dusty. How the hell did Daddy know about the writer who'd tried to assassinate his character?

"That Sally woman called me up a week ago to ask a whole bunch of questions. You been holding out on me, boy. Since when did the county decide they wanted our land?"

"Since about a year ago."

"Why the hell are you giving them a hard time about this? I say we cash in now."

"Daddy, you don't own this land anymore. I bought it from you eight years ago. It's *my* land they want."

"You think I'm a fool, don't you? That cash you gave me wasn't near enough for this land, boy." His father took a menacing step forward, balling up his fists the way he always had. "I owned this land before you were ever even born. And I'm here to get my cut of the sale price."

Daddy came at him like he'd done a million times before. Only this time Dusty didn't let him win. This time Dusty gave him a hard shove. Daddy backpedaled and slipped on the rain-slicked decking. He tumbled back and landed hard. He didn't get up.

For an instant Dusty wondered if he'd finally gone off and killed his old man. Upon closer inspection, Gregory Dustin McNeil Sr. was still alive. But the dude might not be for long if Dusty left him out in the rain. So against his better judgment, he picked the old man up and hauled him inside the little house that had been built small on purpose so that Daddy would never have a place to come home to.

❧

Amy's Bec & Bridge dress hugged her hips, and the surplice neckline made the most of her minimal boobs. Accessorized with a plain gold chain, hoop earrings, and her Valentino black patent T-strap shoes with the three-inch stiletto heels, Amy had done her best to please Aunt Pam.

Too bad she'd forgotten to steal one of the umbrellas in the front hall closet this afternoon when she'd gone home to get her stuff. The skies had opened up, and the hard spring rain had undone her grooming efforts. She tried to fix the damage in Aunt Pam's first-floor powder room, but it was hopeless.

Of course, Pam was on her the moment she entered the family room. As always, her aunt's hugs were warm and loving and reminded Amy that her aunt—as difficult as she could be—loved her family fiercely. But before the hug ended, Pam whispered, "There are two TV cameras recording everything, so be careful what you say. And I wish you'd made an appointment at Glamorous You. Your hair is a disaster."

Pam ran her fingers through Amy's hair, trying to fluff it up a little. "I've got to run and check on Lydia and dinner," Pam said. "Danny's at the bar, and I trust you understand what you need to do." Pam gave her arm a resolute squeeze before she hurried off.

Amy pivoted toward the bar and found her prodigal cousin gazing at her out of surprisingly serious brown eyes. "Hello, Amy. You've grown up."

He lounged on one of the barstools with a long-necked Sam Adams in his hand. The California sunshine had burned away all traces of his East Coast origins. Sunbronzed skin, a bright orange and blue Hawaiian shirt, and a long ponytail down his back made him stand out in the mostly blue and gray worsted crowd.

Amy wanted to rush right into his arms, but Danny wasn't alone. A stranger with a scraggly beard and a video camera stood beside him, his telephoto lens trained on her, ready to catch whatever emotion she let fly.

"Danny," she said in a cool and calm voice, trying her best to channel Aunt Pam. She crossed the carpet, holding out her arms, and gave him a quick kiss on the cheek, afraid to show the emotions that knotted up in her throat. She'd missed him so much.

For a long time Danny had been her wingman and champion. As kids, they'd been the closest cousins in age and temperament. Neither of them was of the same genius caliber as the rest of the clan. So naturally they'd gotten into adventures—and trouble—together. They'd also watched each other's backs until he'd found the courage to tell his father, Uncle Charles, that he didn't want to be a lawyer, hated Harvard, and wanted to work in film. Uncle Charles had reacted to this news by telling Danny that if he wanted out of Harvard and into film school, he could damn well pay for it himself.

And since Danny had a very large trust fund, set up by his maternal grandfather, paying for tuition had been no problem. He'd left home, gotten his degree, and even produced several arty films that had gotten critical notice at Sundance but had failed financially.

Still, in his early years out West, he'd gotten some notice as a serious filmmaker, and then his affair with Mia Paquet, the reality TV celebrity, had sidetracked his career and his life. At least, that's what Amy thought. The rest of the family thought Danny deserved whatever trouble he got into because he'd dared to break out of the family mold.

"Wow, what happened to the little girl I remember?" Danny asked.

"I'm still little, but now I wear higher heels. And you look kind of rad with the ponytail."

"Yeah, so I've been told." His gaze shifted to Uncle Charles, who stood by the French doors talking politics with Uncle Mark and David. Amy gave the room a quick scan. Most of the family had yet to arrive, and David had come without Willow and Natalie. Not a surprise, given that Natalie had school tomorrow and Willow had a house full of guests.

Aunt Julie sat on one of the couches across the room playing with the most adorable toddler Amy had ever set eyes on. Beside Julie sat the infamous Mia Paquet—

glamorous and beautiful, like a Barbie doll with boobage out to here and legs down to there. Danny had always appreciated the girls with the biggest racks, so of course he'd hooked up with Mia.

Gathered around Mia and her baby were two other women Amy immediately recognized as Mia's girlfriends and the other stars of the *Vegas Girls* reality TV show. Ivory of the chocolate-brown skin and pink-streaked hair. And Pearl with the incredible cheekbones and the blue-black Asian hair coiled around her head. In the presence of these gorgeous, put-together women, Amy faded away to invisibility.

"I'm tending bar at the moment," Danny said, pulling Amy's attention back where it rightly belonged. "What can I get you?"

"I'm sure there's some Bella Vista Merlot back there." She took one of the empty stools as he snagged a glass from the rack above the bar and poured her a glass of the family wine.

"You know, the producers will cut out the product placement. But nice try," Danny said.

"I wasn't trying to advertise the family vineyard." She glanced at the photographer. "And to be honest, I'm ticked off at you for putting everyone on television. It's invasive."

"I'm sorry about that. But I wanted to introduce the baby to the family."

"You could have brought Scarlett back for a visit with her family without the cameras."

His eyebrows lowered in the signature Lyndon scowl—the one every male member of the family had inherited from William Lyndon, the man who had built Charlotte's Grove and whose portrait glared down from above the mantel in the formal parlor. "Without the wedding, Scarlett will never legally be a Lyndon," Danny snarled.

"No? Can't you make a declaration or something in Nevada?"

"I can, but it's not the same as being married to Scarlett's mother." The tension across his shoulders and the harsh tone in his voice suggested that Danny was wound tighter than the grandfather clock in the front hall. He might be wearing a carefree Hawaiian shirt, but the happy-go-lucky guy she'd known as a kid had disappeared. This Danny seemed more like her brothers and cousins. More serious. More focused.

She glanced uneasily at the cameraman waiting like a giant predator to pounce on her the moment she said something juicy and full of conflict. There were so many things to say, starting with the admonition that in the twenty-first century he didn't have to marry Mia to claim responsibility for his daughter.

Danny noticed the direction of her stare. "You don't have to be coy. Everyone knows why I'm here. I've been trying for the last two years—from the moment I found out we were going to have a baby—to make Mia my bride. So right now I'm asking everyone in the family to make this wedding all it can be. I want all of you to be happy for me. And for Scarlett."

Unfortunately, Danny didn't sound happy for himself. But, then again, Lyndons were a failure when it came to marital bliss.

Amy regarded the people in the room with a critical eye. She doubted Pam and Mark had married for love. She couldn't remember ever seeing them kiss or hold hands. Aunt Julie and Uncle Charles almost never spoke to each other. And Mom and Daddy's marriage hadn't been a bed of roses.

Amy would fail if she tried to talk Danny out of marrying Mia. But at least she could try to talk him out of turning his loveless marriage into a sideshow that would suck the rest of the family in.

She turned back toward him. "Ambushing the family and putting them on television isn't a good way to get them on your side or even to make them happy about your choices. A better way would have been to invite them all to a private ceremony with a party afterward."

Danny shook his head. "Amy, I know Pam thinks you can change my mind about this, but you can't. Mia will never agree to a private ceremony. She wants the moon and the stars and the whole world watching. That's the quid pro quo, as Dad would say. The only way I get her to the altar is to sacrifice everyone's privacy."

Amy glanced at the cameraman and thought about what she could possibly say to convince Danny to give up this idea, and she came up with absolutely nothing. Danny seemed committed to his plans, and if she challenged him here, it would only create the kind of drama the TV show fed off.

She'd need to get him in a private moment, and even then she didn't think she had much chance of changing his mind. It suddenly occurred to her that having the family depend on her for this important task was, maybe, not such a great thing. In the end, she'd be blamed for failing them.

She was angsting over this when the boys swept into the family room with the usual fanfare. The boys, as everyone called them, consisted of Danny's brothers, Jason and Matthew, and Amy's brothers, Andrew and Edward. And like a wolf pack, these urban-dwelling, well-educated, good-looking, politically connected alpha dudes always made a big statement when they showed up en masse.

The arrival of all that male beauty immediately engaged the cameraman, who turned away from ordinary Amy to capture Danny's reunion with his brothers and cousins. Being left aside didn't bother Amy in the least. For once being invisible had its merits. The camera crew ignored her all through cocktail hour. And she managed to avoid Aunt Pam as well by hanging out with Aunt Julie and playing with Scarlett, who was a joy.

At dinner, Uncle Mark, the most alpha in a pack of alpha men, took charge, dominating the table conversation—a turn of events that clearly annoyed Mia, her girlfriends, and the executive producer.

No doubt Uncle Mark had carefully chosen the most boring topic possible—a discussion of the bipartisan criminal justice reform bill under consideration before the Senate Judiciary Committee. And once Uncle Mark seized a conversation, no one could ever get it back. His nickname—Bulldog Lyndon—summed it up nicely.

All through the salad and main courses, Uncle Mark pushed the conversation so down into the weeds that the camera crew lost interest and stopped recording. His masterful performance might have completely thwarted the television people were it not for the fact that Uncle Mark had to take a phone call just as dessert was being served. Apparently the bipartisan negotiations over the very bill he'd been discussing had hit a snag, and Bulldog Lyndon was needed.

No sooner had Mark left the table than Mia took charge,

exploiting the opportunity as only a reality TV star could, by dropping two gigantic bombshells.

"I have some fabulous news," Mia said in her breathy Marilyn Monroe voice. "We just got word that our wedding is going to also be a *Say Yes to the Dress* special. We're scheduled for a shoot at Kleinfeld in New York on Wednesday. And since we're doing this on a quick turnaround, I'm expecting there to be a lot of drama over the dress selection."

Mia almost squealed, as if wedding-dress drama was the best thing ever. She turned toward Aunt Pam. "I can't wait to try on dresses. And, Pam, I'd be so pleased if you would come with us to New York. I need your fashion advice."

Pam blinked a few times. "*Say Yes to the Dress*?"

Pearl, Ivory, and Mia's jaws dropped in unison, as if none of them could fathom how a twenty-first-century woman had never heard of the reality show where brides choose their dresses while their friends and family kibitz.

But the Vegas girls didn't know Aunt Pam. She watched public television and cable news, and that was it. The rest of the time she entertained herself by reading—mostly history. Amy could no more imagine Aunt Pam appearing on *Say Yes to the Dress* than she could see her aunt attending a Miley Cyrus concert, with or without the twerking. Her aunt just didn't do popular culture.

Amy had to rescue Aunt Pam before she said yes to dress shopping. "Aunt Pam, *Say Yes to the Dress* is a reality show where brides try on wedding dresses while their family members ridicule and judge each selection."

"Good God. Why?" Aunt Pam said.

"Because it's fun to watch," Pearl said.

Quite true, and Amy could well imagine how an episode

featuring a showgirl and a senator's wife would be fraught with make-believe drama. Ivory and Pearl would urge Mia to buy a mermaid gown with a neckline down to her navel, and Aunt Pam would suggest something a little more formal.

Uptight even.

Yeah, it was a train wreck in the making and would probably boost the show's ratings. But it would be bad news for Uncle Mark's reputation and his next election.

Pam glanced at Julie and then Amy and then back at Mia. She straightened her spine. "Don't you think it's more appropriate for you to invite Julie? After all, she's your future mother-in-law."

Way to go, Aunt Pam. She'd sidestepped the invitation and backhanded the ball into someone else's court. No doubt she'd learned this as a killer on the tennis courts down at the country club.

But Julie was a low-handicap golfer, and she knew how to hit a ball a long way. "Oh, don't bother about me. I'm a fashion disaster. I'll stay home and babysit Scarlett." The twinkle in Julie's eye suggested that she'd watched *Say Yes to the Dress* once or twice. Who knew?

"Oh no, you can't do that," Mia said. "Danny will stay home with the baby. He's devoted to Scarlett." Since Danny had done diaper duty, and bottle duty, and was even now holding the baby in his lap, this pronouncement went unchallenged.

Julie turned a mother's adoring smile in Danny and Scarlett's direction. "Yes, he is," she said, the candlelight flickering in her dewy eyes. "But I'd still like to stay home and help. Really, Mia, if you want someone from the family to go with you, you should take Amy. She's got a wonderful sense of fashion. And she's helped several of her sorority sisters choose their dresses."

Oh shit. How had the ball landed in her court? Damn. She sucked at tennis and golf and every other sport known to man or woman.

Mia turned her critical gaze in Amy's direction with a look so sharp it hurt.

"I can't," Amy blurted before Mia said a word. "I have to work."

Pam rolled her eyes. Julie's mouth dropped open. The boys reacted as if Amy had just dropped in from another planet.

"Since when do you have a job?" Andrew asked.

"Since a few days ago. I—"

"She's working for Willow at the inn," Pam said, shooting David a daggerlike look.

"For real?" Mia cocked her head. "What do you do there? Can you help me plan the wedding? That would be so fun, having Danny's little cousin Amy help with the arrangements. He talks about you all the time."

"That's a wonderful—" Pam started, but Amy interrupted.

"I'm a gardener," she said, sitting up straight in her chair. "I help maintain the grounds and set up for events. I love it. For the first time in my life, I'm independent."

"You are not independent," Pam said in that holier-than-thou tone that Amy hated. "You're relying on Willow's kindness, and you're living in Thomas's cabin. You don't even have enough income to get your hair done. You need to stop this foolishness and call Grady right now and say yes to his marriage proposal. Then you and Mia can both go to Kleinfeld and shop for dresses together."

Amy's face burned hot and then cold. How dare Aunt Pam criticize everything, including her job? She wanted to scream at her, but of course she couldn't do that with the cameras rolling. Hell, she couldn't do that, period.

So she took a huge breath and tried to think of something to say that would de-escalate the conversation. Before she could say anything, Mia spoke again, her girlish voice turning hard. "The shoot in New York is only about *my* dress, Amy. I'm sorry, but—"

"Wait a second," Andrew interrupted. "You didn't say yes to Grady's proposal? He's told everyone that you're getting married."

"Then he's a liar. I told him no. Quite emphatically."

"But you've been together for more than a year," Andrew pointed out like Captain Obvious.

"Yeah, and he's worth millions, which makes him perfect for you." Edward's follow-up comment put the hurt in the one-two brotherly punch.

Mia's mouth dropped open. "You said no to a man worth millions?"

"I did."

"Why?"

"Because I don't love him." Amy gave the cameraman a quick, nervous glance as he zoomed in on her. Why had she signed the release form that the *Vegas Girls* producer had shoved at her earlier in the evening? This was bad. The producer looked like she'd just had a shot of caffeine. All boredom had fled, and suddenly Amy's love life had turned into a subplot in a reality TV show.

She needed to change the subject, but her public declaration of independence turned into a full-on family discussion in which her brothers, cousins, aunts, uncles, and three

Vegas showgirls offered their opinions about how Amy should grow up, recognize the truth, and say yes to Grady Carson, hedge fund manager and millionaire.

The final humiliation came when Ivory said, "Honey, if you don't want that man, can you give me his number? Mia's found herself a rich sugar daddy, and I want me one too."

Chapter Nine————————————

Amy excused herself from the table the moment the dinner conversation turned back to Mia's appearance on *Say Yes to the Dress*. She pretended to go to the bathroom but instead made a mad dash through the rain to her car. Thank goodness the synthetic material of her Bec & Ridge dress was water-friendly.

She had no idea how long it took before the family discovered her missing because her cell phone had been turned off and the fishing cabin didn't have a phone. And since the weather had turned downright stormy, no one followed her up the road either.

So she was fine.

Except for the fact that she had no clue how to start a fire in the woodstove, and without her iPhone, she couldn't exactly ask Siri for help. She made several attempts, but they produced more smoke than fire or warmth. So she and Muffin curled up together in the small bed in the back room with three heavy quilts that she'd found in the old chest at the foot of the bed. They were warm.

After a while.

Muffin turned out to be a super alarm clock, too, even if walking her in the early morning without a caffeine fix required more dedication than Amy had ever shown to anything in her life. It was a drag, quite literally, since Muffin pulled incessantly on the leash and had her own ideas about where to go, usually into mud puddles left by the rain.

Waking up to walk the dog had one saving grace—Amy got to work early enough on Tuesday to discover that Antonin, the head chef at Eagle Hill Manor, kept a pot of coffee going all day for the staff. So she was properly caffeinated when she reported to the barn at 9:00 a.m., ready to work and feeling surprisingly in charge of her life.

The "in charge" feeling disappeared the moment she laid eyes on Dusty. Her mind went back to that moment with a wiggly dog in her arms and soap in her eyes. She totally needed to cut out the memory of that particular lust-filled moment. And she had to stop thinking of him as *Dusty* and get back to thinking about him as *Mister McNeil*.

He made it easy when he scowled at Muffin "Why is she here?"

"I couldn't leave her alone. I did that last night, and she howled the whole time. She's been traumatized and abandoned before. And besides, I don't have the gas money to run back and forth between here and the cabin in order to walk her."

His mouth twitched, but his dimples didn't come out this morning, as if they were hiding behind a big rain cloud. Mr. McNeil's shoulders also seemed tense, and the dark circles under his eyes suggested that he hadn't slept well last night.

"Are you okay?" she asked.

His brows drew together. "I'm fine." The words exploded from him like bullets from a machine gun, conveying the unmistakable message that he most definitely was not fine.

"What's wrong?"

He stood up. "What part of 'I'm fine' did you not understand? Come on, I need you to spread mulch and compost this morning. I'm afraid it's going to be muddy work after last night's downpour."

He walked right past her with his long-legged stride, and once again she found herself rushing after him, her own legs pumping hard to keep up. Muffin thought they were playing chase. She woofed and nipped at her heels a couple of times.

Uh-oh, not good, because that earned both of them another thunderous look. "If you want to bring that dog to work, you have to keep her on a leash and teach her manners. Get a book on dog training."

"I will, as soon as payday comes."

Dusty stopped, turned, and jammed his hands onto his hips. "Amy, have you ever been inside a library?"

"Sure. They had one at the college I attended even if it wasn't an Ivy League school."

"That's good to know because you'll find the Jefferson County Library on Washington Avenue near the county courthouse. And if you go down there, the nice librarian will give you a library card, which costs nothing. And then you can borrow books."

"Cool. I didn't think about that. I guess I should have. There are a lot of things I'm learning about, you know, like the dollar menu at McDonald's."

"Yeah, I guess." He turned and continued striding off to the garage area of the barn.

"You think the library would have a book on how to build a fire in a woodstove?" she asked to his retreating back as she jogged to keep up. "Because I'm a total dud at that. I tried last night, honestly, but I couldn't get the fire going."

He stopped again and cocked his head in her direction. Something changed in his bright blue stare. "You didn't have a fire last night?"

"I was okay. Muffin and I snuggled under the covers. The dog gives off lots of body heat."

He exhaled sharply as though he'd lost his patience with her, although she couldn't see why he should care whether she had a fire or not. Still, Amy had to choke back the "I'm sorry" that wanted to come out of her mouth. What was she sorry for, exactly?

Good thing she didn't say it because Dusty—Mr. McNeil—surprised her by saying, "After work I'll come up to the cabin, split some wood for you, and give you a lesson in how to start a fire in a woodstove, okay?"

She couldn't help it, she grinned at him. "That would be so nice, thank you. You've been..." She lost the ability to speak. An emotion much deeper than lust lodged under her heart. She wanted him, yes, but more than that, she *liked* him. Dusty was a kind human being.

"I've been what?" he asked.

"Kind and helpful. And I appreciate it."

"Yeah, well, whatever." His quick dismissal raised the

same hurt inside as Aunt Pam's derision of her job and her choices last night.

She chided herself for that slipup. Dusty McNeil didn't act out of kindness. Like everyone else in the world, he served his own agenda. And now that she thought about it, it only made sense that Willow had asked Mr. McNeil to be nice. Maybe Willow had actually *hired* him to babysit Amy.

Danny and the *Vegas Girl* entourage breezed into Eagle Hill Manor around midmorning. Amy saw them arrive, the camera crew swarming around the stars. An hour later, Danny turned up at Amy's elbow as she hauled mulch from the pile behind the barn. The minute Muffin saw Danny, her little tail wagged like a flag.

"Hello," he said, squatting down to pet the dog. "What's your name?"

"Muffin. I found her a few days ago. She was abandoned."

"You have a dog? I'm surprised." Danny stood up.

"Like I said, it's a recent thing."

"And you bring her to work?"

Yes, she did, because she didn't have any other option and also, probably, she got away with it because Willow had paid Mr. McNeil to look the other way.

"Yeah," she said, spreading the compost and mulch.

"What on earth are you doing?"

"Taking care of the azaleas." She said the plant name with authority. "Mr. McNeil says these plants are very thirsty, and the mulch will help them retain water, especially after they bloom."

"Dusty McNeil?" Danny said in a voice chilly with disapproval.

Amy straightened and leaned on her rake. "Yeah. He's my boss."

"That's actually funny."

"No, it's not."

He shrugged. "Yeah it is, sort of—the idea of a McNeil bossing around a Lyndon."

Amy saw red. "Danny, if you want to ruin your life and marry that showgirl, go ahead and do it. But don't come here and judge me, okay? Daddy locked me out of the house and told me to marry Grady or get out. I chose the latter. And since, unlike you, I don't have a trust fund to fall back on, I had to get a job. And since I'm not qualified to do much, this was the best I could do. So get used to it."

"Amy, come on, don't be so dramatic. You have other options. In fact, I'm here because everyone thinks it would be a fabulous idea if you would help Mia with the wedding plans."

"Everyone? Really?"

"Well, Aunt Pam suggested it."

"Aunt Pam wants me to convince you to have a small, private ceremony. I think Aunt Pam is right, so if I took this job, I would be in constant conflict with your bride. And, of course, the producers would try to make my non-relationship with Grady a part of the story line."

"Uh, well, I guess…"

"You guess? Look, Danny, I think you should break up with Mia."

"Come on, Amy. Be reasonable."

"No. I don't want to be on TV. I don't want a job you've

arranged for me. And I'm not going to help you plan a wedding so you can marry someone you don't love."

He blinked at her. "What are you talking about? Of course I love Mia. And besides, I have to consider Scarlett."

Amy turned her back on him and continued spreading mulch. "Okay, whatever, be like everyone else in the family. I never thought I'd see the day when that happened. But here's a news flash for you. I don't have to help you screw up your life or embarrass the family."

"Amy, we're not talking about me. We're talking about you. Explain to me why you're willing to walk away from a nice, rich, smart guy who wants to marry you. And why you think working as a gardener is a better deal."

She gripped the rake and thought about braining her cousin with it, but she didn't do violence. Besides, he towered over her and always had.

"You know what? I like being a gardener." Amy said the words like an affirmation. Maybe mulching azaleas wouldn't bring world peace, but from the azaleas' point of view, getting mulched was a big thing.

"Amy, come on," Danny said. "I can give you a loan, and we can find you something better. Something more—"

She turned on him. "I don't want a handout. I want to explore my options on my own. Can't anyone understand that?"

"I do understand, but being a gardener is not a real option."

"How do you know? Come on, Danny. You're the one who made a stand and went off to do something different. I loved you for being brave and doing the thing that you wanted most in life. But I don't see you making films right now."

He paled slightly, and Amy wished she could take her angry words back.

"You don't know anything about my life," he said. "So stay the hell out of it."

"Danny, I'm s—"

He put up his hands, palms out. "I get it," he said before turning away and heading in the direction of the Carriage House, where Mia and her entourage were making plans for turning his wedding into the greatest show on earth.

Morning came and went, but Dusty's foul mood stuck around. He'd started his morning dragging Daddy out of the Murphy bed in the A-frame's tiny living room, handing the old man a cup of coffee in an old travel mug, and showing him out the door.

Daddy didn't force the issue for once. Maybe the bump on his head had knocked some sense into him. Dusty didn't really care. He only hoped the bastard would go someplace else and never darken his door again. But Dusty knew that was wishful thinking. Daddy would turn up tonight drunk as a skunk.

Maybe Daddy's return was a message. Maybe the time had come to give up the fight, pull up stakes, sell the damn land, and move far, far away, where people didn't know his sad story. Someplace Daddy could never find him again.

The fishing in Montana was good. He'd always wanted to go there.

On vacation. Not to live.

Dammit, Dusty had been fishing the streams that fed

into the Potomac and Shenandoah Rivers all his life. He'd learned where the trout hid in the deep pools during the spring season. He could find the bass in the summer. He could pick the right flies and lures for winter and fall. If he wanted to start a fishing camp and guide service, he needed to do it here, not someplace he'd never been.

These thoughts tumbled around in his head as he trimmed the boxwood hedge using a pair of old-fashioned hand shears instead of a power trimmer. The quiet back here on the terrace soothed him as he worked until someone bellowed, "Yoo-hoo, cute gardener guy."

Being called "cute gardener guy" annoyed him since he'd worked his way through Virginia Tech, earning a degree in horticultural science. He glanced over his shoulder. An Amazon on spike heels with pink hair, coffee-colored skin, and an enhanced chest waved at him. "Bombshell" didn't even come close to describing this woman. She was built curvy and her legs were so long she could have gotten a tryout with the Rockettes. The beading on her tight little tank top sparkled in the afternoon sun, momentarily blinding him.

"Can I help you?" Dusty asked.

She giggled. "I declare, you Virginians are all so polite," she said in a stupid, fake Southern accent. He swallowed back his annoyance. Guests were always right, even when they were wrong.

He put down his garden shears and faced her but said not a word. She was a beautiful specimen of womanhood, but he resented the way she flirted with him as if he were a Virginia mountain cabana boy.

"Hi," she said, with a showgirl simper that didn't attract him in the slightest. "I'm Ivory. Mia Paquet's girlfriend?"

Was he supposed to be impressed by this information? He had no idea. "Yeah?"

She batted her eyes a few times, and when that didn't get her what she wanted, she frowned. "Antonella, our executive producer, sent me to talk to the gardener about making some changes. You're the gardener, right?"

He nodded.

She pointed to the stand of Portuguese laurels that he'd planted last fall in order to create drama for brides getting married out at the gazebo. The laurels screened the walkway to the house, allowing weddings to be staged and brides to make their appearance in grand style. "Antonella wants you to remove those shrubs."

"Why?"

"Because we have to put the cameras there so they can get a long shot of Mia walking down the footpath in her wedding dress."

Dusty almost shook his head. It was amazing the things brides asked for. And when their requests were refused, they often turned meaner than pit bulls.

He had no desire to prolong this encounter, so he put on an I-just-work-here expression and said, "I can see that, but you'll have to ask Willow Lyndon to authorize that."

She responded by tottering forward on her screw-me shoes and using her sex appeal like a weapon. "So, what's your name, honey?" she asked.

"Mr. McNeil, and I have work to do."

She seemed surprised that he didn't bother looking at the boobs she'd shoved at him. But he'd seen plenty of fake boobs in his day, and they'd always turned him off. His girlfriends might have been mostly cocktail waitresses and blackjack dealers, but he'd always insisted on real ta-

tas. He had standards, and in his opinion, a handful was enough.

His mind wandered to that morning when Amy Lyndon lost her beach towel. He would never forget the sight of her all nude and perched up high on that fence. That woman defied all his expectations. She had a natural charm about her that made him want to laugh and kiss her at the same time. Like this morning when she got all grateful for his help and all eager to learn the names of the plants he'd asked her to mulch. She didn't look down on him or his occupation. She didn't treat him like a cabana boy.

Whoa, wait a sec. He'd lost his train of thought. And while he'd been woolgathering, Ivory had gotten right up on him in a cloud of spicy perfume that made him sneeze.

"God bless," she said, patting his face. "Whatcha doing after work, honey? I think you and me could be friends. In fact, with a face like yours, I could probably get you a role on the show."

He was about to tell Ivory to back off when chaos descended in the form of Sven the labradoodle, who had apparently escaped from his state-of-the-art kennel behind the barn and was now in hot pursuit of Muffin the cockapoo. The dogs came racing around the blind curve of the boxwood hedge. Muffin, small and agile, avoided colliding with Dusty and the showgirl, but the goofy Sven tripped over himself and knocked Ivory right into Dusty's chest. He caught her, of course, and she sagged against him.

Just then the itty-bitty and adorably sexy Amy Lyndon rounded the corner and skidded to a stop in her oversized hiking boots. She paused long enough to take in the sight of Dusty and Ivory while a fetching blush ran up her cheeks. "Oh, uh, I'm sorry...I, uh—" She shut her mouth and tore after the dog.

"Muffin, you come back here," she yelled as the dog made a wild circuit of the patio with her floppy ears flying and her pink leash dragging across the flagstones. The dog scampered by her mistress and then hightailed it around the boxwood and out toward the western wall, with Amy clunking behind in her ridiculous boots.

Dusty set Ivory back on her high heels, pivoted, and dove for Sven, but he missed badly and ended up skidding across the flagstones on his knees. Ow, that was definitely going to bruise, but he had succeeded in cornering the dog. At least for a moment.

Sven made a quick change of direction in a move worthy of any first-rate NFL running back. He evaded Dusty's tackle and busted loose, heading after Muffin once again. Dusty pushed from the ground and gave chase, skidding around the boxwood just as Muffin cut a swath through a group of people out on the lawn a few yards in front of her.

Muffin's passage through the knot of people caused barely a ripple except for the fact that the camera crew panned in Amy's direction as she clumped along in her ridiculous work clothes. In fact, everyone turned toward Amy and her dog, a move that proved fatal.

Sven might not be as gigantic as his reindeer-sized namesake from the movie *Frozen*, but he still had a good fifty pounds on Muffin. So when the dog put on speed and hit the crowd, one cameraman went down and everyone else disbursed in a dozen different directions.

Yup, good ol' Sven was the epitome of a reverse sheepdog. Instead of herding people together, he scattered them and knocked them down like duckpins.

Dusty stepped it up a notch just as Amy laid herself out and snagged Muffin's leash. She landed with an audible *ooof*, the dog jerking to a stop. A moment later, a somewhat amorous Sven made his move. Their little X-rated dog show was almost amusing, but maybe not to everyone.

Dusty arrived on the scene, breathless, the knees of his khakis stained with blood. He grabbed Sven's collar and pulled him away.

"Ew, that's gross. Stop," Amy said, pulling Muffin in the opposite direction.

Willow arrived on the scene. "What the hell is going on here? Why is Sven out of his kennel?"

"Uh, well, um..." Amy said. "It was sort of my fault."

Willow turned her green-eyed stare on Amy, and the little-bitty woman wilted right on the spot. Willow could be intimidating as hell sometimes, and Amy's downward glance and the defeated slope of her shoulders said it all. The poor thing expected to have her head handed to her.

"No, it wasn't Amy's fault," Dusty said on a cough. "The latch on the gate's been loose for weeks, and I haven't gotten around to fixing it. Anyone leaning on that gate could open it up. I'm sure that's what happened."

Amy raised her head, surprise in her eyes. "But—"

"You did lean on the gate, didn't you?"

She hesitated a moment and then nodded her head.

Willow turned on him. "Well, no harm done, I guess, since it was Danny and his cockamamie celebrity girlfriend up there. To be honest, if Sven's antics have upset them, maybe they'll decide to get married someplace else, because I cannot believe what that woman wants to do."

Dusty nodded his head. "I heard she wants us to remove the Portuguese laurels."

"It's worse than that. She wants to turn the Carriage House into a circus tent because members of the Cirque du Soleil touring company will be putting on a special show during the reception. Which, you'll be pleased to learn, is supposed to take place in three freaking weeks. The woman is insane."

"Three weeks? We're all booked up for the next three months."

"On weekends. But Mia is happy to accommodate us. This wedding is taking place midweek. On April twenty-sixth."

"You could always tell her no," Dusty said.

Willow shook her head. "No, I can't. David has asked me to be nice. For the family and Scarlett's sake. Besides, you have to admit that the publicity will be good for business. Honestly, Dusty, I know we joke about how these weddings sometimes turn into circuses, but Danny's wedding will actually *be* one."

Chapter Ten

The Jefferson County Public Library sat at the corner of Washington Avenue and Third Street and stayed open every day until 5:30 p.m., giving Amy plenty of time to leave work at 4:00 p.m., drop Muffin at the cabin, and then return to scope the place out.

Who knew the Jefferson County Library had such a fount of knowledge readily available for free? She was amazed to discover that the library had free Internet with workstations that she could use to double-check the various Virginia registries of lost dogs. She scanned through the lost dog notices, but none of them matched Muffin's description.

With a sigh of relief, Amy concentrated on getting herself a library card, and then the wonderful librarian, Donna Carlton, helped her find a book on dog training. Donna also introduced her to the extensive and almost overwhelming collection of gardening books.

Wow, Shenandoah Falls appeared to be the home of a boatload of garden enthusiasts, judging by the number of books and their well-used condition. After half an hour of perusing various volumes, Amy finally settled on a small paperback guide to trees and shrubs in the mid-Atlantic region. She figured she could carry it around in her back pocket at work and learn the names of all the trees and shrubs growing on the inn's grounds. She couldn't wait to impress Mr. McNeil with her horticultural knowledge at work tomorrow.

The sun hadn't yet set by the time she returned to the cabin, so she settled down on the porch with a cup of ramen noodles and started the book on dog training. She had just made it through the first chapter when the sound of tires crunching on the cabin's long gravel driveway interrupted her.

Uh-oh, company was coming—probably Aunt Pam on a mission to give her another pep talk about her life. Muffin must have picked up on Amy's annoyance because the dog jumped up and started to bark like her visitor was a serial murderer or worse. But when Mr. McNeil's blue pickup truck pulled into the driveway, the dog shut up and started wagging her tail.

Was this good or bad? Amy couldn't decide. Dusty McNeil was not Aunt Pam, but then again, he had probably been paid to look in on her and report back. So either way, the family had decided to spy on her. At least they'd sent a nice-looking spy.

The late-afternoon sun back lit his hair, giving him a godlike halo. He came striding up to the screen door carrying a brown paper sack. "Hey," he said. "I stopped by the diner on my way. I got bacon and egg sandwiches."

He said this while frowning down at her half-eaten cup of ramen. "I'm glad I did. Ramen noodles are not a sufficient dinner."

Yup, he'd been hired by someone to babysit her. She might not have a lot of work experience, but she knew that bosses didn't usually come around bearing free meals and nutritional advice. Amy decided to give him the cold shoulder. She turned back to the *Idiot's Guide to Puppy Training*.

"You need protein if you're going to work the way you did today," Mr. McNeil said. He pulled a sandwich out of the paper bag, and the mouthwatering scent of bacon filled the air.

It was a known fact that Muffin would do almost anything for a piece of bacon. The same could be said of Amy herself. She snatched the sandwich from Dusty's outstretched arm. "Thanks," she said, totally aware that her self-righteous need to be self-reliant had crumbled in the face of a bacon and egg sandwich.

"There are some hash browns in the sack. Help yourself. I came to chop wood," he announced. "I'll be out back by the woodpile."

He dropped the sack on the small wooden table by the Adirondack chair, gave Muffin a little scratch under her chin, and then strode away, his boots sounding sharply on the porch's floorboards, the screen door slamming behind him. A moment later, he pulled a long-handled ax from the bed of his pickup.

Substitute a war hammer and Dusty McNeil could be a stand-in for Thor. It almost hurt to watch him cross the yard. Amy longed to follow, but that would be unwise. So she settled back in her chair and devoured the yummy food while she worked at ignoring the heavy *thud, thud, thud* of Dusty chopping wood that echoed from the backyard.

Her imagination dreamed up something from right out of a smoking-hot porno movie starring Dusty, shirtless and sweaty, swinging that ax, his glistening muscles rippling with every stroke. Who knew she had such naughty Norse god–lumberjack fantasies?

This was bad. She needed to get up and clear her mind. "C'mon, Muffin, let's take a walk."

She snapped the leash on the dog's collar and, armed with a handful of dog kibble, headed outside to begin her first training session. The book said that good dog owners taught their dogs leash manners. And since Muffin had no manners whatsoever, Amy could only surmise that Muffin's original family had not done well by her. Muffin was lucky to have been abandoned because she was a Lyndon now, and all Lyndons had impeccable manners.

Following the book's instructions, Amy said "heel" a few times and tried to get Muffin to behave. The dog made some progress, but every few seconds she'd sit down and look longingly at the path to the woodpile with her head cocked to one side. So in the end Amy let the dog drag her around the corner to investigate.

Holy crap! Dusty had taken off his shirt. And he'd most definitely worked up a sweat, which darkened his blond hair and glistened on his chest in full-out beefcake calendar mode. He sure could swing an ax and get results. He was a machine when it came to turning big pieces of wood into little ones.

Amy came to a standstill, and her mouth dropped open. She might have drooled a little. Muffin barked.

And Dusty stopped swinging his ax. "What?" he asked.

"Uh, nothing...I mean, thanks for the sandwich and, uh, thanks for chopping wood...And..." She stopped, took a breath, and started again. "Mr. McNeil—Dusty—I get that Willow is paying you to be nice to me. But you shouldn't have taken the blame for the whole Sven debacle today. There wasn't anything wrong with the latch on the kennel. I went back there to get a three-pronged rake, and I saw Sven, and he looked sad and lonely. And I thought I needed to get over my fear of him, you know? And I also thought that maybe he and Muffin could be friends, and so I opened the gate, and the next thing I knew, Sven made a move on Muffin. He was all over her kind of like you were all over Ivory out on the terrace this afternoon. I had no idea that Sven was a doggie Casanova."

She ran out of words again just as she realized she'd been babbling.

He leaned the ax against the chopping block and took a few steps forward, displaying all the beautiful musculature of his chest, which, she noticed, also had a few golden hairs around the nipples. He reminded her of the Michelangelo statues Daddy had insisted she see during that trip to Italy they'd taken after Mom died. She hadn't been all that blown away by the marble, but in the flesh, Dusty sure did impress.

"I was not all over Ivory," he said.

"No?" Her spirits soared.

He shook his head. "Sven knocked her into me. And for the record, no one is paying me to be nice to you."

"Then why are you being so nice?"

Amy had just asked the question Dusty had been asking himself from the moment he'd taken the blame for the dog fiasco. Why the hell had he done it?

Simple answer: Amy Lyndon had settled down in the back of his mind like one of those commercial jingles that sticks with you. She was hard to forget. And he needed a distraction from the reappearance of his father in his life.

She stood with arms folded, looking adorably kick-ass in her goofy, oversized work clothes. So he took another step forward and stooped down to get to her eye level. Her breath hitched a little as he invaded her space, and she bit her lip. No doubt about it, the attraction was mutual. The dark, heavy-lidded look in Amy Lyndon's eyes gave him all the permission he needed to move in. Not that he needed permission—not even of a Lyndon.

He cupped her head and pulled her up into a kiss that he wanted to keep soft and reassuring. But the moment their lips touched, it morphed into something hot and confusing. Amy's kisses were immediately intoxicating. They blew his mind like the moonshine his grandpappy used to distill out in the woods down by Liberty Run. The first time Dusty tasted that stuff, it lit up the inside of his mouth and made him dizzy as hell.

Wow. She packed a wallop. The next thing he knew, she'd jumped right up into his arms, wrapped her legs around his middle, and pressed all her sexy soft spots into all his hard ones. He ran his hands down her backbone and stopped when he got to her sexy ass.

Her moan sounded like heavenly music, and he lost himself for a little bit, until Amy broke the kiss and locked gazes with him. "Is Willow paying you?"

"No. Shut up. That's insulting."

She cocked her head. "Is it?"

He pressed kisses along her cheek to her ear. "It is," he murmured. "I've been thinking about you this way ever since that morning when you lost your towel." He nuzzled the tender skin under her earlobe, and she pressed into his touch. "Because you turned me on that day."

"You're not just being nice?"

How could Amy Lyndon be so unsure of herself? She'd grown up with a silver spoon, been pampered and petted and kept safe all her life, and spoiled rotten. How could she not know her own worth?

Clearly she didn't, though, and that raised a whole passel of issues he didn't want to deal with. A guy like him shouldn't even think about messing around with a woman like her. She was way, way out of his league and didn't even realize it.

If he took this any further, it would be the same as taking advantage of her. And he couldn't do that. The women he hooked up with, like Zoe, were worldly and wise. Amy was neither of those things.

He gently pried her from his body and put her back on the ground. Then he took a giant step backward. "Amy, I'm sorry I started this. It's a mistake."

"No, it's not. We could—"

"Nope. We can't. And I better go." He pivoted.

"So it *is* true, then?" she said to his back. "They're paying you to be nice to me, right?"

"No!" he said over his shoulder before striding all the way to his truck without another backward glance. He was halfway down the mountain when he remembered that he'd left his ax and hadn't taught her how to burn all that wood he'd split.

Dammit. He hated the idea of her being cold and alone up on that ridge. But he hated the idea of her throwing herself at him even worse. She deserved a better man.

Mia and the crew departed for New York and the Kleinfeld shoot early Wednesday morning, leaving Daniel behind to deal with Mia's insistence that her groom and groomsmen be dressed in formal cutaway jackets and morning suits. Everyone in the family owned a tuxedo, but that wasn't good enough for Mia. She pointed out on numerous occasions that Kate Middleton's father wore a morning suit at her wedding, and nothing less would suit Mia, who increasingly saw herself as the princess bride.

Renting the morning suits would have been the cheapest way to go, but Mia wanted only the best. And since the producers refused to pay for handmade morning suits, Danny stepped up and offered to pay for them. So on Wednesday afternoon, he left Scarlett with her doting grandmother and met his brothers at one of the best bespoke tailors in downtown DC.

"So glad we're camera free," Jason said as the tailor measured his inseam.

"No one wants to see a guy getting measured for a suit, bro," Matt said as he checked e-mails on his smartphone. "And if you've seen one suit, you've pretty much seen them all, right? Not like wedding dresses."

The tailor lifted his head and gave Matt a long, sober stare, but Danny's brother missed it because he'd returned his attention to his phone. Danny had to agree with the tailor. At more than thirteen hundred dollars a pop, these suits were something special, but neither he nor his brothers had any need for a suit of morning clothes. He doubted any of them would wear the suits again, unless they followed in Uncle Thomas's footsteps and joined the diplomatic service. Or scored an invitation to Ascot.

"Do you have to rush back to Shenandoah Falls or is Mom okay to babysit?" Jason asked Danny.

"No. Mom's in heaven. I have the night off."

"You're sounding seriously pussy whipped, dude," Matt said, continuing to work his iPhone.

Danny refrained from responding. Matt was twenty-five and unattached, so he didn't understand fatherhood. Danny's love for his baby girl knew no bounds, and if that was the definition of being whipped, then so be it.

"Cool," Jason said. "Let's have dinner together."

"I'll text the gang," Matt said. "How 'bout we meet at Jack Rose for happy hour?"

"Who's the gang?" Danny asked.

"Andrew, Edward, Brandon, Grady, Laurie, and Roxy. You know, family, roommates, fiancées," Matt said.

"Is one of you engaged to Roxy?" Danny asked, surprised.

"No, but she's practically family," Jason said. "Brandon is the engaged one. You met Laurie the other day."

Jason held out his arms while the tailor took measurements. "Maybe we shouldn't invite Grady or the Kopps."

"Why not?" Matt asked, still studying his phone.

Jason rolled his eyes. "Because it might be awkward, that's why."

"Awkward how?" Matt asked.

"Because Amy turned Grady down. Let's just say it's a family thing."

"And what about next time? If Amy's too stupid to realize that Grady is a great guy, then that's her problem. Not that Amy is the brightest light in the chandelier, if you know what I mean." Matt finally raised his head.

Danny wanted to pull the damn iPhone out of his brother's hands, get right up in his face, and remind him that Amy belonged to the family and deserved respect. But he refrained. He'd come home to mend fences and rebuild the bridges he'd foolishly burned eight years ago. So popping his brother in the face was out.

But Jason evidently felt no such constraint. "You know, Matt," he said, "sometimes you're a total dickwad. Amy is family. You ought to stand by her."

"Yeah, and Grady is our landlord and friend. It's too late anyway. I've sent out texts to everyone. If you want my opinion, we should be trying to fix this thing with Amy and Grady."

"Are you out of your mind?" Danny asked. "When I talked to Amy yesterday, she wanted nothing to do with the guy."

"She's going through a phase," said Matt. "She'll get over it."

Danny wasn't so sure, but before he could make any judgments, he needed to meet this Grady guy. An hour and a half later he got his chance.

By the time Danny and his brothers finished with the tailor and arrived at Jack Rose, the "gang," as Matt and Jason referred to them, had already settled into a half-circle booth at the back of the trendy restaurant. Extra chairs had been drawn up for the large crowd, and Danny found himself sitting right beside Roxy Kopp and across from a guy with sandy brown hair and a receding hairline who, by process of elimination, must be Grady Carson.

Danny had been living in LA and Vegas for the last eight years, so naturally he judged Grady on the externals first. His narrow sloped shoulders, thin, mousy hair, and pale washed-out complexion screamed geek and nerd. He was squirrely, and everyone knew that a guy like that could catch a beautiful woman if he had a big enough stash of cash.

But apparently Amy couldn't overlook Grady's hairline or bad teeth, because she'd made it clear that Grady's millions didn't impress her. Either that, or Amy really was a dewy-eyed romantic who still believed in true love.

Danny had checked his innocence at the door when he'd moved to Tinseltown eight years ago, but somehow he couldn't help feeling that Amy deserved someone with a more vibrant personality. And after talking with Grady for five minutes, mostly about today's stock market developments, Danny concluded that Grady Carson had a personality like wet tissue paper.

Having satisfied himself that Amy was, as usual, smarter than anyone in the family gave her credit for, he turned to his right and proceeded to admire Roxy Kopp. In her gray suit and white silk blouse, she looked the epitome of the young DC professional. Danny especially liked her blouse. She'd unbuttoned the top few buttons, enough for a hint of lace to show at the V of her neckline.

Yeah, she had a chest. And it turned him on.

What was wrong with him? He was about to be married, and Roxanne Kopp was practically a member of the family. As a kid, she'd been a total pest, the absolute bane of his existence who'd tattled on him with impunity. Of course he'd picked on her unmercifully, teasing her, pulling her pigtails, and a lot of other stupid stuff. Roxy was so easy to bait, and getting her all flustered had been pretty amusing for a troublemaker like himself.

In fact, it might be fun to see her flustered now, as a full-grown woman.

He let that thought linger as he ogled her cleavage and then mentally backed away. Scarlett's father should behave like a gentleman, not a thirteen-year-old. The thought sobered him because he knew damn well that he was the closest thing to an adult in the crazy world that Scarlett had been born into.

So he leaned back and took a sip of his bourbon. "So, how've you been, Roxy?" he asked.

"Why don't we bypass the family chat, okay? You aren't interested in my dull and boring life." Roxy flipped her dark hair over her shoulder. Man, she was one beautiful woman. Why the hell didn't she have a steady boyfriend?

"I am interested in your life," Danny said. "Matt told me that you work for a nonprofit raising money for kids with disabilities. That sounds like a good cause to me."

She nodded. "Yeah. I guess I grew up to become a do-gooder. The truth is, I'm real good at hitting people up for money. And that's the beginning and end of it."

She gazed at her martini, the picture of a dissatisfied, unhappy woman. He wanted to explore that, to punch her buttons. "You haven't ever forgiven me for the frog incident, have you?" he asked.

She looked up, blinking. "I'm surprised you even remember it."

He laughed out loud and shook his head. "Roxy, you have no idea, do you?"

"About what?"

"I put that frog down your shirt hoping you'd get so freaked out that you'd take off your blouse. I had this deep need to see you naked from the waist up."

"What?" She straightened in her chair and stared at him for about fifteen seconds while a blush crawled up her face.

"I wanted to get that out in the open, you know, because I didn't pick on you because I hated you. I did it because I was a dickwad of a thirteen-year-old and you had a nice set of boobs even when you were only twelve."

"I have to go." She picked up her purse and dug in it for a moment, coming up with a twenty-dollar bill, which she placed on the table. Then she turned and headed through the crowded dining room.

Danny picked up the bill and followed her, catching her right before she slipped through the door. He handed the twenty back. "Your drink's on me. And you don't have to leave. I'm just being the same dickwad I always was."

Her coffee-colored eyes grew bright. "I hate it when you tease me, Danny. So please stop. And I can pay for my own drinks."

With that, she slipped through the door, leaving him standing there wanting more. But he couldn't follow. Scarlett depended on him, and he would never let his little girl down.

Chapter Eleven————————

Amy couldn't even manage to have a one-nighter with the Casanova of Shenandoah Falls without screwing it up. Had her kisses not been good enough for him? Or what?

She didn't buy his line about the consequences of hooking up. Since when does a Casanova ever think about consequences?

Like never.

It had to be the whole boss-employee thing, which could get complicated, and both of them needed their jobs. Still, his retreat had humiliated her.

So on Wednesday morning she braced herself for her first glimpse of him, sure that she'd get all tongue-tied and stupid. It would take a while to forget the taste of his mouth or the caress of his broad, working man's hands on her backside. Unfortunately, all that hotness was indelibly burned in her mind and libido. And while her mind could work on forgetting, her libido had a memory like a steel trap.

Her angst proved unnecessary because Mario informed her that Dusty had the day off. Mario didn't elaborate on the reasons, and Amy didn't want to ask too many questions. So her imagination ran wild.

Was he sick? Was he a coward? Was there a family emergency? Had Willow found out about the kisses and fired him as a babysitter? She wanted to know the details right now, but that wasn't in the cards.

So she shoved Tuesday's kiss to the back of her mind and concentrated on doing her job to the best of her ability. She spent a lovely spring morning pruning and raking, while also consulting the Jefferson County Library's field guide to shrubs. She managed to successfully identify half a dozen specimens.

She also gave Muffin a few leash-etiquette lessons at the same time. By lunch the dog had stopped pulling on her leash altogether, so Amy didn't worry about taking Muffin into the dining hall. The dog settled down at her feet and took a nap.

Amy had just taken her first taste of the baked ziti on today's menu when Courtney Wallace found her. "I gather from Dusty that you're the one who fixed the centerpieces for the Ganis-McQuade wedding last Saturday," Courtney said as she sat down in the chair across the table.

Oh great, that again. Couldn't a girl enjoy her lunch without being chewed out by someone? Apparently not. "I'm really sorry, Courtney. I thought I could help out, but clearly I—"

"Wait, what? You did help. You pulled my ass out of the fire. I'd called at least a dozen florists that day, and I couldn't find a yellow rose to save my life. I had been trying to come up with some plan to save the day when I went back to the workroom, only to discover that my prayers had been answered. The bride and her mother thought the addition of the forsythia was so dramatic. Where did you learn to arrange flowers like that?"

A deep, satisfying warmth percolated through Amy's midsection. "I don't know, exactly. My sorority sisters used to say I was a good improviser. But that's mostly because I'm a genius at screwing things up and have to constantly figure out fixes for all of my many disasters. The truth is, I may have fixed the centerpieces, but Mr. McNeil bawled me out for taking the daffodils from the pool house flower beds."

"Oh, don't worry about him," Courtney said with a dismissive wave of her hand. "Dusty's bark is worse than his bite. On the inside, he's a marshmallow. But don't get any romantic ideas. I know he's like some unholy cross between Brad Pitt and Heath Ledger, but he's commitment phobic. You should see the house he lives in. It's a tiny A-frame he built for himself after tearing down the old house he'd grown up in. It's just big enough for him and his fishing gear. I took one glance at that place and ran."

Crap. That was more information than Amy needed to know. Had Dusty hooked up with Courtney? If he'd done that, then why not with her? Or had he hooked up with Courtney before the two of them came to work for Willow?

Dammit, she wanted details. The more she thought about last night, the more insulted she became. Why the hell had he run away? What was wrong with her?

"So," Courtney said, leaning forward, pulling Amy from her obsessive thoughts, "I'm up to my eyeballs in weddings—especially your cousin's circus-themed extravaganza. I was thinking I could maybe ask Willow if you could help me out on some things."

Amy hesitated before responding. Up until today, Courtney had said maybe three words to her. Why suddenly was she sitting there suggesting that Amy could avoid working on the grounds crew?

"Let me think about it," Amy said carefully.

"Well, if you want me to, I'll put in a good word for you with Willow."

Could it be that Courtney's praise was genuine? It really seemed to be true. "Thanks," she said.

On that note, the rest of Amy's day floated past. By the time she settled down for bed, she'd learned the full Latin names of more than a dozen shrubs and trees, had trained Muffin to heel without the leash, and had managed to get a fire going in the woodstove.

On Thursday she decided to expand her dog training horizons. She grabbed her lunch on the run and headed out to the kennel where Sven spent his days. She had to pass the kennel numerous times during the day, getting or returning tools to the barn. And every time she passed the kennel's gate, Sven's loneliness made her feel sad.

Mario said that Dusty paid some attention to the dog, but for the most part, Sven spent his days alone until Natalie came home from school. And even then, Natalie had after-school activities that kept the dog from getting the attention he needed.

Amy approached the kennel carefully and opened the gate only wide enough to let her and Muffin pass, so this time Sven didn't escape. Besides, the dog seemed happy to have human and doggie company.

It was funny. Amy had completely lost her fear of the dog once she'd come to realize that his bad behavior stemmed from his loneliness. She decided right on the spot that she would do something about that by eating her lunch here with him every day.

She did more than eat lunch on Thursday. She worked on some of the lessons from the dog training book, and after an hour of playing fetch and working with both dogs, she had Sven sitting on command. He still had trouble with "stay" and "heel," but it was a start.

She made sure both dogs had water and left Muffin in the kennel to keep Sven company before she reported to Mario for her next assignment. Dusty still hadn't returned to work, and no one on staff seemed to know why.

Was he staying away because of her? Amy didn't think so. He must be sick.

A weird desire to make him some chicken soup settled into her head and heart. Not that she'd ever made chicken soup, except for heating up the kind that came from a can, but still.

The more she thought about it, the more she wanted Dusty's kindness to be genuine and not something bought and paid for. So maybe she should repay his kindness with some of her own.

In the wee hours of Wednesday morning, Curtis Warner, the owner of the Broken Spoke Roadhouse, had awakened Dusty from a not-very-deep sleep to let him know that Daddy had gotten himself into a brawl and landed himself in the Winchester hospital.

Daddy deserved a comeuppance at the hands of a younger and meaner biker dude, but Dusty found no comfort in that. He called in sick and hightailed it to the hospital like the dutiful son he wanted to be, consumed by guilt and worry.

And right on cue, Daddy used that guilt like a weapon, blaming Dusty for his concussion, broken collarbone, and fractured radius. Daddy always blamed Dusty for everything that went wrong in his sorry-assed life.

The cops claimed they were still searching for the guy who'd beaten the crap out of Daddy, but Dusty doubted that Chief LaRue gave a rat's ass about anyone with the last name of McNeil. So it was unlikely that Daddy's assailant would be brought to justice.

The Winchester Medical Center had kept Daddy overnight on Wednesday, long enough for the docs to poke and prod him further and discover that Daddy had a failing liver, diabetes, high blood pressure, bad cholesterol, and a dozen other ailments that needed meds and attention. So when the hospital finally released him early Thursday morning, Dusty had no other choice but to call in sick for a second day and bring the old man home. He settled him down in the Murphy bed that took up every square inch of his tiny living room.

"You know, there would be room for me if you hadn't torn down the old house," the old man whined at least twenty times in the first two hours of his convalescence.

Dusty didn't want his father home on a permanent basis, no matter how his conscience tweaked. He'd scheduled an appointment for Friday with a Jefferson County social worker. Since Daddy was older than sixty-five and had nowhere to go, Dusty hoped the county could find him a place in a nursing home, or maybe a drug treatment program.

And if Daddy couldn't qualify for long-term care under

Medicaid, then Dusty would have to face reality—sell his land and use the money to set up a trust or something to help his father for a while. He figured Jamie Lyndon might be interested in buying the property at a price equal to what the county might give him. Then Jamie could deed the land to the county for a park, get a huge tax deduction, and once again be hailed as the town's biggest philanthropist.

Dusty was up in his loft, hunched over a computer screen reading about Wyoming and seriously thinking about bailing out on his current life, when someone pulled into his driveway. The sound of tires on gravel served as Dusty's doorbell out here in the meadow by the stream.

He scooted down the narrow staircase and around the bed where Daddy snored, fast asleep on the painkillers he'd been prescribed. Dusty opened his front door to find Amy Lyndon and her dog, Muffin, standing on the deck. She carried a paper grocery sack in one arm and had changed out of her baggy clothes and back into those holey jeans she'd been wearing the first day on the job—jeans that hugged her body a whole lot tighter than those ridiculous pants.

The spit dried up in his mouth, and lust pooled deep behind his navel. She was precisely the diversion he needed from the sucky mess his life had suddenly become.

He stepped through the door and shut it behind him.

"Hi," she said with unmistakable concern in her voice. He warmed to that tone and lost himself in the spark that burned deep in her dark chocolate eyes.

"You look tired," she said. "Did you catch Mario's stomach flu? I brought chicken soup."

He almost laughed out loud. "You made chicken soup for me?"

"Uh, well." She cocked her head to one side. "I didn't

exactly make it. But it turns out that two cans of chicken soup were affordable...barely. But tomorrow is payday, right? And besides, I owe you for the dog leash and food, and an apology for thinking that you were only being nice to me because Willow was paying you. So a couple of cans of chicken soup is really small, you know? As a way to show my appreciation for your kindness."

Except it wasn't small at all. He figured she'd probably spent half of her cash on hand for a couple cans of soup. And for some reason, the magnitude of that generosity blew him away. He stood there not really knowing how to respond.

He ought to send her home. But he didn't want to.

"I know," she said on a sigh. "You probably don't want me hanging around. But honestly, I'm not one of those women. I don't think I have any sort of hold on you because of what happened on Tuesday when you came to chop wood. I was worried because no one at the inn seemed to know why you needed two days off, and I..." She stopped abruptly. "I'm babbling, aren't I?"

He stepped forward and plucked the bag from her arms. "Thank you. I'm not sick, but I appreciate your kindness."

He stared down into her big brown eyes for a long, breathless moment, feeling like a goofball teenager who'd just discovered the opposite sex. How the hell did Amy Lyndon manage to scramble his brains every time he looked into her eyes? Right now he just wanted to strip her naked and bury himself in her.

She'd be the perfect diversion, but he couldn't do that. Not with Daddy here.

"What's the matter?" she asked softly.

He ground his teeth as the urge to tell her about Daddy's

return came over him, almost as if he'd been waiting for someone to come knocking on his door asking if he might need help. Sharing his feelings about Daddy wasn't something he did on a regular basis.

But instead of blowing her off, he said, "It's my daddy," and his voice wobbled. He needed to get a grip.

"Oh no. Is he okay?"

"Yes. No. It's complicated."

"I can heat soup, and you can tell me. I'm sure I can relate to difficult father issues."

He almost laughed. "I doubt it, Amy."

"Okay, but I'm a good listener. People tell me that all the time. I think it's because I don't usually have much to say, you know?"

Except when she babbled like a brook. That thought worked its way right through the worry and the anger and the guilt that had swallowed him up the last couple of days. "I got a better idea," he said. "Let's go to your place and start a fire and heat up the soup."

She blinked up at him. "Courtney told me you lived in one of those tiny houses that only had room enough for one person. But it doesn't look that small."

"It only appears larger because you're so small. Trust me, we don't want to hang out here."

"Okay. Let's go build a fire. But for the record, I built one for myself yesterday. I don't know if I did it right, but it burned okay."

He had to stifle another laugh. "Honey, I think you have the potential to be a great fire starter, among many other things."

Chapter Twelve————————

Amy had to coax the story out of Dusty. About how his father had gotten into a fight and ended up in the hospital. About how his father was sick and needed a place to stay. He spoke about his father in a monotone, as if he were trying to hide his feelings, but Amy could see the deep emotions shining from his troubled baby blues like a neon light.

"What are you not telling me?" she asked as they sat at the small table in the cabin's tiny kitchen, empty soup bowls between them.

Dusty cocked his head. "What makes you think there's more?"

"Because there is." She brazenly touched the back of his hand. His skin, warm and rough beneath her fingers, sent a sexual rush through her. She wanted him to turn his palm over so she could hold his hand.

Instead he pulled back as if she'd scalded him. "You don't know a thing about me." He dropped his hand into his lap.

"That's true. But I'd like to know more."

"About my father? There's nothing much to know. He's a bastard and a drunk. And don't think just because your daddy locked you out of the house that you have some deeper understanding of my life. You don't."

"I never said I did. So, does that mean your father locked you out of the house when you were younger?"

He let go of a long, deep sigh, as if he were exhaling all the trouble in the world. "Yeah, he did, all the time, whenever he got drunk. Willow's mom used to watch out for me. I crashed at the Jaybird Café all the time, and sometimes out at her farm. And sometimes I had to make a fire in the old warehouse and sleep there on the dirty floor in a sleeping bag.

"But I got the last laugh, or so I thought. I bought him out eight years ago and kicked him out of his own house. I handed him more than a hundred grand in cash, and it was worth every penny because I thought he'd go and never come back. God alone knows what he did with that money, but he sure came running the minute he read Sally Hawkes's article in the *Winchester Daily.*"

"He came back because of that?"

"Yeah. He thinks he's entitled to a payday even though the land's no longer in his name." Dusty paused for a long moment, giving Amy a deep, sober glance that melted her heart. "I've spent my whole life trying to convince folks that I'm not my father. And I've failed. This whole fight with the county is all because of who I am. If I had a different last name, do you think the Jefferson

County Historical Society would've come up with their plan? No. And that's the point. As far as anyone is concerned, I'm white trash."

"That's crap, Dusty. Everyone at Eagle Hill Manor respects you. A lot."

"Maybe, but that's just a handful of people." He shoved back from the table and stood. "Amy, you'll never know how much I appreciate the fact that you spent your last couple of dollars on this soup. But I really shouldn't be here with you. I should get going."

"No, wait. I get that you think you shouldn't be here because you're my boss. And if that was your reason for walking away from me on Tuesday, I'll accept it. But if you walked away because you think you're not good enough for me, that's just BS."

Dusty replied with silence.

"Damn it all. Why is it that the entire world wants to treat me with kid gloves? I can't even have a no-strings, bad-boy experience without the bad boy himself getting all noble on me."

"Amy, don't be ridiculous."

She got up and moved to stand right in front of him. "I. Am. Not. Ridiculous. I'm so tired of people accusing me of that. If you respect me, don't treat me like I don't have a brain in my head. Treat me like you treat any other woman."

They stood there for a long moment staring into each other's eyes while a coil of sexual desire twisted through Amy. Did she dare go after what she wanted?

Would he let her?

There was only one way to find out.

He started to turn away, but she grabbed him, lacing

her hands behind his neck. "So, you said something about teaching me to make a fire."

She pulled his head down to her level. He gave her only token resistance, and when their lips met, his resistance vanished, and the kiss, which started as a soft dance of lips and tongues, turned hard and hot.

She leaned all the way into his rock-hard chest as his hands came down to her hips and pulled her close. His noble reticence fled as he pressed himself against her, cupping his broad palms on her butt like a proper bad boy should. She groaned out loud at the delicious sensations his touch unleashed.

And then Dusty took charge.

He hitched her up as if she weighed nothing and flipped her so that she was cradled in his arms. "Before we take this to the next level, Amy, I need to make it clear that no one is paying me to be nice to you, okay? And right now I'm not really thinking about being nice at all."

His words set off a riot of anticipation inside her, especially when he strode off in the direction of the cabin's bedroom. Now, this was more like it. A Casanova needed to take charge.

"I like naughty," she said.

"Really?"

She nodded. "I have lots of fantasies about stuff."

"Why does this not surprise me," he said in a dry tone, and then followed with, "I like a woman with a good imagination."

He carried her into the bedroom and gently put her down on her feet, and then he cupped her head and started with the kisses again. His tongue knew things about kissing that Amy had never experienced before. Everywhere he touched, her cells came alive as if they'd been living a pretend life until right this minute. He awakened her in every sense of the word.

But when he freed her from her shirt and bra and got a good, long look at her puny breasts, she braced for his disappointment. Dusty was too kind to say anything, but...

Oh, wait. He put his talented tongue to work on those nonexistent breasts and ignited an all-consuming lust that almost took her away right then and there. She groaned out loud, and damned if he didn't answer her with one of his own.

He was turned on. For real. Wow.

The idea that she could turn on a guy like Dusty McNeil gave her a strange sense of power she'd never known before. She didn't have to wait for him. She didn't have to play this any way other than the way she wanted it. She didn't have to be nice or restrained or quiet.

So she tackled his belt and his zipper like a kid set loose in a candy store. He let her play while he deftly freed her from her jeans. Eventually he picked her up and tossed her on the bed like she weighed nothing. He followed after and proceeded to make every one of her bad-boy fantasies come true.

Dusty was gone in the morning, and Amy told herself she didn't want it any other way. A girl couldn't expect more than what she'd gotten from the Casanova of Shenandoah Falls. But he hadn't gone without leaving her something. Not a sappy note, but a fire burning in the woodstove.

And that was fine. She didn't need sappy notes. She'd gotten everything she needed from him, and she hoped she'd given him something back. Maybe a little space, given the father issues he was working through.

Still, there was the whole boss-employee issue between them, and Amy didn't quite know how she would react to him at work, so she was relieved when Courtney pulled her away from the grounds crew almost as soon as she arrived at the inn on Friday morning. Instead of raking and weeding, Amy spent the morning working on the flower arrangements in the chapel and didn't come face-to-face with Dusty until lunchtime, when he sneaked up on her in the dog kennel.

"I've been searching all over the place for you," he said in that deep voice of his.

She turned to find him leaning against the chain-link fence in a loose-limbed male stance that immediately fired up her hormones. Damn, it almost hurt to gaze upon all that tanned, golden-haired goodness. She almost had to squint when he smiled out of the corner of his mouth and his baby blues lit up like a Broadway billboard.

"It's payday," he said. "Did you forget?"

Damn. She had forgotten. How could she forget? After she bought the chicken soup yesterday, she had only four dollars and a couple of pennies left—not even enough to do all her laundry at the coin wash.

Dusty held up an envelope. "It ain't much, honey, but you've earned it. Courtney is raving about you. Mario wants to adopt you as his daughter. And it's clear that Sven thinks you are a dog-obedience goddess."

She wanted to ask him what he thought about her, but that would be out of line. And probably immature. She didn't need to beg for compliments from him. After all, she'd earned respect from Mario and Courtney without sleeping with them.

Still, somehow his opinion of her mattered more than anything.

So she turned her back while she checked Sven and Muffin's water bowls, which were already full, and gathered her composure before she ducked through the kennel's door. "I've been leaving Muffin here with Sven to keep him company. I hope that's okay, because the kennel is really big. And I was thinking that Willow ought to advertise it, you know? Like for guests who want to bring their dogs on vacation. Maybe she could hire someone to be the doggy day care person. Like a cruise director for canines. Someone who could make up games and train them and, I don't know, do fun stuff."

She was babbling again. Damn.

"I see you've gotten over your fear of dogs."

"Yeah, I guess. I had a bad experience when I was little."

"Here." He handed her the paycheck, and their fingers inadvertently brushed in the exchange. A shock wave of lust traveled up her arm and right to her nipples. Good thing her oversized Eagle Hill Manor golf shirt hid the reaction, but she could have sworn that Dusty noticed anyway. He hesitated for a moment while his ears turned an adorable shade of red and his baby blues darkened. Wow. She'd made Casanova blush.

You'd think, after all the stuff they'd done to each other last night, they'd be satisfied. They'd be over it. But no. Apparently not. They hovered for a long moment as a force as old as time pulled and tugged at them. Amy's pulse rate climbed as their mouths moved slowly toward each other.

Her girl parts began to anticipate the kiss, and a surge of excitement rushed through her.

And then an unwanted and thoroughly recognizable voice interrupted. "Amy, where the heck are you hiding? You can't really be back here with the dogs," Aunt Pam shouted from somewhere around the corner near the front of the barn.

Dusty jumped away from Amy so fast that by the time Aunt Pam rounded the corner and came into sight, he'd turned his back and was walking away. That had been a very close call, and all the more troubling because Willow followed in Pam's wake, wearing an unhappy expression that turned darker still when she encountered Dusty on the path. They exchanged an ominous glance fraught with meaning.

Uh-oh. Not good, especially when Willow turned to watch Dusty as he continued on his way toward the entrance to his office with a frown on her face.

As usual, Aunt Pam had missed the exchange entirely. Amy steeled herself for Pam's inevitable comment about her dirty clothes.

"Amy, enough is enough. I'm desperate for your help."

Wow. No comment about the dirt? She had definitely come up in the world. Since when had Pam ever been desperate for anyone's help, much less hers? "You need *my* help?" Amy asked, her words laced with genuine surprise.

"It's Danny," Pam said in a flat voice.

"What, is he okay?" Worry pooled in Amy's stomach. Danny might be misguided, but she loved him with all her heart.

"He's fine physically. But that woman is about to drive us all crazy with her wedding plans. Thank God she and her girlfriends have decided to stay in New York for the weekend. Which is why I need you. We have the whole weekend to talk Danny out of this wedding. And I can't think of anyone better than you to make this happen. He listens to you."

"No, he doesn't. Not on this score. I already told him not to marry someone he doesn't love."

"What?" Pam's eyes almost bugged right out of her head. "Amy, don't be ridiculous. Of course they have to get married. They have a child together."

"So?" Amy tucked the envelope with her pay into her back pocket.

"My God, Amy, do I have to explain the way the world works to you?"

Amy pressed her lips together and refrained from getting all up into Aunt Pam's face. No one in her family thought she had a brain in her head. No one thought she could manage on her own. No one valued her in the least. She was a problem everyone wanted to solve, and she hated it.

And maybe that's why Dusty McNeil attracted her. He'd allowed her to be someone else last night—a naughty, worldly girl who could choose to indulge her fantasies without strings. What's more, Dusty McNeil knew all about her shortcomings and her ignorance about some things. But he didn't think she was stupid. And he trusted her to do things for him and for herself. Hell, he'd even sent her out snipe hunting—an activity that had forced her to face a lot of her fears. And even if she'd failed to catch the snipe, the experience had been worth it.

So really, if she was so ridiculous, why had Pam come seeking her help?

Her courage fully stoked, Amy turned on her aunt. "I'm sure there's some law in California or Nevada that would allow Danny to legally claim Scarlett as his child. And I'm sure he and Mia can work out some kind of custody arrangement. He doesn't need a marriage license to be financially responsible for the baby. And I got the impression that the only way he got Mia to agree to marry him was to put the whole thing on television. Besides, it's pretty clear that she's only marrying Danny for the TV ratings and his trust fund. She could care less about him. Or Scarlett. And Danny doesn't love her either."

"Amy, what has gotten into you?"

"Nothing," she said, swallowing back a million things she wanted to say out loud but couldn't. "But I don't have time to help you, Aunt Pam. Lunch is over, and Mario has me scheduled to plant a few *Rhododendron ferrugineum* in the new bed down by the chapel." The Latin rolled off her tongue as if she'd been saying it all her life.

She turned and started down the path, but Willow stopped her. "Did Dusty teach you those plant names?" she asked.

Amy shook her head and pulled the Jefferson County Library's field guide to trees and shrubs out of her back pocket. "Nope. I figured it out from this book. And I really need to thank you for the job, Willow. I love it. I love getting dirty. I love being outside all the time. I love working with flowers and plants. And dogs. Who knew I had secret talents for gardening and dog training?"

Pam's face paled. "Amy Jessica Lyndon, are you out of your mind? A gardener? Really? That's beneath you. All of this is beneath you. Don't you realize that?"

Amy gave her aunt a long stare. "No, I guess I don't.

But then you know me. I'm dumb and ordinary, and I always screw things up. All of that is probably true, but one thing isn't, Aunt Pam. I am not ridiculous. I know how things work.

"Like, for example, I know Danny has been brainwashed like everyone else in the family. He's determined to do the right thing for Scarlett and marry Mia whether he loves her or not. Just like Daddy married Mom. Just like Uncle Charles married Aunt Julie. It's a pattern in this family. Everyone gets married for the wrong reasons, and the kids have to put up with it. I feel sorry for Scarlett. She's going to have to live in a house where her parents hardly speak, and I know what that's like." She stopped when her voice wavered, surprised by the hurt that still lived down deep.

Amy turned her back and took several steps before she realized that her last statement needed one small amendment. She stopped and turned. "Uh, Willow, what I just said? It doesn't apply to you and David. You guys really love each other, and Natalie is a lucky little girl." She glanced at Pam. "If you want to know what I want, Aunt Pam, it's not Grady Carson and his fat bank account. I want what Willow and David have. I want someone who loves me for who I am, brown hair, flat chest, dirty clothes, and all."

Chapter Thirteen

Willow strolled into Dusty's office and settled into the chair beside his desk. "I don't mean to pry, but what's going on? You never miss a day of work."

Dusty scrubbed his hands over his jaw and filled her in on his father's return, the fight down at the roadhouse, Daddy's injuries and maladies, and the fact that the old man seemed to think he was entitled to more money.

He blew out a long sigh. "And I'm stuck. I can't kick him out because he's hurt. I've got him sleeping on the Murphy bed for now, but I have an appointment with a social worker this evening. To be honest with you, I just want to dump him somewhere, sell the land, and run away."

Willow had the good sense not to say a single word. They sat together in silence for a long while, like they used to do when they were kids. Willow had always been there to listen, never to pass judgment, and always ready to come to his defense or beg him a bed at the run-down farm where she'd grown up.

"Where would you go?" she finally asked in a soft, heartbreaking voice.

"I've been thinking about Montana or Wyoming. Fishing's good, and there aren't a whole lot of people up there."

"No, I guess not, just a lot of snow in the winter. What about your plans?"

"You mean for the *resort*?"

She smiled. "I know you hate that word. I was merely suggesting that you market your fishing camp as a resort because it sounds better. It's all in the marketing, Dusty. And to that end, I sent you a whole bunch of information on how to write a business plan. Did you get my e-mails?"

He nodded.

"Are you going to do something about them?"

"I don't know." He shook his head.

"I'd hate it if you moved to Montana. I'd miss you."

"I'd miss you, too, but I have no clue what to do about Daddy."

"I do."

"What?"

"Kick him out the way he kicked you out."

"But—"

"I know. It's cruel. It's unkind. And you're one of the kindest people I know. But you can't back away from your fight with the Historical Society. I won't let you. And I won't let you give all your money to that man. It's not right. It's not fair."

"I can't kick him out."

"Okay. I guess I understand. But promise me you won't

go running off to Montana. I need you. Which is another reason I darkened your door."

"If you're here to ask me if I'll re-landscape the grounds so that reality-show girl can get a long camera shot, we're likely to come to blows."

"That's not why I'm here. I'm here about Amy. Pam is really putting the screws to David about her, and David thinks I'm being mean making her work on the grounds crew when she's so obviously not suited for it. And then Brianna quit yesterday when Courtney had one of her profanity explosions. It wasn't directed at Brianna, but I gather Brianna is a born-again Christian, which probably disqualifies her from working with Courtney, the f-bomb queen. Courtney desperately needs an assistant, and for reasons that have everything to do with Amy's quick thinking last Saturday, Courtney wants Amy for the job. And since Pam would prefer that Amy work inside, you can see my problem."

"So you're here to tell me you're reassigning Amy?"

"I would have thought you'd be thrilled." The expression on Willow's face was easier to read than even the big letters on the eye charts at the eye doctor.

"Does she want to be reassigned?" he asked, trying to keep his cool.

"I don't know. Given that she's learning the Latin names of plants and has told Pam that she likes gardening, probably not. But, honestly, I don't see Amy as a gardener long term. Do you?"

Willow's eyebrow arched, and she leaned forward and gave him her what-kind-of-idiot-do-you-take-me-for look.

"I had no idea she was learning plant names. But that's the way she is. She throws herself into things body and soul. You know?"

Willow shook her head. "No, I don't know. According to David, Amy is a spoiled featherbrain without aim or purpose or even strong opinions about much. Although a minute ago she stood up to Pam, and I almost found myself applauding her."

"Let's face it, Willow. We both adore David, but he's never been one of the most observant guys in the world."

"He says everyone in the family thinks she's a lightweight. Until a minute ago I shared that opinion. How on earth did I miss her steel backbone?"

"Maybe because she hid it under her designer clothes. Maybe you had to strip her naked or something to see it." His mind wandered back to last night. Oh yeah, she had a really nice naked bod.

"Have you seen her naked?" Willow asked.

"Was that a rhetorical question?"

"Dammit, I told you to stay the hell away from her. She's your employee, and—" Willow jumped up from the chair and started pacing. "If David ever finds out you played around with his cousin, he's going to punch you in the nose."

"Why?"

Willow turned and made eye contact. "Do you want me to lay it out for you?"

"No, please don't. Believe it or not, I get how you'd be concerned about sexual harassment or whatever, assuming I *played around* with Amy as you put it. But why would David be so upset? Are you saying I'm not good enough for her?"

"Come on, Dusty, stand down. This has nothing to do with status. It has to do with the fact that you don't ever commit—to anyone. You string women along, and you break their hearts. Amy is innocent and sweet and, oh, I don't know, ditzy or something. She would be easy to hurt."

"She's not ditzy. Amy is smart as a whip; she just sees the world differently. I don't even know how to explain it."

Willow stopped pacing. "You like her."

"Of course I do. What's not to like about someone who rescues an abandoned dog and gives it her whole heart? Or someone who . . . ?" He stopped before he mentioned the two cans of chicken soup she'd bought for him with almost her last dollar.

Willow said nothing but stared at him as if he'd lost his mind.

"Maybe you never realized it until today, but Amy has a lot more grit than most people think," he said into the silence.

Willow sat down again and leaned forward on the edge of his desk. "Wow. I never thought any woman would ever get to you."

"Get to me? What's that supposed to mean?"

"It's supposed to mean that you care about her."

"I do care about her. But not the way you think."

Willow shook her head. "No, Dusty, you're lying to yourself. You've slept with her, haven't you?"

He said nothing, and his silence spoke the truth.

"If you break her heart, Pam and David will never forgive you. And I might have to fire you."

"I'm not going to break her heart. I'm pretty sure it's made of unbreakable steel, same as her backbone. If she were that easy or that dumb, she would have gone off with that guy everyone wants her to marry. But near as I can tell, Amy isn't interested in any long-term relationships. With anyone."

"No?"

"Absolutely not."

"I'm sorry, Dusty, but you're wrong. She just gave an impassioned speech about how much she wanted to find someone who loves her, and you're not that man. So for your own good as well as hers, I'm going to reassign her. And I want you to keep your distance."

He nodded. "Sure, whatever." But something down deep in his chest hitched. He would miss Amy's ready smile and her baggy pants and the sweet, hot, crazy things she dreamed up between the sheets.

"You need to promise me, okay? I'm not kidding. You can't make Amy Lyndon your girl of the moment. If her father finds out you've been sleeping with her, he won't be happy, and Jamie Lyndon has the means to do terrible damage to your life. He could easily give a donation to the county that would allow them to move forward with the park plan. You don't want that to happen, do you? You need to get going on that business plan and give the county an alternative."

He nodded. "Yeah, I get it. I promise."

Amy spent most of the day working on the new landscape being installed at the Laurel Chapel's cemetery. She had just finished planting a rhododendron when Willow and Courtney came strolling down the path from the manor house, dressed like well-put-together professionals.

"Wow," Willow said. "The new plantings look wonderful. You've done a nice job."

"Yeah, well, Dusty planned the bed, and Mario dug the

holes. I just put the plants in the ground," Amy said, brushing the dirt off her baggy work pants, which now sported holes in both knees. Her golf shirt dripped sweat, and black earth rimmed her broken fingernails. She was a mess, but she stood straight-shouldered and proud of the labor she'd put in today.

"Is there something you need me to do?" Amy asked.

Courtney grinned like the Cheshire cat. Willow not so much. In fact, Willow's expression suggested that Amy was in need of pity, or maybe an intervention. Crap.

"I have some good news," Willow said without a smile. "You know that event planner job you wanted? Well, it's—"

"Brianna quit on me, and I'm desperate for help," Courtney interrupted, her eyes sparkling with excitement. "And I think you'd be perfect for the job. You have mad skills with cut flowers, and I'm sure you'd much rather work with centerpieces than haul chairs or plant shrubs. I need you, Amy. I'm overwhelmed with too many things to do."

Courtney's words lit a little fire inside Amy. No one had ever wanted or needed her before. A week ago, she would have jumped at this opportunity, but the look on Willow's face argued for caution. Something was up. "Did Aunt Pam put you up to this?"

Willow shook her head. "No. I know she hates the idea of you working on the grounds crew and would be pleased if I moved you into event planning, but I'm offering this job to you because you've earned it. Courtney came to me the minute Brianna quit to ask if you could be promoted."

Amy glanced at the smiling Courtney. She would have hugged her right there if she hadn't been all sweaty and covered in dirt. Still, for some reason, she didn't want to say yes to this offer. She needed to prove something to *Mister McNeil*, even if she'd slept with Dusty. And there was always the chance that, regardless of what Willow said, Aunt Pam had manipulated this.

"What if I told you I wanted to continue working on the grounds crew?" Amy asked.

"I'd say you were insane," Courtney responded. "The planner job is permanent, and it pays better. Plus you don't have to wear baggy pants and work boots and you can go out after work to the Jaybird for happy hour without taking a shower."

Willow gave Courtney one of those I'm-the-boss looks. "Um, Court, could you give me a minute here?"

Courtney leaned in toward Amy. "You need to take this job, okay? I'm not going to take no for an answer, no matter what Willow says." Then Courtney turned toward Willow. "I'll be inside checking on the altar flowers. But don't let her say no."

When the chapel's front doors had closed behind Courtney, Willow folded her arms and assumed the stance of a woman who intended to have her way. "I need you to take this job," she said.

"You *need* me to take it or you *want* me to take it? There's a huge difference."

"Let me rephrase. I'd like you to take the job. Courtney would be overjoyed to have you—and that's saying something because she goes through assistants like some people go through M&M's. The event planner job isn't easy either. You'll work your ass off, and there's a ton of stress that goes with it. But Courtney wants you, and that's important to me."

What? Wait. No one had ever expressed that much faith in her abilities. Willow had to be lying. So Amy folded her arms over her chest and mirrored Willow's badass posture. "Am I getting this job because the family thinks I'm too good to be a gardener?"

Willow's mouth quirked at the corner. "Absolutely not. I don't look down on people who work with their hands, Amy. My own mother is a farmer, and I spent a lot of time shoveling goat manure in my time. Besides, I value everyone who works here, from the front desk to the grounds crew."

"Okay, I believe you. But the family wants me to give up this job. And there's a small part of me that doesn't want to, just to prove something to Daddy when he gets back from his vacation."

"Amy," Willow said in a commanding tone, "is this reticence on your part about putting your father in his place? Or is it about impressing Dusty McNeil? Because if it's either of those reasons, then you're probably making a mistake. I'm offering you a stepping-stone to a career where you could excel. Think about what *you* want for *you*, not what anyone else wants or expects of you. If you truly want to become a gardener, then go for it. I won't stand in your way. But I don't think that's what you really want."

Amy continued to stand her ground. "Did you pay Mr. McNeil to be nice to me?"

"Of course not. What gave you that idea? Besides, he hasn't exactly been nice to you."

"Yes, he has."

Willow shook her head. "Amy, I know he's handsome and charming at times. But the fact that he sent you on a snipe hunt means he doesn't exactly respect you."

"You know about the snipe hunt? He told me not to tell—"

"I'm not surprised that Dusty didn't want me to know," Willow said. "But he happened to mention the hunt to David, and David told me all about it. But here's the thing. There is no such animal as a snipe. A snipe hunt is a prank someone plays on a naive and uninformed person. It's a huge sign of disrespect."

"There's no such thing as a snipe?"

"No. So if Dusty has been nice to you since the snipe hunt, it's probably because he feels guilty. Dusty's a careful man and he's already locked in a battle with your aunt Pam over his land. The last thing he needs is to tick off your father or anyone else in the Lyndon family, including my husband."

How could Amy have been so stupid? Her stomach cramped up, and the muscles along her shoulders quivered while anger corkscrewed through her. How could he have fooled her? Easy. She'd been thinking with her hormones, not her brain.

"Okay, I guess you have a point about Mr. McNeil," Amy said in a tight voice. "I'll take the job."

❧

A kind of madness seized the staff at Eagle Hill Manor on Saturdays, especially in the spring. Every Saturday was a wedding day for at least one bride, and sometimes two, depending on the size and timing of each wedding.

Amy's first day on the job as an assistant event coordinator was a Saturday. Courtney was super busy with all kinds of details, but she put Amy in charge of the Carriage

House setup for the Leblanc-Afolayan wedding, a one-hundred-and-fifty-guest affair with a spring-garden theme.

Amy spent hours working with the waitstaff on setting up the tables and futzing with the centerpieces—tall twenty-four-inch-high crystal vases each filled with three dozen white tulips. That added up to six hundred stems in all, which had been shipped from a tulip supplier in Holland in plastic shipping boxes filled with water. Amy had to make sure each vase looked appropriately casual, as if the tulips had been freshly cut and just tossed into the vase. It took a lot of time to make sure each blossom draped appropriately.

Each round table had one of the tall centerpieces and six smaller crystal vases filled with white carnations—more than a thousand of them. And once the flowers were in place, a hundred and fifty etched-glass votive candles had to be distributed among fourteen tables and a dais.

Courtney gushed over the flowers when she came to check on Amy, and her approval made Amy feel all grown up and competent in a way she'd never felt before.

"You are such a godsend," Courtney said, giving her a warm hug. "I knew I didn't have to worry about anything here. The room looks gorgeous. I only wish the bride looked as nice."

"What's the matter?"

"Boob drama." Courtney rolled her eyes. "Honestly, you would think that a bride would check to make sure that her underwear and wedding dress are compatible before the wedding day. But no, Megan bought a gorgeous lace bra for her gorgeous lace dress, but the bra shows above the neckline. And, unfortunately, Megan is not what I'd call well endowed. She can't go braless, and while her bikini bra doesn't show above the neckline, she can't wear a swimsuit under her wedding dress. She's sent her sister off to the Victoria's Secret store in Tysons with instructions to buy every A-cup push-up demi bra in the store."

"Why?"

Courtney frowned. "Because she doesn't fill out the dress without—"

"I know. I heard you. But she doesn't need another bra. All she needs is some duct tape and maybe a pair of socks."

"What?"

Amy grinned. "Courtney, I know every boob hack there is. When you're born with nothing on top, you figure these things out. Go tell the bride to relax. I'll be up in just a minute."

She hurried out the French doors and headed for the barn. For the last week, she'd been in and out of the warehouse where the garden tools and equipment were stored. Mario had a special shelf with electrical tape, masking tape, painter's tape, and lots and lots of duct tape in various colors, including bridal white. A business like Eagle Hill Manor needed duct tape on a daily basis for all kinds of things.

This might be the first time it was needed for a bride's cleavage.

She hurried into the building and came face-to-face with the last person she wanted to see.

"What are you doing here?" Dusty asked, and then he gave her a slow up-and-down look, as if he didn't quite know what to make of her all dressed up. The look unleashed her hormones. So annoying given the fact that their relationship was based on his pity.

"I need some duct tape," she said, raising her chin.

"For what?"

Heat climbed up her face. He did not need to know the true reason. "I need it for the table linens," she said, improvising.

"What's wrong with the table linens?"

"They're slipping. Look, I'm in a hurry. Are you going to guard your duct tape like a mean dog with a bone or are you going to work with me here?" She put her hands on her hips.

His mouth twitched, as if he were laughing at her. "No, no problem. Take as much duct tape as you need."

She snatched a roll of the white tape. "Thanks."

She turned, and even though a part of her wanted to glance at him over her shoulder, she forced herself to put one foot in front of the other. Dammit all. Why did he have to be so handsome and sexy?

She pushed that impossible question out of her mind and scooted into the library and up the grand stairway to the Churchill Suite, where Megan Leblanc, the flat-chested bride, was holed up with her bridesmaids and her mother.

Amy knocked on the door, and Courtney answered. "Um, they're in a snit right now. I might have mentioned duct tape, and that suggestion was met with more than a little skepticism. Are you sure you know what you're doing?"

So much for Courtney having faith in her. Well, this wouldn't be the first time no one believed her. She stared Courtney right in the eye. "Trust me on this. And if you don't trust me, just look up boob hacks on YouTube. The knowledge might come in handy for future emergencies."

Amy stepped around Courtney. "Hey, everyone," she said in a happy tone as she strode into the room, taking in the long faces and the shine of tears in the bride's eyes. "I'm here to fix things."

"With duct tape?" The bride looked horrified.

"Well, that would solve the problem."

"Yes, but what happens afterward? I mean when... You know..."

"Oh, that... Well, think of the fun he'll have unwrapping you. Maybe with his teeth?"

The bride stared. Her mother giggled.

"Okay, so maybe instead we could use makeup on your cleavage. Do you have some matte bronzer and powder? Some bronzer between the boobs and a little glittery highlighting on the top can really make the girls pop, you know? Although that might be risky with a white dress.

"Maybe we should just go for the classic fix—a pair of balled-up socks. Don't tell me you never did that when you were a teenager."

Megan looked guilty.

"There's nothing wrong with giving nature a little helping hand," the bride's mother said. "And, honey, I know you had this idea about wearing a beautiful lace bra, but the bra you bought isn't going to work. Why don't you let Amy help you out, okay?"

Megan bit her lip and nodded.

"I promise, we won't use the duct tape unless absolutely necessary."

"How does that work, exactly?" Megan asked, the worry on her face morphing into curiosity.

Amy whipped out the cell phone Willow had given her yesterday as a perk of employment. She pulled up her Internet browser and searched for a specific video starring a drag queen named Cherri Bomb. "Take a look," Amy said, handing over the phone. "But basically, you squeeze the girls together and someone tapes them from right to left and then left to right. Just watch the video. If a drag queen with no boobs at all can use duct tape to make himself look like a C cup, just imagine what we could do with you."

Chapter Fourteen

Dusty awakened on Sunday morning to find himself alone in his tiny house. Daddy had left, and not just for a walk or a drive. The old bastard was good and gone—took his clothes and his truck and even stripped the Murphy bed of its sheets.

Maybe their meeting last Friday with Samantha Fry, the Jefferson County social worker with a take-no-crap attitude, had put the fear of God in him. Samantha made it clear that Daddy needed to get himself sober, and she was going to find him a low-cost recovery program come hell or high water.

That hadn't gone over too well. As usual, Daddy had blamed Dusty for everything. For tearing down the old house. For building a new one that was too small. For investigating Medicaid options. For not selling the land. Even for Daddy's addiction to booze. The list of grievances went on and on.

Why the hell did Dusty allow himself to feel one iota of guilt about any of it? Daddy hadn't ever shown one moment of remorse for repeatedly throwing Dusty out of the house—even on cold winter nights. But Dusty felt nothing but guilt when he discovered his father missing. Inevitably, the guilt gave way to worry and then to anger. Why the hell should he be all torn up with worry for a man who'd never, ever worried about him?

He tossed that thought around like a dog with a bone and finally concluded that he wanted to be the sort of man who worried about things like this. The sort of man who took care of his family—even someone like Daddy. So he swallowed back his anger and called the cops, but Officer Pierce told him the SFPD couldn't do a thing about the situation since Daddy was an adult of sound mind.

So, bottom line, Dusty was a free man once again. Free to be alone.

And for the first time, his tiny house seemed way too big, even for him. He felt caught in the middle of his life, caught in limbo. He would be thirty-five next November, and he hadn't really accomplished much. Maybe he needed to forget about Daddy and figure out what to do about the rest of his life. Maybe he should read Willow's e-mails again and do something about a business plan.

But the minute he pulled up Willow's messages on his laptop, he lost faith in himself. Willow's suggestions for his business plan were like Greek to him. He didn't have the first idea about how to write a business plan. And even if he wrote one, he didn't know how anyone put a plan into action.

He had worked his tail off to become a horticulturist, and he'd spent his whole life learning to fish. He wasn't a businessman. Writing a business plan intimidated the crap out of him.

He made himself a pot of coffee and sat out on his deck for a little while, listening to spring birdsong and trying to figure out what he should do next—go searching for his daddy, start working on a business plan, go fishing, or something else?

The something else took the form of an X-rated image of Amy Lyndon, and the more he tried not to think of her, the more her memory stuck in his head. Amy embraced her problems. She wore her own lack of experience and knowledge like a badge of courage.

She'd accomplished so much in such a short time. And yesterday he'd admired her even more after seeing her all turned out for her new job in a sexy little dress and hearing later how she'd somehow saved the day for a bride with that roll of duct tape she'd borrowed from the barn.

He wasn't alone. Everyone at Eagle Hill Manor had fallen utterly in love with her because she had a ready laugh, a willingness to learn, and a wickedly smart imagination. That thought left an uneasiness in its wake. No, he didn't love Amy Lyndon. Much.

He put his coffee cup down on the deck and rubbed his temples where a headache had started to bloom. Shoot, if Amy Lyndon could face the world fearlessly, why couldn't he do the same thing?

So what if he didn't know what the term ROI meant when Willow used it in her e-mails. He could learn. And hadn't he told Amy that everything she needed to know could be found at the Jefferson County Public Library?

Yes, he had.

Yesterday had been exhilarating and exhausting. Amy had put in twelve hours on the job, and she'd succeeded in so many ways. Not only had she fixed Megan's boobs, but she'd also fixed the best man's too-tight rental tux pants with a rubber band, and solved a problem with the champagne fountain with a bobby pin. It turned out that she had a talent for fixing things.

Even so, all that fuss and stress over a wedding made Amy suddenly wonder if she wanted anything so grand when she finally found Mr. Right. Maybe it would be better to elope, or have a small wedding, like the one the family wanted for Danny.

Not that Aunt Pam would ever allow Amy to have a small wedding. Pam had been denied the chance to plan David's and Jeff's weddings, so she'd be all over Amy's wedding, and regardless of what Amy might want, Pam would turn her wedding into a gigantic affair fit for an American princess.

Unfortunately, princesses always had to wear poufy ball gowns and endure boring and obnoxious wedding guests for the sake of the kingdom. Princesses lived in high castle towers and got told how to behave. It wasn't much fun being a princess, she'd discovered.

Maybe she could throw the family for a loop by finding a pirate or even a cute gardener to run off with.

She turned that thought around in her mind for a long time before setting it aside and labeling it "wishful thinking." She didn't know any pirates, and the cute gardener in her life had pranked her and lied to her.

The whole snipe-hunting thing had been boiling inside

her for a couple of days. So on Sunday, after she'd returned her library books, she sat down at one of the library's long tables, fired up her new business phone, and Googled the words "snipe hunting."

She'd just started reading the list of URLs when the hairs on the back of her neck stood up. At the same time, the library got uncomfortably warm. What the hell?

She glanced over her shoulder and found the explanation for the sudden atmospheric change. The dishonest Dusty McNeil leaned his long, athletic body against the information desk as he chatted softly with Donna Carlton. He wore a blue fishing shirt with the sleeves rolled up to expose ropy muscles along his forearms. Tangled blond hair fell across his forehead in a sexy bed-head look that had Amy's insides revving. She turned back to her phone, determined to ignore him.

Her search results for "snipe hunt" were displayed on the screen. The Wikipedia definition at the top of the list started with the words "a fool's errand" and contained phrases like "practical joke" and "gullible rube." Links to various web pages with snipe-hunting instructions followed. There was also an obscure reference down at the bottom of the list to a bird called the Wilson's snipe, which apparently lived somewhere in Louisiana.

She followed the first link, and there it was, all laid out for anyone who ever wanted to send a so-called friend for a snipe hunt: the sack, the pinecone, and the peanut butter.

Dammit it to hell and back again. Wikipedia had it right. She'd been a total sucker, not just for going snipe hunting but for believing that Thursday night had been anything other than pity sex.

It was time to get out of the library.

But fate or bad luck or whatever interceded. Dusty finished his conversation with Donna and turned toward the stacks just as Amy got up from the table and turned toward the exit. Amy realized too late that they were on intersecting trajectories.

He altered his course to intercept her. He even put on one of his gorgeous smiles, complete with dimples this time. "Hey," he said in a voice pitched low and quiet, "I saw you when I came in. Courtney told me you saved the day yesterday with the duct tape you borrowed, but she said the problem had nothing to do with table linens like you said it did, and now I'm—"

"I was just reading Wikipedia's definition of snipe hunting," she interrupted, too angry with him at the moment to discuss anything work-related. Or, really, anything at all.

His beautiful sun-bronzed skin paled. "Oh?"

"Yup. Now, if you'll excuse me, I need to get back to Muffin."

She stepped around him, but damned if the man didn't follow her right out of the library's front doors.

"Uh, wait," he called. "Let me explain."

She turned. "No need to. I get it. I'm dumb and naive. But it's mean when you set up a person to fail and then laugh about it."

She turned and tried to run away from him, but he had much longer legs. He caught up in no time, grabbed her arm, and halted her forward progress. His touch should have revolted her, but instead it sent an electrical jolt right into her core.

"Amy, you are not dumb, okay?"

"Yeah, sure." She tried to shake him off, but instead of letting her go, he tugged her around so she had to face him.

"Look at me, Amy."

She didn't.

"C'mon, honey, look at me."

She finally peeped up at him. It was a gigantic mistake because his baby blues were full of concern, and she so wanted that kind look to be real and not a figment of her overactive imagination.

"You. Are. Not. Dumb," he said. "And I was wrong to send you snipe hunting. I realized my mistake the next morning when I discovered you were homeless and desperate for money. I've been homeless a time or two. I know how it goes."

"A few days ago you told me not to draw any comparisons between our life experiences."

"Okay, I was wrong to say that too. But the thing is, that morning, when I found out you had tangled with some kind of animal out there in the woods, I needed to do something to make up for the fact that I may have put you in danger. In retrospect, I'm pretty sure the animal who scared you that night was Muffin, but it could just as easily have been a mean raccoon or a bear or something."

"You should have told me the truth."

"If I'd done that, I wouldn't have been able to pay you. And you needed money. So . . ." His voice faded out.

"So the money and the breakfast were just handouts."

He shook his head. "No. I paid you for the work I asked you to do in a fair exchange even if my initial motives were unkind. I'm really sorry, okay? But I'd like to make one thing clear. I didn't send you on that snipe hunt because I thought you were dumb. I did it to teach you a lesson about asking dumb questions."

"You didn't like my questions?"

He shook his head. "No, just the opposite. That first day on the job you were trying so hard to impress me and make me think you knew stuff that you clearly didn't know. You tried to BS me about the weeds and look what happened with that. So I tested you by sending you snipe hunting. If you'd asked me what a snipe was, I would never have sent you on a wild-goose chase.

"But it backfired on me, Amy. And then you turned around a few days later and surprised the hell out of me and everyone else by bringing that field guide of trees and shrubs to work. A dumb person wouldn't have done that. I don't know how it happened, but somehow you discovered the value of asking questions. You see, Amy, the lesson I wanted to teach you was that there's no such thing as a snipe...or a dumb question. Every question is worthy of an answer."

She pulled her arm free but made no move to escape. His words had paralyzed her.

"You want to know something else?" he asked, but hurried on before she had a chance to answer his rhetorical question. "This morning I was reading a bunch of e-mails Willow sent me with advice on how to write a business plan. Not one of them made any sense to me. I don't know anything about ROI and things like that. All that jargon made me feel stupid, and I was about to give up on the whole thing, but then I thought about you."

"Me?"

He nodded and smiled in the most adorable way, with the corners of his mouth impishly curling. Amy's anger began to slip away.

"Yeah," he said. "I thought about you, and I said to myself, 'Amy didn't know squat about dog training, but she went to the library and she learned from a book, and now Sven sits on command.' "

A smiled tugged at her mouth. "Yeah, I guess that's true."

"So, see? You aren't dumb. You're brilliant. And you're an inspiration. You're the reason I decided to double down on my fight with the county. I need to find a book on writing a business plan, and I need to do what Willow has suggested for months—write an alternative plan for my land."

"Oh, good. I love it when people stand up to Aunt Pam."

"Do you?"

"Yeah, but don't think I've gotten over being mad at you just because you're making Aunt Pam's life difficult." She paused, trying to find the words that wouldn't totally bare herself to him. "The thing is, I don't want pity sex from you or anyone."

He blinked. "What?"

"You heard me."

"Honey, if you think what happened on Thursday night was pity sex, then you need to think again. I stayed because I wanted to. There is no other reason. I think you're a beautiful, smart, desirable woman."

She stood there blinking up at him. Was he feeding her a line, like a good Casanova, or was he telling her the truth? She couldn't tell. "Is that really what you think?"

"Of course it is. Didn't I just tell you that I came here to the library because you inspired me?"

"Yeah, you did. Wow. I don't think I've ever inspired anyone before." Should she trust him? Should she forgive him? Her brain wasn't sure, but her heart tugged her in that direction.

"There's a first time for everything," he said.

An incredible rush of warmth spilled through her and pooled in her midsection when her heart finally won the fight with her head. Maybe having sex with him hadn't been such a mistake. She'd like to do it again, but maybe not right this minute. After all, he'd come to the library to find a book on writing a business plan. She'd read Sally Hawkes's article in the *Winchester Daily,* and that had lit a fire under him. Willow was right; Dusty needed an alternate plan.

"So, um, you want some help?"

"In standing up to Pam or writing my plan? Or did you have something else in mind?"

"Both. And then we can take Muffin for a walk."

Chapter Fifteen

With Amy's enthusiastic help, Dusty found three business plan books, which he checked out of the library. Then they bought a couple of bacon and egg sandwiches from Gracie's Diner and headed up to the fishing cabin, where they spent the early afternoon on the screen porch reading the books and talking through Dusty's ideas for his fishing guide business.

She helped him cut through the details in his head to frame up each idea in a way that made rational sense. Once he got all his thoughts laid out on a piece of paper, each one numbered in order of importance, the project didn't seem so overwhelming.

"See?" she said after they'd been at it for a while. "The only way to get through something this complex is to make a list of all the smaller steps. I used to do that all the time when I planned events for my sorority. I'm just not smart enough to deal with planning anything without breaking it down into a to-do list, you know?"

"I hate it when you say stuff like that," he said, looking up from his notebook.

"What stuff? You don't like to-do lists?"

"Stuff like 'I'm not smart enough.'"

"But I'm—"

"Stop. You do that all the time, and it's not true, Amy. You're an extremely intelligent person. I don't understand why you think you're not."

"Try living with the Lyndons for a while. They're all brilliant."

"I've been friends with David for a long time, and he's smart, but I don't think he's any smarter than you are. Maybe he and Willow have advanced college degrees, but neither of them could get Sven to behave himself. You checked out a book from the library, read it thoroughly, and inside of a week, you've changed that dog's life. Sven might get to spend more time inside with Willow now that she has some confidence that he won't jump all over the guests."

A smile as bright as sunshine opened up on Amy's face. "Yeah, I know. I'm so happy for Sven. It's like the book says, a well-trained dog is a free dog." Her voice carried an earnest ring to it that almost made him laugh. She had no clue about herself. Not a one.

Running into her at the library had been a stroke of luck. He glanced down at his notebook where an outline was taking shape. He'd never have made it this far without Amy's help. He probably would have given up an hour ago and headed out to the stream for some fishing. Amy had helped him focus, had helped him drill down, and had helped him lay out the problems one by one.

Anyone could slip and fall into something serious with a woman like her. She was good company, like a fishing buddy or something. He wanted to spend time with her even though he'd promised Willow to stay away. But if he stayed here admiring her, he'd end up taking her back to bed, and that would definitely break his promise. But maybe there was another way. Maybe they could be friends without benefits, the way he was friends with Willow.

"I think we've made a lot of progress this afternoon," he said nonchalantly. "But it's a nice day, and Muffin's getting antsy. Let's take the dog fishing."

"Now?"

"Yeah."

"But I don't know how to fish."

"How is that possible? Your family is crazy about fishing. I see your dad and uncle out on the stream all the time. And David lives to fish."

"It's definitely possible," Amy said. "In my family, it's one of those unstated rules that the boys go fishing and the girls go shopping."

"Really?"

She nodded. "Yup. And please don't tell me it's unfair. When I was little, I remember wanting to go fishing with Daddy, but Mom always said I'd have more fun shopping. She was right about that. I like shopping. A lot."

"I bet you do."

"The thing is, up until the last two weeks, I mostly shopped with other people's money, and I've come to understand that doing that is soul-sucking."

"Soul-sucking?"

She nodded. "Yeah. I've come to the conclusion that the best thing that ever happened to me was when Daddy locked me out of the house. I've accomplished so much in two weeks. I have Muffin, I've made friends with Sven, and I saved the day yesterday for a flat-chested bride."

"What?"

She giggled. "Oops. I didn't mean to divulge that."

"How exactly did you save the day for the flat-chested bride?"

"With the duct tape I took from the barn. It's a godsend for those of us who have no cleavage." Her cheeks turned pink the minute that word left her mouth.

"I'm suddenly intrigued. How exactly do you—"

"Never mind. I believe we were talking about my shopping habits, and we're not changing the subject. And I've learned the value of a dollar. So shopping doesn't seem like so much fun anymore."

"I can assure you that fishing will not damage your soul."

She tilted her head and regarded him out of a pair of eyes that twinkled with mischief. "Oh, I just had an awesome idea," she said.

"About fishing?"

"Well, sort of. It's about fishing and your business. What if you were to target women who wanted to learn to fish as customers? You could create an environment where they wouldn't feel intimidated. Women would flock to you because you're handsome and experienced and, you know, the whole package."

The temperature on the porch went from early spring to late summer.

"I've never taught a woman how to fish," he said as the heat crawled up his neck.

"No?"

He shook his head.

"You can practice on me."

"Okay," he said slowly. "I'd love to practice on you." But what did he want to practice? That was the important question. Right then he wanted to pull her out of that chair and carry her back to the bedroom, where they could continue what they'd started Thursday night.

So much for the idea of them being friends without benefits. Maybe he should stop thinking with his dick.

"I'll go get some rods out of the truck," he said, and escaped the porch.

He regrouped out at the truck, where he sorted through his fishing gear and assembled a couple of fly rods. He needed a clear set of dos and don'ts when it came to Amy Lyndon.

Teaching her to fish would be innocent enough. He could justify that on the basis that he might need to teach the wives and girlfriends of his future clients. But flirting with her, kissing her, touching her, or taking her to bed were all forbidden. It went without saying that he needed to avoid falling in love with her.

But the boat may have sailed on that one.

❧❧❧

Amy hadn't expected fly-fishing lessons to be so... intimate. They stood together in a small clearing in the forest where meadow grass grew thick, punctuated here and there with stands of white and yellow wildflowers that Dusty called fleabane. Not far away, Liberty Run bubbled and splashed on its way down toward Shenandoah Falls. The stream was no more than ten feet across, but the water moved swiftly, churning over rocks and swirling in places where, according to Dusty, the trout liked to hide.

Dusty didn't start Amy's lesson off by casting into the stream. Instead, he tied a piece of bright orange yarn on the end of her fishing line and made her practice her cast on dry land. He stood behind her with his arms wrapped around her and his front side heating her backside even though they weren't touching. His scent spilled over Amy like warm honey. His voice feathered in her ear as he murmured instructions in that deep voice of his.

If she hadn't been so determined to learn how to fish, she might have turned around and kissed him. But right now Dusty had a lot riding on this fishing lesson. He needed to practice his teaching skills, and she needed to learn. So kissing was out.

"Here's how you hold the rod," Dusty said, showing her his firm but gentle grasp on the cork at the end of the fly rod. "Basically it's like you're shaking hands with it, see? You try."

She took the rod from him, surprised by the way it balanced in her hand.

"Don't strangle it," he said, and his left hand came around her rib cage to make adjustments to her grip. It would be so easy to lean back and settle into his sturdy frame, but that would defeat the purpose of this lesson. So she mentally told her heart to stop beating erratically, but her heart didn't listen.

"All right," he said, stepping back, taking his scent and warmth away. "Now, I want you to pull out some line—maybe seven or eight feet." He leaned over and showed her how to grab the neon green line and pull it from the reel.

"Won't it get tangled?" she asked. "I thought I had to move the rod to get the line to play out."

"Nope. In fly casting, the line is heavy, so you have to pull it from the reel and feed it down the rod. It's not like spin casting. You can throw that light fishing line directly from the reel on a spin rod. This requires a lot more skill and patience."

This made no sense to her, but she refrained from asking any questions, dumb or otherwise, because she figured she'd learn by doing.

"All right, now I want you to hold the line in your left hand." He showed her how, which required him to step closer again, sending her temperature soaring.

"When you move the rod back and forth, it's going to bend, and that's what creates the energy that feeds the line out. That's called 'loading the rod.' To cast, move your arm back and then forward, keeping your wrist straight and pivoting from your elbow, which is going to sit on an imaginary shelf on your hip."

He stopped and grabbed her right arm and positioned it next to her body. His touch awakened all her girl parts, and the rush of blood in her ears drowned out the sound of the stream.

"I'm showing you a side cast method to start with. I think it's easier to control the line, and learning it this way will come in handy when you fish along the run. There are a lot of good fishing spots where you can't make an overhead cast because the trees get in the way."

Once he'd positioned her body, he said, "Okay, you've got the stance right. Now I want you to move your hand back and then forward without breaking your wrist. The secret of the cast is that your arm is going to accelerate to a stopping point in back and then come forward in the same way. People sometimes call this a snap action, but I think it works better if you imagine that you're holding a paintbrush filled with paint and you're trying to fling the paint off the end of the brush."

Keeping all that in her head made Amy dizzy, but she tried to do as he'd instructed, and to her utter astonishment, the line she'd taken out of the reel traveled down the rod as she moved her arm back and forth, imagining a paintbrush.

"Gorgeous," Dusty said.

"What? Who? Me?"

"Yeah, you're cute, but that was a beautiful cast. Did you see the loop the line made?"

No, she hadn't. She'd been concentrating on flinging paint.

They continued like this for the next half hour, with Dusty always patient and kind and sweet. He had a knack for teaching even if he talked too much, and she got the hang of casting pretty quickly.

He made learning fun. He never criticized her mistakes. He gave her confidence, so she ended up enjoying herself doing something everyone had always told her she would hate.

"You're good at this," she finally said.

"Of course I am. I learned to fish when I was really young. I've been doing it a long time."

"No." She shook her head. "You're good at teaching people."

"I am?" He seemed genuinely surprised.

Her chest swelled up with an emotion she couldn't even name as it occurred to her that Dusty McNeil had taught her all kinds of things that had nothing to do with fly-fishing. Dusty might be the only person in her life who'd ever allowed her to stand on her own two feet. And while they'd gotten off to a rocky start with the daffodils and the snipe hunt, in truth, Dusty didn't criticize her mistakes the way Aunt Pam did. Aunt Pam made every mistake about Amy's shortcomings, but Dusty used every mistake as a teachable moment.

The minute that idea popped into her head, it became impossible to contain herself. She angled the rod down onto its handle and stepped right up to him, taking his face in her hands.

"Thank you," she said, "for everything. For believing in me. For teaching me stuff..." She had a lot of other things she wanted to say, but her voice got wobbly, so instead of talking, she pulled him down for an innocent enough thank-you kiss.

But the moment their lips brushed, the little kiss went awry. His mouth, warm and gentle, unleashed a craving in her that would only be satisfied by taking the kiss carnal. She wanted to drink him up like a bottle of Bella Vista's special vintage wine.

Suddenly the rod between them was more barrier than either of them could stand. They had just jettisoned it and were two seconds away from dropping to the meadow grass when Muffin started barking her head off.

Clearly the dog believed that they were in danger.

"What?" Amy turned just as Muffin hunkered down and growled at someone making his way down the path from the cabin. One glance at the intruder and Amy's newfound confidence disappeared.

Daddy had returned from his vacation. And by the grumpy scowl riding his forehead, he was not a happy man.

Chapter Sixteen————————

Muffin, leave it," Amy commanded, and her brave little dog sat down but continued to watch Daddy as if she thought he might be a master villain. Two weeks ago Amy would have given anything for Daddy's return. But now she shared Muffin's opinion, especially since the scowl on his face spelled trouble.

"Whose dog is that?" Daddy asked.

"It's mine."

"Since when? You're afraid of dogs, just like your mother."

How many times had her family compared her to Mom? A million? More? She'd always taken it as a compliment before, but these last few days had changed her perspective. Maybe her family constantly compared her to Mom in order to keep her in line and limit her options. Mom had married a rich man, and the jury was out as to whether she'd done it for love or money. What was a known fact is that she chose to stay with Daddy despite his infidelities. Had she done that out of love, or had she been too scared to live life on her own, without Daddy's money?

Amy had loved her mother dearly. But it suddenly occurred to her that Mom had lived a half-life. She had never stood on her own two feet. She'd been afraid of her shadow. She'd spent her days shopping, trying to fill up the hours.

Amy wanted no part of a life like that, so she planted her feet wide apart, put her hands on her hips, and firmed her chin. "Everyone has always told me that I'm afraid of dogs, but I can't remember how that happened. And then I met Muffin and discovered that I like dogs. Maybe Mom's fear of them was projected onto me. You think?"

Daddy ignored the rhetorical question. In fact, halfway through her speech, he'd turned to stare at Dusty. And Dusty stared right back at him while the testosterone level climbed into the stratosphere.

"What are you doing here?" Daddy fired the words in Dusty's direction as if he were skeet shooting and Dusty was the target.

"I—"

"He was teaching me how to fish with a fly rod, Daddy. Don't be so dramatic," Amy said.

"It didn't look like he was teaching you to fish, Amy. Besides, the idea of you going fishing is hilarious."

"Hilarious how?" Dusty asked, stepping forward a few paces and folding his arms across his chest. "She's a quick study. I bet I could have her double hauling before the afternoon is out."

Amy had no idea what double hauling was, but a powerful sense of accomplishment swelled inside her.

"I doubt it," Daddy said. "She's not very athletic. Now, do us both a favor and leave."

"Daddy, Dusty is my—"

"I don't give a rat's ass what you were doing with him, Amy. It's time for you to grow up, quit screwing around, and get with the program, okay? And believe me, Jeff is going to hear from me. He's not doing you any favors allowing you to camp out here."

"What program exactly did you have in mind?" she asked.

"The program that has you marrying Grady Carson." He sent a killing glance in Dusty's direction before continuing. "I'm not too happy with Willow either. How could she allow you to work at the inn—as a gardener no less? And how could she allow you to spend time with him?" Daddy nodded in Dusty's direction. "It goes without saying that Willow will hear about this. I'm sure she won't like the idea of this man hitting on one of her employees."

She stood there hoping Dusty would stand up for himself, maybe punch Daddy in the nose or something. Or better yet, rescue her from her life as a princess by swearing his undying love for her.

Unfortunately, Dusty didn't do any of those things.

It was a known fact that no one ever stood up to Daddy. He owned more land in Jefferson County than anyone else, and the world sucked up to him. As for undying love, she and Dusty might have enjoyed some incredible sex, but sex wasn't a sign of undying love.

So she tried not to be disappointed when Dusty picked up his fishing equipment, nodded his head in deference to the Big Man, and said, "I was just leaving, sir."

The sight of his retreating back demoralized Amy. Her chest tightened with indignation. She turned on her father. "Why did you do that?" she asked.

"Because he's not the kind of man you want in your life, honey. Now, I brought the SUV, and I'll help you move your things back into the house. I'm sorry I kicked you out. I thought for sure you'd run right to Grady. But don't you worry. I'll help you fix the problems I created."

"Fix the problems? Daddy, there are no problems here."

"Of course there are. You're living in a cabin without central heating, out here in the boondocks where you're not safe. You're working as a laborer, and the fact that you're spending time with riffraff like Dusty McNeil only underscores my point. Honey, that man has gone through more women than—"

"Don't say one more word. First off, I'm happy living here. Second, I've been promoted to an assistant wedding planner. And third..." She couldn't think of a third thing because she was angry. So she turned away from him. "Muffin, heel," she commanded, and the dog padded right to her side and followed her as she set off down the path toward the cabin. A part of her wanted to run so she could stop Dusty from leaving, but she held herself and her heart in check. This fight with Daddy and the rest of the family was about more than Dusty McNeil.

What if she decided, right here and right now, to stop letting her family define her? What if she stood on her own two feet the way Mom never had?

She stopped in her tracks and turned around. "I'm not moving back into the house. I do not want to marry Grady Carson. I will sleep with whomever I choose. And Dusty McNeil may be a consummate player, but he is not riffraff.

And if you do anything that jeopardizes his job, I will never speak to you again."

She turned around and picked up her pace.

"Amy," Daddy bellowed from behind, "you're being ridiculous."

Oh, how she hated that word.

She stopped again and faced her father. "I am *not* ridiculous. You need to quit calling me that. And I'm not my mother, so quit treating me as if I am. Throwing me out of the house was the best damn thing you ever did for me. I thought you did it so I would learn to stand on my own. But now, it appears, it was just some ploy to get me to say yes to Grady Carson. But I've said no, Daddy, and I'm not taking it back."

"And what about Dusty McNeil? Is he a ploy to get back at me? He must be ten years older than you. Honestly, Amy, did it not occur to you that McNeil is only interested in your money?"

"What money are you talking about? I don't have any money. That's why everyone says I need a rich husband, so he can keep me the way you kept Mom for all those years."

Daddy shook his head. "No, that's not the reason. Honey, one day, when I'm gone, you and your brothers will inherit what I've built. My kids will get majority ownership of the vineyard and the orchards and the apple-processing businesses. You'll be a wealthy woman in your own right. You think Dusty McNeil hasn't figured that out?"

She stood stock-still. She had never thought of this before, probably because she had never even considered the possibility of Daddy dying one day. "Daddy, you're as healthy as a horse, and I'm not going to live my life worrying about the day when you're no longer with us. I want to live my life now, not tomorrow."

She turned and tramped through the meadow grass with Muffin following dutifully. Dusty was long gone by the time she arrived at the cabin, and he'd taken his notebook and the books he'd borrowed from the library with him.

Daddy spent the better part of half an hour pacing the screen porch and raging at her while she sat calmly in the Adirondack chair with her arms folded. She didn't argue. She didn't say one word.

"Jesus, Amy, what the hell has gotten into you?" he finally asked.

"Independence," she said.

He stared at her for a long moment, clearly confused. Then he turned and slammed through the screen door. But as he left she heard him mutter, "Maybe Pam knows what to do about you."

Amy almost smiled at that. Pam didn't have a clue either. And besides, her aunt was obsessed with her own set of problems involving Danny, Mia, and a reality TV show.

❧

Dusty peeled out of the cabin's driveway and headed toward town. He should have told Jamie Lyndon where to shove it. But how could he? Amy's father was the most powerful man in Jefferson County. What Jamie Lyndon thought about a person mattered.

And to make it more complicated, Jamie Lyndon had a sterling reputation as a good guy who gave money to charity and local causes. Everyone liked and respected him because he listened to people, was humble, and even funded

Linda Petersen's secret effort to buy Christmas presents for needy kids every year.

So Dusty couldn't hate the guy, even if he wanted to deck him. Success in this town required Dusty to make friends with everyone, including the Lyndons. In short, his future depended upon Dusty being the exact opposite of his old man.

And yet, even after years of Dusty being respectful and avoiding fights, Jamie Lyndon—and a lot of other folks in town—still held him in contempt because of the legacy of failure and addiction that had been handed down to him. And just to prove the naysayers right, Dusty left the fishing cabin and went running straight to the Jaybird Café, his favorite watering hole. As he strolled into the restaurant, he made a promise not to drink himself into a haze no matter how ragged his emotions.

The café was semi-deserted on a Sunday afternoon in the early spring, with just a couple of sports fans watching the Nationals lose to the Mets on the flat-screen TVs. He snagged a seat at the bar, and before he could even order a drink, Juni Petersen, Willow's little sister and the bar's manager, came over, studied him a moment, and then said, "Your aura's off."

"Can I have a Sam Adams Boston Lager, please."

Juni pulled the beer and slid it across the bar to him. He took a long swallow of the bitter brew while Juni continued to eye him.

"Hey, what's up with you, Dusty?" she finally asked into the silence. "Usually when I read your aura, you immediately make some comment about how aura-reading is bullcrap." Juni leaned on the bar right across from him, her dark eyes smiling.

In so many ways, Juni was like a little sister. He never would have made it through his childhood if it hadn't been for the kindness of Juni and Willow's mother. Linda Petersen was an eccentric, but she had a heart of gold and had raised two wonderful, independent, and *nosy* daughters.

"The usual," he said on a sigh. "Daddy's come back, wanting me to sell the land and give him the money. And then he got drunk and picked a fight and got all busted up. And the docs told me he's got a bad liver and diabetes and shit." He took another slug of beer.

"I was trying to find him a place," he continued, "a recovery home or something. But he took off. And now I don't know where he is. And I shouldn't even care."

Juni reached out and patted his hand. Like any good bartender, she combined a talent for mixology with common-sense psychology. "That's not what's eating you, Dusty."

He looked up from his beer. "No?"

She shook her head. "No. You've always had this bright yellow thread in your aura that's all about your dad. I can see it's brighter than it has been recently. But I'm more interested in the pink."

"Pink? In my aura? Juni, when you say stuff like that it makes me want to roll my eyes."

"Roll away, but it's true. There's someone new in your life, isn't there?"

"What?" Juni had mastered this guessing game so well that a lot of people never figured out that the whole aura-reading thing was a sleight of hand that distracted while she pried out all the juiciest bits of gossip.

She smiled and raised her eyebrows. "Oh, let me guess. It's one of Mia Paquet's girlfriends. I think Pearl is beautiful, don't you?"

"You watch *Vegas Girls*?"

She laughed. "No, but the whole cast came in here a few days ago. Spent a lot of money and talked a lot of smack. It's funny how Daniel Lyndon was the only one missing. I gather from the conversation, he stayed home with the baby."

"And you think I belong with one of those women?"

"No, Dusty. That's why I'm so intrigued by what I see in your aura."

Dammit. He'd just been played for a fool.

"I'm not talking about this." He took another swig of beer.

"Okay, but you should know that you usually have this red color, which goes with your reputation as an unrepentant bachelor. But all that's disappeared entirely, and suddenly there's this pink everywhere."

"What does that mean?" he asked. Man, she was reeling him in like a fat trout.

"You've fallen in love." She stepped back a pace. "And then there's the fact that you're here drinking a beer on a Sunday afternoon when you'd usually be fishing. Obviously something has gone terribly wrong in your life. Your equilibrium has been unbalanced. And I know your daddy's return is not the cause. There's a woman, am I right?"

Well, damn. Nothing like getting psyched out by Juni Petersen. "How much for the beer?" he asked, standing up.

She waved her hand. "It's on the house. And so is my advice. Dusty, if you have a chance for love, then don't be an idiot. Love is a lot like playing poker. Even with a winning hand, you're going to lose if you don't risk something. You know?"

Chapter Seventeen ———————

On Monday morning, Amy woke early after a fitful night's sleep in which she dreamed about Dusty and Daddy having a knock-down, drag-out fight that left them both bloody. The nightmare left her shaking and deeply disturbed.

Dusty may have disappointed her yesterday by walking away from a confrontation with Daddy, but maybe her subconscious was trying to tell her that he'd done the right thing. She didn't want Dusty to stand up to Daddy as much as she wanted Daddy and Dusty to respect each other.

Like that could ever happen in the real world. So she shoved the whole Daddy-Dusty problem into the back of her brain, took Muffin for a long walk, and went to work.

Mondays were usually so slow that the event staff took the day off. But not today. Willow had called a midmorning summit in the dining room with all the principal Eagle Hill Manor staff as well as the *Vegas Girls* stars and production team. The purpose was to discuss the Paquet-Lyndon wedding scheduled for April twenty-sixth.

By all reports, this meeting promised conflict and drama, even though it wouldn't be taped for the show. Everyone at Eagle Hill Manor, Willow included, had completely lost their patience with Mia Paquet and the show's producers. Courtney, upon whom most of the ridiculous requests had fallen, was especially put out. The summit would undoubtedly turn into an f-bomb festival if Mia asked Courtney to do one more stupid thing.

Amy would have given anything to be there when Courtney blew a gasket, but Courtney needed her to cover a meeting with Brandon Kopp and his fiancée, Laurie Wilson, whose wedding was scheduled for August.

Amy already knew a lot of details about this event, even if she'd been on the job for only a few days. Brandon was practically a member of the family, so of course she'd met Laurie on many occasions. And Laurie had been planning her wedding for at least two years. She was so obsessed about every detail that it was all she ever talked about.

Even so, Amy took a moment before the meeting to review Courtney's notes on the event. She was reading through several pages of minute detail when Aunt Pam strolled into her tiny office on the third floor of the manor house and sat in the straight-backed chair by her desk.

"We need to talk," she said.

Uh-oh. By now Pam had probably heard all about the whole Dusty-giving-Amy-kisses-while-teaching-her-fly-casting situation. If Aunt Pam had blown off the summit meeting to come up here, then Amy was in trouble.

"Is the summit meeting with the *Vegas Girls* people finished?" Amy asked.

"No, but Willow seems to have things well in hand."
Pam leaned in. "There are many things I do not admire
about David's wife, but I must say she has a backbone
made of steel. She started the meeting by telling Mia to
take her wedding and shove it."

"What? You mean the wedding isn't—"

"No, the wedding is on, unfortunately. But no landscaping
will be torn out to accommodate camera angles." Pam
let go of a long, mournful sigh.

"To be honest," she continued, her shoulders drooping a
little, "I'm resigned to the fact that Danny is going to trot
us all out to be ridiculed."

"You could convince him not to marry Mia."

"I wish I could. The more time I spend with that woman,
the less I like her. She's indifferent to the baby. It's quite
sad."

"That's why he decided to marry her. To protect Scarlett."

"There are dozens of ways he could protect Scarlett without
tying himself to that woman." Pam settled back into her
chair as if she had just discovered this obvious truth.

"Right, but he's not listening to that particular line of argument.
I know. I've tried."

"We need to try harder." Pam showed no signs of leaving.
Damn.

"Okay, I'll try. But right now I'm about to go into
a meeting." Amy loved being able to tell her aunt that.
Maybe she'd get a clue and leave.

"I know," Pam said curtly, busting Amy's balloon. "I
thought I'd help you out with Laurie and Brandon. I gather
she's bringing a crowd with her to this meeting."

Amy wanted to scream. Did Pam think she needed help

to do her job? But instead of yelling or pitching a fit, she took a breath and said, "According to Courtney's notes, this meeting is just with Laurie."

"Well, Courtney doesn't have all the facts. Roxy called last night. She, Brandon, and Andrew are all coming with Laurie because she wanted her groom, best man, and maid of honor's opinions about the final details. She's really become quite OCD about this event."

"Andrew took a day off from work to help Laurie plan her wedding? Really?"

"I guess she needed reinforcements. So, are you prepared?"

Amy gave her aunt a cheesy smile through her clenched teeth. "Yes, I am."

"Good. Now, in the five minutes we have before they get here, I need to talk to you about Dusty McNeil. Really, Amy, you've taken your rebellion quite far enough."

"I'm not rebelling. I'm taking a principled position," Amy replied in a tight voice that barely masked her anger.

"Amy, don't take that tone with—"

"You know, Aunt Pam, courtesy goes two ways. I don't want to hear what you have to say about Dusty McNeil. And I don't need to hear about how Jeff's cabin is not safe or how I am incapable of doing this job. I'm getting my life together. Courtney and Willow trust me to manage this meeting with Laurie. I'm fine up at the cabin, but I don't plan to be living there for that much longer. I already posted my name on an online roommate-matching site. I need to find a place that accepts pets, and I—"

"You put your name on a public roommate service? Oh my God, Amy. You're so naive. You could end up rooming with a serial killer. Honestly, you're being so..."

"Ridiculous? Yes, I know I'm being ridiculous, Aunt Pam. And you know what? I'm enjoying it."

Aunt Pam's mouth dropped open.

Amy willed herself to be civil as she continued. "I know Daddy asked you to talk with me. And I know exactly what Daddy thinks of Dusty because Daddy said it right out loud so that Dusty could hear it. Daddy's words were ugly and cruel, but Dusty was the better man. He walked away from the fight, even though Daddy tried to goad him into one. So when you report back to my father, please tell him that I expect him to apologize to Dusty McNeil."

Danny would have been happy to avoid Willow's summit at Eagle Hill Manor. He wanted no part in the minutiae of planning this wedding. He'd ceded all that to Mia, and he'd opened his checkbook and paid for the stuff the studio wouldn't go for.

He would have avoided the showdown at all costs except that Mia had a fake-crying jag, accused his family of being snobs (the truth), and insisted that he had to make a choice between her and them.

He tried to explain that Willow Petersen could be pushed only so far, but Mia wouldn't listen. His Vegas girl truly believed that if Danny threw a temper tantrum, his family would do as he demanded. She had no clue.

And so Mia was in for a rude surprise when Willow started the summit by making it clear that Eagle Hill Manor would not be hosting the wedding for free; nor would she waive the usual event contract.

This unleashed more drama than *Vegas Girls* had seen in three seasons, and it was a pity that Willow had banned all cameras from the powwow, because Mia had a full-fledged tantrum.

Willow remained unmoved by Mia's hysterics. Apparently she had a lot of experience dealing with distressed brides. She handled the tantrum by gathering up her papers and saying, "Well, I guess that's that. I'm sorry we couldn't accommodate your needs."

She started toward the door before Antonella jumped up and said, "Wait. I think we can work things out."

Willow was no dummy. She'd learned negotiation at Wharton, and she had all the leverage. The studio had already invested too much time and money in this location. Besides, the story line required Eagle Hill Manor because Pam had refused to let them use Charlotte's Grove. The producers needed the historic manor house.

Willow stopped and turned toward Antonella. "Let me make one thing clear, Ms. Mastriani. There will be no changing of the inn's landscaping. No holes will be drilled in the two-hundred-year-old reclaimed barn-wood beams holding up the Carriage House roof. If the circus aerialists need rigging, they need to figure it out without damaging or defacing any of the interiors."

"Sure, no problem," Antonella said.

At which point Mia pitched another fit, turned on Danny, and demanded that he fix the situation.

"For chrissake, Mia, you can't expect people to destroy hundred-year-old hand-hewn beams so you can have the Cirque du Soleil perform for our wedding guests. This isn't Vegas, baby. The stuff here isn't made of plastic. It's real, and it can't be replaced if it's broken. So sit down and shut up."

Mia's mouth dropped open. So did Antonella's. It was stunning to know he could still raise his voice to Mia. But what else was he supposed to do?

Mia sat down, folding her arms across her chest. Her fury didn't disappear; it morphed into a barely suppressed resentment as the meeting moved on to a discussion of other items on Mia's list of must-haves, starting with her wish to have two dozen white doves released from two six-foot-tall, white wire birdcages on either side of the gazebo.

"We're not doing the doves," Courtney Wallace said.

"Oh, for goodness' sake, are you willing to do any of it? What's the problem with the doves?" asked Antonella, who had clearly lost her patience.

"Releasing doves bred in captivity is inhumane. Those doves will be easy targets for hawks out here. They won't survive. And I don't think you want the animal rights people getting on your case. Besides, we have a corporate responsibility pledge that you can read on our web page that makes it clear that we do not allow the release of doves or the use of rice, paper confetti, or glitter in the ceremony toss. In case you're wondering, we encourage the use of birdseed, lavender petals, or dried-flower confetti for the ceremony toss, and we have lots of ideas of how to make sure your wedding guests are prepared for that wonderful moment." Courtney smiled a perfect wedding-planner smile after delivering this speech, which sounded rehearsed to Danny's ears.

But he had to hand it to Courtney. The moment she said "lavender petals," Mia perked up and asked a dozen questions.

After that, the conversation got even further down into the weeds, at which point Scarlett, who had been sitting on his lap, got bored. Danny would have left the baby with Mom this morning, but Mondays were Mom's golf league at the country club day, and Mom regarded golf on Monday the way some people regarded church on Sunday.

"She's being a total brat, Danny. Make yourself useful and get her out of here," Mia snapped, when Scarlett started to whine.

The members of Willow's team, all of whom had behaved like consummate professionals, turned their collective gazes on him. He hated the pity in their eyes.

Most of them had seen Mia in action by now. They knew how she snapped at Scarlett and Danny every time things didn't go her way. And that, in a nutshell, provided all the reason Danny needed to continue supporting this freak show. So he didn't argue with his bride. He merely left the meeting carrying his eighteen-month-old baby on his hip like an old hand. They made their way out to the west lawn, where Scarlett practiced her newly found ability to run, chasing after butterflies and bumblebees on her stiff-kneed toddler legs and filling the morning with her joyous laughter.

When she lost interest in the insects, Danny carried her down the footpath to the Old Laurel Chapel. The stone building perched at the edge of a small woods, on a sloping meadow awash in purple violets and yellow buttercups. When he reached the clearing, he put Scarlett down and let her toddle forward while he took in the view of the Shenandoah Valley and the rolling purple ridges of the Allegheny Mountains to the west. He drew in a deep breath, inhaling the unmistakable scent of early spring in a verdant land. The sound of birdsong filled the air.

God, it was beautiful here. He'd forgotten how green Virginia was. Living in deserts for the last eight years, he'd grown accustomed to shades of brown and drought-tolerant landscapes. This green place resonated down in his soul, whispering to him that he belonged here in these hills, in this meadow.

He turned his gaze on the newly restored chapel and was surprised to find Roxy Kopp sitting quietly on the church's steps, her gray slacks and sweater camouflaging her against the building's fieldstone façade. She smiled at Scarlett, who had covered more ground on her little legs than he'd expected.

"Hi," she said.

"Hi," he answered.

Silence stretched between them. They hadn't parted well the last time they'd met.

"Uh," Danny said, jamming his hands into his pockets, "I need to apologize for being a jerk the other night. I didn't mean to drive you away. I'm very, very sorry for the frog and my uncouth behavior as a thirteen-year-old... and the other night."

Roxy continued to watch Scarlett as the baby toddled in her direction. She didn't raise her gaze or make eye contact with Danny. "Apology accepted," she said in a husky voice that reeked of sex appeal.

"I'm surprised to see you here," he said.

She stood up, dusting off her slacks. "Oh, I took a day off from work to come out here with Brandon and Laurie. Laurie is a little too involved with her wedding plans, but sometimes she has a lot of trouble making up her mind. Anyway, she wanted me here for moral support or something. And Andrew too. I have no idea why the best man and maid of honor need to be consulted about the flowers in the chapel. But she's a good friend, so here I am."

She pointed her thumb over her shoulder. "She's been in there with Amy for ages. Andrew gave up about thirty minutes ago. He headed off to the manor house to get himself a Coke. I gave up too. Honestly, I can't understand how anyone can talk about flower arrangements for more than an hour. When I find Mr. Right, I'm definitely going to elope."

He chuckled. "I wish I was eloping," he said. "Mia is back at the manor discussing the exact color of blue—chambray or indigo—she wants for the reception table linens. I don't even know the difference between those two colors. Do you?"

When Roxy smiled it felt as if the sun came out from behind a cloud. "Well, I think chambray is lighter than indigo. But they're both a shade of denim."

"See, it's a girl thing. To me, blue is blue."

Roxy took a few steps forward, then dropped down to be on Scarlett's level. "Aren't you a pretty girl." She spoke in a high singsong voice. The kind of "baby talk" most women used when they addressed Scarlett. Most women except Mia.

Mia had been indifferent to the baby almost from the beginning, sending Scarlett off to the nursery without so much as a second glance just minutes after the delivery. To this day, his fiancée obsessed about her stretch marks.

Danny had been the one to give Scarlett her first bottle. Danny had been the one on diaper duty. If it had been left up to Mia, Scarlett would have been handed off to a parade of nannies while Mia went about executing her career plan. Mia wanted a lucrative Hollywood film contract, and nothing, not even a child, was going to get in her way.

She was also seriously delusional about her acting skills, but that didn't seem to matter. Hollywood had a way of elevating the hollow and untalented, which was why he'd become jaded by the cult of celebrity. Somehow he'd lost his way in Tinseltown.

Roxy continued to interact with Scarlett, and in a matter of moments she'd earned the child's trust, even though the baby had entered her "stranger anxiety" phase and had been exceptionally clingy the last week or so. But it must have been love at first sight, because Scarlett gave Roxy one of her drooly, but irresistible, smiles.

"Oh, aren't you precious," Roxy said, holding out her hands, palms up. "You want to come see the flowers?" she asked.

Scarlett forgot all about her stranger anxiety and took one of Roxy's hands. They walked together out into the meadow, where Roxy hunkered down again, her head close to Scarlett's as she showed his child how to smell the buttercups. They finally sat down in the field while Roxy braided a garland of buttercups and violets for Scarlett's head. And Scarlett babbled in her own nonstop adorable fashion, speaking words that weren't real but listening intently to every word spoken to her.

This. This was what he wanted. A woman who would braid wildflowers for his baby's head and talk to her as if having a real conversation. Roxy may have been a pest and a brat as a child, but she had grown into a beautiful and kind human being.

He'd forgotten about kindness. Mia didn't have a kind bone in her body. And he didn't even blame her for that. She'd had a rough childhood that had taught her how to be tough and strong and to ask for more.

In contrast, Danny had enjoyed every advantage money, position, and power could buy. Once upon a time, he'd thought that he could complete Mia, give her the life she wanted. But what she wanted couldn't be given. Now he wondered if it was selfish for a man like him—born with every advantage—to ask for more.

He didn't want to marry Mia. He wanted to run away from her. He wanted to come home, back East, where it rained.

But how could he ask for all that and still protect Scarlett? Mia might not give a rat's ass about the baby, but the minute he made a play for custody, she'd do her best to deny him. She liked his money and would think nothing of holding the baby hostage.

Chapter Eighteen

The summit with the *Vegas Girls* production people didn't break up until nearly 1:00 p.m., making it one of the longest pre-event meetings ever. In Dusty's opinion, the entire thing was a waste of everyone's time since it mostly involved telling Mia to sit down and shut up. He strolled back to his office, intent on checking his messages before he headed out for an afternoon of fishing. Mondays were technically his day off—not that he didn't put in plenty of overtime on Mondays when the inn got busy. But today he needed the alone time down on the run, and he resented having to spend almost four hours doing battle over every minor detail of the event setup—from the PA system to the placement of outdoor propane heaters.

At least Amy hadn't been present at the meeting. Because if she had been, he might have foolishly suggested a continuation of the fishing lesson. But Dusty needed to avoid a fight with Jamie Lyndon, even if a wild, irresponsible part of him wanted to drive up to the vineyard and challenge the dude to a confrontation.

No. If he wanted people to treat him with respect, he needed to be a man worthy of respect. Even if that meant taking an insult and walking away. Maybe that made him a wimp in some people's eyes, but the majority of folks in Jefferson County wouldn't approve if he took a swing at Jamie Lyndon.

So it was ironic that, the moment he committed himself to nonviolence, someone grabbed him from behind, spun him around, and laid a wicked right cross to his face that missed his nose by millimeters. The punch slammed into his cheekbone, forcing him to stumble back a few spaces while black dots swirled in his vision.

What the hell?

"You stay away from my sister," someone said.

Dusty brought his hand up to test his cheekbone. Yup, there was a cut below his eye. He turned toward the guy who'd blindsided him, his slow fuse suddenly flaring to life.

Andrew Lyndon, Amy's *big* brother, stood there breathing hard, as if laying one sucker punch had winded him. Oh boy, Dusty would have to treat the sonofabitch with kid gloves. Hadn't he made it clear that he didn't want a fight? Apparently not.

"That's a chickenshit way to punch a guy," Dusty said. "If you wanted to discuss my relationship with your sister, we could have used words instead of fists." He moved his jaw from side to side.

"Okay, but it's chickenshit for a man with your reputation to take advantage of an innocent girl who's at least ten years younger than you are." Andrew's hands curled into fists. He may have been dressed like a gentleman for the ninth hole at the country club in carefully pressed khakis and a Ralph Lauren polo shirt, but by the color in his cheeks and the scowl on his face, Dusty figured Andrew Lyndon had truly lost his temper.

Dusty had to hand it to the guy. Sucker punch or no, at least Andrew was trying to protect his sister.

"I admire you for caring about Amy," Dusty said, taking a step forward, keeping his hands open and down at his sides. "But where were you when she was sleeping in her car? Oh, and by the way, Amy's not a girl and I'm not ten years older than she is; she's a woman, and—"

The minute Dusty came within range, Andrew took a wild-ass swing.

Dusty sidestepped and turned his shoulder as Andrew stumbled past. The guy clearly had no clue how to fight. Probably because he'd been raised a little rich kid whose father never took swings at him.

Andrew turned and came at him again with another wild roundhouse swing. Dusty stepped aside again, but this time he deflected the punch with an open hand, then grabbed Andrew's right wrist and yanked him forward.

Amy's brother lost his balance and took a dive right onto the gravel footpath. He landed with an audible *oof* of escaping air and lay there spread-eagled for a moment, catching his breath. Yeah, it was a bitch when you landed on your solar plexus. Dusty had had plenty of practice enduring that sort of thing as a kid.

Andrew eventually rolled over, the palms of his hands scraped and bloody from his fall, his eyebrows lowered in the Lyndon scowl.

"It always amazes me that some people swing first and

ask questions later," Dusty said in his calmest voice. "I suggest you have a talk with your sister before you consider further violence."

Dusty turned his back on the guy and strolled down the footpath to his office, where his small refrigerator contained a couple of emergency cold packs. He snagged one, laid it against his cheekbone, and sank into his chair, his head pounding.

The front door slammed open. He winced, preparing himself for round two. But instead of Andrew, his little ol' sister, wearing a furious frown of her own, marched into his office. "What the hell did you do to—oh my God."

She rushed forward in full Florence Nightingale fashion. "Let me see," she said, sitting on his desk and pulling his hand and the cold pack away from his cheek. "You're bleeding." Concern sparked in her chocolate-drop eyes, and damned if Dusty didn't fall a little more in love with her right then. Her outrage warmed him from top to bottom.

"We should take you to the emergency room," she said.

"I'm fine, really."

"What can I do to help?"

He was tempted to suggest that she kiss it and make it better. But that might hurt.

"I'm okay," he said stoically.

"I can't believe you let Andrew punch you. Andrew doesn't get into fights. He's like the calmest guy in the world."

"Really? Because he didn't seem that way to me, and for the record, I didn't let him punch me. He coldcocked me from behind. But once he did that, I sure didn't let him punch me a second time."

"Oh no, did you hurt him?"

"Only his pride, but that's what he gets for starting a fight."

"I'm going to kill him," she said, standing up. "And after that I'm going to give him a piece of my mind. And just so we're clear, I don't want you retaliating by fighting with my father or my brothers or anyone from my family. I had a nightmare about this. I want everyone to be friends."

Good luck with that. Dusty would never be friends with Andrew Lyndon. That was the important takeaway from this experience.

"Amy," he said in a weary voice, "we need to learn something from what just happened."

"What? That my brother has lost his mind and his iron-clad composure?"

"Well, I suppose that's one lesson. But if your brother has lost his composure, that's an ominous sign that maybe you and I don't belong together." Like Dusty hadn't realized this was fated from the start. What on earth made him think he could have a relationship with anyone, much less Amy Lyndon?

Her mouth turned down at the corners, and her dark eyes grew round with surprise. He didn't want to hurt this woman, but he was going to. Wasn't that what Willow had been trying to tell him from the start? They didn't belong together, and no matter how much he'd come to admire Amy, he still couldn't blow a lifetime of work trying to rehabilitate his family name by challenging the Lyndons, especially if they were lining up, taking swings, and accusing him of abuse.

Even worse, he couldn't fault her daddy or her brother. Hell, if he had a sister, he sure wouldn't want her hanging out with a guy like him. So for her sake, because he loved her, he needed to call it quits now. But when Dusty tried to speak, something tangled up inside his chest, choking him. Damn. This was harder than he'd expected. He had to suck in a big breath before he managed to say, "It's over, honey. It was fun, but I never promised—"

"I never asked for any promises," she interrupted before he could finish. And she was right about that. Amy had made it clear from the start that she'd been looking for fun times with a "bad boy."

"So you're good with this?" he asked, his throat so tight the words almost stuck there. What the hell? He'd never had trouble ending a relationship, and really, when viewed rationally, this particular relationship consisted of one hot hookup and an unfinished fishing lesson.

She bit her lip as if trying to keep from saying something painful. Thank God she stayed silent, because it wouldn't have taken much for him to change his mind.

But after a long moment, where the silence and his fate hung in the balance, Amy nodded her head. "Yeah, we're good," she said, hopping down from his desk. Then she leaned over and kissed his forehead, branding him forever with her lips. "It was fun, Dusty. While it lasted. And I'm sorry about Andrew. But don't you worry. I'm going to give him a piece of my mind."

And then she turned and left him, alone.

Amy had known all along that her crush on Dusty McNeil would end this way. She'd known it even before her father and brother started throwing punches and making threats. But she sure wished her family had stayed the hell out of it.

Resentment and frustration lodged in her throat. If her family thought picking fights with Dusty would change anything, they were wrong. Amy wasn't going back to the way things had been before Daddy threw her out. So what if she was a little heartbroken right now? A grown-up, fully realized woman needed a little adversity in order to build character.

So when Amy entered the inn, the last people she wanted to see were Andrew and Brandon, standing around in the lobby, clearly waiting for Laurie, who had insisted on speaking with Courtney once the summit was over.

Good. There was no time like the present to have a serious conversation with her brother about his surprising behavior. But as she approached, she heard Brandon say, "Pushing people around is exactly what you'd expect from a guy like McNeil."

Amy lost it. She stalked right up to Andrew. "What's the matter with you? Since when do you pick fights with people?" Then she turned on Brandon. "And for the record, Dusty didn't push anyone around. He simply responded to a sucker punch and defended himself."

"Amy, don't be dumb. Dusty McNeil is a loser," Brandon said.

"Are you saying I'm stupid?" Her hands came to rest on her hips.

Andrew threw his hands up palms outward. "Amy, please calm down. No one is saying you're—"

"I. Am. Not. Stupid," she said, getting right up into Brandon's face before turning on her brother. "If you told Brandon that Dusty picked that fight, then you're a liar.

And I never thought I'd see the day that you behaved so badly. Andrew, really, this is none of your business."

"Amy, I'm–"

"You screwed with my life, Andrew. And I don't like it. What gives you the right?"

Brandon sounded off before Andrew could get a word in. "Amy, you turned down Grady for a loser like McNeil. In my book, that makes you an idiot."

She wanted to strike back at Brandon, but Andrew stepped between them. "Look, Amy, I'm sorry, but you can do better than that guy."

How could someone she loved be so blind? He'd messed up everything. The tears came rushing to her eyes and took control of her throat. She couldn't speak, and maybe that was just as well.

Instead, she fled to her third-floor office, where she allowed herself exactly five minutes to get the anger and sadness under control. She actually channeled Aunt Pam, a woman who had impeccable control over her emotions. It surprised Amy to realize that she'd learned something from a lifetime of observing and dealing with Pam.

Dusty, Andrew, Daddy—none of them would rain on her parade. If she wanted to be independent, she'd have to take the good with the bad, and the only way to show her family she could manage her life by herself was to *just do it.*

So for the next week, she threw herself into her job. There was plenty to do. Eagle Hill Manor had no less than three weddings scheduled for the following Saturday, plus all the work involved in the *Vegas Girls* wedding shoot only two weeks away. She crossed paths with Dusty on a regular basis, but she kept her head down and avoided eye contact because it hurt way down deep every time she gave in to her desire. She didn't want to behave like Zoe. She didn't want to grovel. She wanted to be strong and show him she'd put him in the past.

In the meantime, she interviewed no less than three potential roommates, none of whom were ax murderers, proving that Pam was overprotective. On the other hand, none of the potential roomies were a particularly good fit. As the days grew longer and warmer, Jeff's cabin seemed more and more like home. She felt lonely sometimes, but maybe she needed the solitary time to figure out who she wanted to be in life. Besides, she had Muffin for company, so she survived and even thrived on her own.

She might have continued along that way except for Easter Sunday. She'd never boycotted the family's Easter brunch. And when Daddy turned her cell phone back on, the family calls started. Andrew apologized profusely and tried to explain that he'd only been trying to protect her, which simultaneously ticked her off and made her love him all the more. At least he cared about her.

Then Aunt Pam called and pleaded with her not to be too judgmental. Sometimes brothers and fathers could do silly things in the name of love.

Finally, Danny called and advised her not to burn too many bridges, and the sadness in his voice made her rethink. If she didn't like the family expressing their views about Dusty, she could hardly turn around and do the same to Danny. Arguing with him about his choices would only make him harden his heart and double down on his decision.

That single phone call rattled around in her head for a couple of days until she remembered something. Last

Monday, the day everything fell apart, she'd caught a quick glimpse of Danny with Roxanne Kopp out in the meadow by the Laurel Chapel. They had been sitting in the grass, their heads together, with the baby between them. They'd been laughing and gazing into each other's eyes, like they were a young family. A husband and wife, deeply in love with each other and their child.

Suddenly the jigsaw puzzle pieces fit together to make a coherent picture. All those years ago Danny had let Roxy tag along on their kid adventures, calling her a pest, teasing her, but never sending her away. Danny had a thing for Roxy. Maybe he always had.

She needed to explore this idea further. And what better way to confirm it than to show up at Charlotte's Grove for Easter brunch. Danny would be there. And the Kopps always came too.

Chapter Nineteen

The rain on Easter Sunday thwarted Aunt Pam's plans for Scarlett's first Easter egg hunt, snarled the traffic on Route 7, delaying the boys' arrival, and caused Amy's hair to go limp and lifeless—a fact that Aunt Pam noted the moment she walked through Charlotte's Grove's door. After accepting the commentary with as much grace as she could muster, Amy entered the family room.

Daddy sat on the love seat with ten-year-old Natalie, their heads together as they focused on an iPhone screen. Daddy was so engaged with his niece that he didn't even notice Amy when she entered the room.

Neither did Uncle Mark, Uncle Charles, David, or his sister, Heather, US Representative for Jefferson County, who huddled in the far corner of the room talking politics. Meanwhile, Roxy Kopp, Aunt Julie, and Willow occupied the larger sofa, their attention riveted on baby Scarlett, who was being her adorable self.

So Amy managed a nearly perfect stealth arrival and made a beeline to the bar, where she found Danny sitting by himself, obviously hiding out as well. He turned on his stool as she approached. "Can I interest you in a drink?" he asked. "We've got Merlot, Cabernet, and Pinot Grigio, as well as beer and hard stuff." Danny left his stool and assumed his post behind the bar.

"I'll take the Pinot."

He poured the wine and pushed the wineglass in her direction. Sometime in the last few days, Danny had gotten a haircut and shaved off his stubble. Even more surprising, instead of a Hawaiian shirt, he wore the standard family uniform: khaki pants, a striped golf shirt, a blue blazer, and tasseled loafers.

"So how does Mia like the new button-down, clean-cut you?" Amy asked.

He sipped his beer and didn't answer.

"Danny, come on, talk to me."

His gaze drifted across the room to where Roxy played patty-cake with Scarlett, the look on his face one part sad puppy and one part dangerous guard dog. Whoa. She didn't need anything more to confirm what she'd been thinking. Danny wanted Roxy—in the flesh. And he hated himself for it.

"So where is your bride?" Amy asked, knowing that she would probably provoke him. But maybe he needed a butt-kicking.

"Upstairs. She says she has a headache."

"And her friends?"

"They've taken off for New York this weekend. They can't wait for this shoot to be over. They're bored out of their minds."

"And you?"

He shook his head. "Not so much. Melissa and Jeff had us over for dinner last night. I like Jeff. A lot. It's a shame his mother kept him away from the rest of us when we were kids. Now that he's here in Shenandoah Falls, it's weird that he won't show his face at Charlotte's Grove. But I guess I admire the way he's taken a stand."

"And I'm grateful he's letting me stay at the fishing cabin rent free," Amy added.

"Speaking of fishing, David introduced me to your friend Dusty. In the wee hours this morning before the rain set in, we skipped church, and he took us to his favorite fishing spot on the Shenandoah River. The guy knows his stuff. I'll give him that. He's also soft-spoken and polite. Hardly the a-hole your brothers and father have tried to make him out to be."

"Thanks for the support. And I hope you're not just saying that so I'll have to come up with something nice to say about Mia. Because that would be a challenge." She gave him a little smile. "I know that's harsh, but it's just how I feel. Even so, I'm not going to try to talk you out of marrying her. Also I should tell you that my brief affair with Dusty McNeil is officially over."

Danny returned to his stool, picked up his beer, and lifted it in a toast. "Guess we're a couple of sad cases, huh?" He gazed across the room toward Roxy, who seemed to be having the time of her life playing with Scarlett. The yearning in his eyes said it all. "The more time I spend here at home in Shenandoah Falls, the more I realize that I want Scarlett to grow up knowing her family. I don't want her to be like Jeff, a stranger who's still angry with his absentee dad."

"Danny, quit kidding yourself. You want more than that, don't you?"

He remained silent for a long time before he shook his head. "What I want doesn't matter. Scarlett trumps everything. I've made up my mind, Amy. I'm going to marry Mia come hell or high water. I don't expect the marriage to last too long, but by the time it falls apart, I hope to have what I need to ensure that Mia loses custody. Right now all Mia wants is to be the center of attention for this shoot. Once she gets her moment in the spotlight, she'll move on to the next thing."

"Who's to say the next thing won't be worse?"

"Amy, I appreciate your concern, but—"

"Danny, look at Roxy. Tell me you don't care about her."

He frowned. "What are you talking about?"

"You cut your hair for her, didn't you?"

"I—"

His response was interrupted by the boys' arrival.

"Hey, everyone," Andrew said in an über-jovial tone as they entered the room. "We made it despite the floods and the traffic. Hope you guys don't mind, but we brought an extra mouth to feed. I think you all know our friend Grady."

A giant-sized expletive escaped Amy's mouth, and everyone turned from Grady to Amy and back again as if they were watching a match at Wimbledon.

Danny leaned forward on his stool and whispered, "Holy crap. This looks like an intervention."

"Count your blessings. If they weren't so hung up on trying to keep me in line, maybe they'd figure it all out and throw Roxy at you."

"Amy. Don't."

"No. You don't. Don't miss out on a good thing. You could fight Mia in court. You don't have to marry her any more than I have to marry Grady. Now, seriously, I gotta get out of here before I make a scene."

She turned away, scouting the room. The only exit that didn't take her in Grady's direction was out the French doors and into the rain. She headed in that direction, but it was too late. Grady had seen her and blocked her escape route.

He grabbed her by the shoulders and gave her a kiss on the lips. Thank God he didn't try to French her or she might have bitten his tongue and made a bloody scene, quite literally.

"You told everyone we were engaged," she whispered the moment his mouth retreated. "But I said no. Emphatically. You embarrassed me."

"I know you said no. The first time. But you're going to change your mind. And don't worry about your dad. I met with him a couple of days ago and made my intentions clear. He's given me his blessing. And Andrew is ready to help us talk this thing out." Grady let her go and pulled a little red Cartier box out of his jacket pocket.

"No. No, no, no, no," she said, putting up her palms and backing away. "No!"

"Marry me," Grady said in a loud voice as he dropped to one knee.

She couldn't speak, but that didn't matter since Grady didn't listen anyway. So this time, instead of refusing politely, she ran. Right out of the French doors and into the pouring rain.

Dusty spent Easter Sunday guiding several fishing parties along the Shenandoah River, where they caught a number of largemouth bass.

By all accounts, the expeditions had been successful, but Dusty felt restless and out of sorts all day. This feeling was nothing new. He'd been consumed with thoughts of Amy ever since he'd broken up with her. It didn't help that he saw her almost daily at the inn, but it was downright annoying that she occupied his thoughts even on his days off.

There were all kinds of things he wanted to tell her about. Like the fact that he'd finished his business plan and had scheduled a meeting next week with Jeff Talbert. He didn't hold out much hope that Jeff would invest in his idea, but at least he'd taken the first steps they'd outlined that day, before her father had returned. He never would have gotten this far without her.

In truth, he wanted to do more than talk to Amy about his plans. He still wanted to teach her to fish. He still wanted to make slow love to her, over and over again.

He was smitten, all right. And on Sunday night he even had a nightmare about her. He dreamed that she'd built a fire in the old Liberty Stove up at Jeff's cabin, but something went wrong. The stove melted down and set the cabin ablaze, trapping Amy and Muffin in an inferno that billowed great clouds of smoke. Dusty's eyes and throat burned as he wandered through the black clouds, unable to find her as his panic mounted.

He jolted awake to the piercing wail of his smoke detector and the acrid reek of smoke. The dream held his consciousness for a few moments as the panic spiraled. He had to find Amy.

No, he had to get out. He jumped up, at first thinking his

tiny house was on fire, but the lurid orange glow coming through his big picture window told him otherwise. The fire burned outside, its light flickering over the barn-wood walls and beamed ceilings of his home.

He jumped into his jeans, golf shirt, and boots, grabbed his cell phone, and raced out the front door in a matter of seconds. For an instant, standing on his deck, looking west, he thought the sky was on fire, so bright were the flames in the darkness.

He soon realized the glow came from the Liberty Furnace building, which burned like a bundle of well-dried kindling. The blaze licked through the broken windows and danced along the roofline, consuming the building's wooden beams and floors and sending out so much heat he could feel it even at this distance.

Sirens wailed as police and first responders arrived on the scene, the lights on their vehicles flashing. He took a step in the direction of the chaos, but his jangling phone halted him. The phone's screen said 4:30 a.m. when Dusty punched the talk button. "It's Dusty," he said.

"Chief LaRue here."

The police chief's angry tone froze him where he stood. "I know the foundry building's on fire," Dusty said. "The smoke set off my smoke detector a minute ago."

"Yeah, boy, it sure is on fire. And your daddy set it."

"What? How do you—"

"I don't know all the facts yet. But here's what I do know. Your daddy was in that building when it caught fire. It's anyone's guess what he was doing in there since the fire marshal condemned that building a year ago. He shouldn't have been there. And you own the building, Dusty."

A familiar guilt seized him. No, Daddy shouldn't have

been there. He should have been camped out in Dusty's living room. More important, when Daddy took off a few days ago, Dusty should have known to look for him in the foundry building, but he hadn't.

"Is he okay?" Dusty asked, his voice shaking.

"No. He's burned and unconscious. We're medevaccing him right now to the Washington Hospital Center's burn unit."

"Damn."

"You better get down there, boy, because I don't think your old man's gonna make it. But maybe that's a blessing, because if he lives I plan to charge his ass with arson and assault."

"Assault?"

"Yeah, assault. Officer Pierce was the first man on the scene. When Ryan realized someone was in the building, he had to be a goddamn hero and rush into it without any protective gear. Damn fool should have waited for the fire department. But he didn't. Probably because he's a goddamn Dudley Do-Right Marine."

"Chief, I'm sorry about this. I—"

"You can keep your apologies for Ryan and his family. Maybe you'll see them up in DC, because he's also been medevacced to the Washington Hospital Center with third-degree burns. He's gonna live, but he'll be living with the scars."

The chief paused for a moment before he said, "If I could arrest you, boy, and hold you accountable for this mess, I would. Honestly, if you'd let the county tear that place down, we wouldn't be where we are right this minute."

Chapter Twenty————————

Jeff's cabin was so back of beyond that Amy didn't have to turn her cell phone off to avoid the barrage of phone calls from her family. There were no bars of service way up on the ridge.

But on Monday morning when Amy ventured into town to do her laundry at the coin wash, her personal phone—the one Daddy paid for—reconnected with civilization and started buzzing like the end-times had arrived. Various family members had left dozens of new voice mails, texts, and e-mails, and they all took her to task for being rude to Grady.

No one took her side except for Danny.

What's more, neither Daddy nor Andrew apologized for the way they'd assisted Grady in ambushing her. Andrew seemed to think he had been doing good work trying to resolve the conflict between Amy and Grady. What the hell?

Did they not listen to her, ever? Andrew, especially, should have known better.

And did Grady think she needed her father's approval to get married?

She and Muffin sat in the Laundromat waiting for her dryer to finish while Amy reviewed her life and her options. By the time she'd folded her laundry, she'd come to a life-affirming conclusion.

Jeff had resigned from the family, and everyone wanted him to come back into the fold. Danny had walked away from the family, and the family seemed perfectly willing to stand by while he married a bitch of a gold digger.

Jeff got their grudging respect. Danny got their grudging indifference. Either of those would be better than the way her family was trying to meddle in her life right at the moment.

Maybe she should divorce the family and see if that changed their behavior. And what better way to send a message to them than to go after the one thing she wanted most? The one thing they disapproved of.

She lugged her laundry basket out to the Z4 and wedged it into the sports car's minuscule trunk. One thing was clear. She needed a bigger, more practical car, one she'd paid for on her own. She could hardly divorce the family if she continued to mooch off Daddy.

Maybe that explained why her father had reconnected her phone and reauthorized her American Express card. Maybe he thought bribing her would keep her in line.

She gave Muffin a little scratch under her chin. "I've been an idiot. You and Dusty are the best things that ever happened to me," she said. Muffin gave her a sloppy kiss and then climbed into the passenger's seat. Amy fired up the Beemer.

"I'm going to get my man," she said to the dog, who woofed her support.

She headed out toward Dusty's place, praying that she'd find him at home but knowing that he'd probably gone fishing today. She didn't care. She'd wait for him. All day if necessary.

She didn't get far down Morgan Avenue before the acrid smell of smoke reached her. A haze of it hung in the air well before she saw the burned-out foundry building. The building's roof had collapsed, taking most of the back wall with it. Blackened bricks and the charred remains of beams had tumbled inward to make a huge, smoking pile of rubble. Yellow police tape ringed the site, and Paul LaRue, the chief of the Shenandoah Falls Police Force, stood near the wreckage with a group of firemen wearing hard hats.

Police cruisers and a fire engine blocked Morgan Avenue, and police were directing traffic toward Second Street. She pulled up to one of the policemen, who immediately said, "You'll need to go around to George Mason Avenue if you're headed anywhere on the east side of town."

"What happened?"

"Old man McNeil set the place on fire. Unfortunately, he got himself caught in the blaze. Officer Pierce ran in to rescue him, but they both were injured when part of the wall collapsed."

"Oh my God. How bad are they hurt?" Amy asked, her pulse running wild.

"Pierce managed to get them both out alive. The old man's in a bad way. Pierce has some burns."

Amy's mind shifted into overdrive. Someone needed to be with Dusty right now. He probably blamed himself for what had happened. "Do you know where Dusty is?"

The policeman sobered. "No, I don't. And I don't give a damn. If he'd been reasonable about that park project, Ryan Pierce would never have gotten himself burned."

Amy wanted to tell the man that the park project had nothing to do with this disaster. The county didn't have the money to buy Dusty out yet, so even if Dusty had agreed to the sale, it wouldn't have changed a thing.

Still, everyone in town would share the cop's viewpoint once they heard the news about Officer Pierce. They would blame Dusty, and the facts wouldn't matter.

"You need to let me pass. I need to get down to Dusty's place, and the only access is off Morgan Avenue."

"Sorry, ma'am, I can't do that. This street is off-limits to all but residents. Besides, I think Dusty's probably in DC right now, since his father was medevacced to the MedStar unit at Washington Hospital Center. Chief LaRuc notified him early this morning."

"Thanks," she said, shifting the Beemer into reverse. She made a quick U-turn and headed in the opposite direction. It took only a few minutes to drive up to the inn, where she settled Muffin in the dog kennel with Sven. She tried to reach Willow but only got voice mail, so she left a message about Dusty and Muffin and then headed east on Route 7 toward Washington.

At ten fifteen on Monday morning, Dr. Lewis found Dusty in the waiting room at Washington Hospital Center and delivered the bad news. Daddy had died, but the cause of death had little to do with the fire.

It turned out that Chief LaRue had his facts wrong.

Daddy had a few burns, none of them life-threatening, according to the docs. But he'd suffered a heart attack. The docs said it was quite possible that if Daddy had been squatting in the foundry building and using candles or building unsafe fires, the heart attack could have caused the fire and not the other way around.

"And Officer Pierce?" Dusty asked, his voice husky.

The doctor's face brightened. "He's doing fine. I don't think there'll be much scarring. But the burns are third-degree."

Dusty nodded. "Thanks."

"I'm sorry for your loss. Did you want to speak with a chaplain?"

Dusty shook his head.

"All right. One of the hospital social workers will come down in a moment with some papers you'll need to sign. She'll have information on what happens next. Again, I'm sorry for your loss."

"Thanks."

The doc nodded and left the waiting room.

His loss? Was it a loss? He couldn't decide. He collapsed back into the hard plastic waiting-room chair, dropped his head into his hands, and pressed his fingers to his eye sockets. He would not cry. Daddy didn't deserve his tears.

The waiting room door swished open, and he looked up, expecting the social worker or chaplain.

"Amy?" He stood up. With her hair pulled back into a ponytail and dressed in jeans and sneakers, she reminded him of the proverbial girl next door. Adorable and sexy. And definitely an angel of mercy.

"I came as soon as I heard," she said in a breathy voice,

as if she'd run all the way from the parking lot. "How is your father? Is he—"

"He died."

The minute Dusty said the word, his voice fractured into a million sharp shards like shattered crystal. All the pain of his childhood, all the fury of his teenage years, all the shame of his adult life came out of him in one long sob that he couldn't choke back.

He turned toward the door. No way he wanted Amy to see him fall apart, but his emotions had another idea, and so did Amy. She intercepted him before he could escape, putting herself right in front of the door. Then she grabbed his arms in a surprisingly sturdy grip. The moment their gazes collided, the hurt he'd kept hidden deep inside burbled out of him.

A hoarse, strangled cry escaped him as a tsunami of pain tried to drown him. But Amy wrapped her arms around his neck and pulled him down so he could rest his head on her shoulder. She became his anchor. His safe harbor. His lifesaver.

She spoke not one word while he wept, but her tight embrace held him up. How the hell had such a little woman become so strong? How could she hold him together when it felt as if he'd come apart at the seams?

"It's okay," she finally said when he'd almost run out of tears.

He didn't want to lift his head or meet her gaze. What would she think about a guy who cried like a freaking baby?

But, as usual, Amy had a few surprises up her sleeve. "Listen to me, Dusty," she said in a fierce tone as she pulled back a little and forced him to raise his head and meet her gaze. "You are not to blame. Not for any of it."

She had the truth of it, but the truth couldn't wipe away the blame. Daddy had instilled this guilt in him as a young boy, and he would never lose it. He tried to push her away, but she wouldn't let go. And her determined grip made him choke up a second time. Dammit all, he wanted to be good enough for her.

"I get it," she said, seemingly unconcerned with the second wave of tears welling up in his eyes. "I understand. You think there's no place for you with me. You think I'm not strong enough to be with you because your father screwed you up. Or because of all the stupid bullshit my father believes about you. But you're wrong. I'm strong enough to love all of you, Dusty. Even the parts your father broke. And I know those parts make it hard for you to commit. But here's a news flash. I don't give a rat's ass about that."

The tightness in his throat disappeared. Damn. Amy had a talent for reading his mind. How did she know all this? How had she become so wise?

Maybe she'd always been that way.

She pointed one of her fingers at his chest and continued. "Dusty, I know you loved your father even though he hurt you. God knows I love my father, but I'm also angry with him. Did you know that he cheated on my mom? Yeah, he did. And they were miserable with each other. So believe me, I didn't grow up in a blissfully happy home either. Not that I can fully understand what happened to you when you were a kid."

"No, you can't," he managed in a still-shaky voice.

"No, I can't. But I can affirm one thing. Your father was not worthy of your tears."

And after she made this pronouncement, she bounced up on tiptoes and pressed her mouth to his. She didn't sweep away his pain. He didn't lose his fear about what her father might do to him if he let her into his life. But he suddenly didn't care about any of that crap.

Amy was his beacon of hope, and maybe it was time to give hope a chance.

❦

Amy hadn't won her war against Dusty's guilt. But when he thrust his tongue into her mouth, turning her sweet, desperate kiss into something hot and carnal, she counted it as a victory in the first skirmish. Maybe she shouldn't use sex to pull Dusty back from the brink. After all, his father had just passed away.

But Amy didn't want Dusty to mourn his father. Not if it meant he would wallow in guilt and shame. The way she saw it, the quicker Greg McNeil was buried and forgotten, the sooner Dusty could move on with his life.

She disengaged from his hungry kiss by linking a few little nips down his chin and neck before raising her head and inspecting him. Lines of exhaustion radiated from his puffy red eyes. His five o'clock shadow had grown into scruff. He needed someone to take care of him.

"Let's find a place to crash," she said.

"No. I should—"

She put her hand over his mouth. "No. You should crash. There's no hurry. Someone ducked in a minute ago while you were having your moment. She left some papers on the chair. I think you probably have to sign some stuff, but that's it. We can take care of that chore together. And we'll call Willow and Courtney and ask them to make the arrangements. They're good at that kind of thing."

"But I should—"

"No. You don't have to do this. Let your friends take care of it while you take a one-day vacation from your life. I suggest we find a hotel. How about the Hay-Adams?"

"The Hay-Adams? Can you afford that? It's gotta be three hundred dollars a night." Dusty's eyebrows knit together.

She gave him her best rich, naughty-girl grin. "So?"

"But—"

"I have Daddy's Amex card. He reauthorized its use because he thinks he can bribe me into behaving. The truth is, I had planned to cut it up into tiny pieces and throw them in his face, but I didn't get the chance yesterday. So now I think I should use Daddy's money for a room at the Hay-Adams."

The corner of Dusty's mouth twitched, as if he wanted to smile but wouldn't let himself.

"It's okay. I know what you're thinking—shacking up with me at the Hay-Adams would be so inappropriate given the situation. But you're wrong about that."

"Come here," he said in a deep voice, settling his hands on her hips and pulling her toward him in a completely possessive way that woke up Amy's girl parts.

"Yes," she whispered, snuggling up into his chest.

"I want you," he whispered.

"So? What's the problem?"

He dipped his head and proceeded to kiss her senseless. When he drew back, his baby blues were heavy-lidded. "I should have my head examined. But I'm thinking that an afternoon with you at the Hay-Adams sounds good."

Dusty left his old blue pickup truck in the parking structure at the hospital because, in addition to implying that Amy would give him her body, she'd also sweetened the deal by letting him drive the Z4, which he considered nothing but foreplay.

Man, that car was fast and smooth and handled like a dream. He enjoyed every minute behind the wheel, but he still couldn't shake the guilt that niggled at him.

He ought to be planning Daddy's funeral. But Amy had taken that job off his hands and handed it to Courtney. He could have stopped her, but he didn't. He just felt relieved.

"You're thinking too much," Amy said from the passenger's side.

He turned in time for her to give him one of her I'm-up-to-no-good grins as her ponytail streamed behind her in the wind. "It's hard not to think," he said.

She nodded. "I can see how that might be the case. So, should I start stripping in the car? Give you something else to think about?"

He laughed, and it broke something inside. How could he laugh at a time like this?

She reached over the console and ran her fingertips up and down his thigh, featherlight, and damned if that touch didn't pull his mind right away from the guilt. Probably because all his blood rushed south.

Oh yeah, driving that car with her touching him counted as foreplay. Suddenly, being alive seemed almost miraculous. His breathing, his beating heart, the wind rushing through his hair, the sun beating down on his skin, the scents of the city, the noise of the traffic, and Amy's seductive touch became one unified affirmation that life goes on and that life should be lived in the moment.

But that heady feeling vanished when Dusty pulled the Z4 into the circular driveway of the Hay-Adams, one of DC's landmarks, located a mere block from the White House. Dusty had never seen the place before, and the granite grandeur of the facade, the polished brass of the front doors, and the crisp uniforms of the bellhops made him uneasy.

The place reeked of old-world money. A small-town boy like him didn't belong here; nor was the Hay-Adams the sort of place that booked rooms by the hour.

He cleared his throat. "Uh, Amy, maybe we should go find a no-tell motel or something."

Amy leaned across the console and gave him a quick kiss that scrambled his brain. "Just remember that your great-great-grandfather was an industrialist and a robber baron, which makes him exactly like the man who originally built the Hay-Adams."

He glanced up at the building's imposing facade and wondered if any of his forebears had ever booked a room here.

"Exactly," Amy said, as if she could mind read. "And besides, I respect you too much to take you to a no-tell motel." She delivered that line deadpan, although something sparked down deep in her eyes.

Another laugh stuck in his throat, just as one of the impeccably uniformed attendants opened the car's door. It was now or never.

He decided to go back to living in the moment and climbed out of the leather-upholstered bucket seat and handed off the car keys. When he joined Amy at the hotel's front steps, she took his hand and practically dragged him into the lobby, which featured ornately carved walnut pillars holding up a vaulted ceiling complete with plaster medallions covered in gold leaf.

The clerk behind the registration desk inspected Dusty's work boots, blue jeans, and fishing shirt and judged him on the spot. His expression remained stern when he shifted his gaze and took in Amy's holey jeans, skimpy cotton tank top, and sneakers. Amy had probably spent several hundred dollars for her ragamuffin look, but the guy behind the desk treated her like she was a bum or something.

The guy's officious attitude chapped Dusty's ass but had zero effect on Amy, who pulled a platinum Amex card out of her purse and slapped it on the counter. "We'd like a room, please. One with a view of the White House, if possible."

The man picked up the credit card, and Dusty fully expected him to give them the brush-off. But instead the clerk inspected the name on the card, and his eyes widened. "Ms. Lyndon," he said, one eyebrow curling upward, "are you related to the senator?"

"He's my uncle. And Representative Heather Lyndon is my cousin. But I don't see why that matters. Do you have a room available or not?"

"Uh, yes, we do. With a view. Do you have luggage?" His gaze bounced from Amy to Dusty and back again.

"No. I have laundry in my car. We'll get it if we need it."

"Right." The guy looked down and started processing their registration.

Amy leaned in to Dusty and whispered, "He's an asshole. He doesn't know that you're the famous fishing guide."

"I'm not famous."

"Not yet. But you will be." She looked inordinately pleased with herself.

The clerk finally produced a key, which opened a hotel room sumptuously decorated in neutral tones with brown velvet tie-back curtains draped over the bed's mahogany headboard like old-fashioned bed hangings.

The room also had a view of the White House, but Dusty didn't get much time to enjoy it because Amy turned toward him, snaked her arms around his neck, and pulled him down for another one of her soft, sweet, intoxicating kisses. He promptly forgot about the fire and the hospital and his own culpability in Daddy's death.

All that guilt disappeared, and in its place something new and amazing blossomed inside him like the most perfect rose. In those kisses, Dusty found a belief that maybe one day he could become a man worthy of someone whose last name unlocked doors. In Amy's kisses, Dusty found a new image for himself. Not the son of a drunk, but a fishing guide with a business of his own. A man who deserved respect, not blame.

Her kisses touched him down deep in the place where his darkest feelings lived, and they made him hungry. He backed her up against the hotel room's door, trying to devour her as she slid her hands down over his shoulders to his ass. She pulled him closer so the curves of her thighs and breasts pressed hard against him. They were so close, and yet she still seemed out of reach. He ground himself against her, an inarticulate sound of frustration and need escaping him.

She broke the kiss. "What do you need?" Her dark eyes had gone black, but the spark of desire burned bright in their depths.

"You're too far away," he murmured.

"Do you want the striptease I promised?"

He shook his head. He didn't want to be teased. Enough foreplay. He wanted to get down to the real action.

She must have figured that out because she lifted the hem of her shirt over her head, baring her breasts without making it a tease at all. And that's when he realized she had gone braless today. No wonder her nipples had been putting on a floor show for him.

He cupped one of her breasts, the perfect size to fill his hand, the nipple hardening against his palm. With his other hand, he pulled the elastic from her ponytail. Her dark hair fell down in soft waves around her shoulders. He buried his nose in it and drank in the scent. Floral and spicy and something unique labeled "Amy." His ability to think and reason disappeared. He needed her. He needed the release. But a part of him—maybe the broken part that longed to be healed—wanted to go slowly.

He lifted his head again. "I want you."

"I know," she said, then bit her lip in the sexiest expression he'd ever seen. His pulse hit the red line as she unbuttoned his shirt and ghosted her hands over his chest in a soft exploration that made him ache all over. He shrugged off his shirt and pulled her tight against him. It was better skin to skin.

He wanted more. "I need you." The words were practically torn from his throat. He didn't like to admit stuff like that.

"I know," she said.

Damn. He bracketed her face with his hands and pulled her up into another amazing kiss that still wasn't enough.

She broke away with a mock-serious look. "Dusty," she said in a soft whisper, "what the hell are you waiting for? I'm not a princess or a virgin."

Okay, he could get with that program. He picked her up and dropped her on the bed and watched her sink into the poufy comforter. She stacked her hands behind her head, giving him a fabulous view of her pert little breasts.

"Ooh, I like this," she said. "And since I'm here and you're there, how about *you* give *me* the striptease?"

He refused to do some candy-ass, *Full Monty* dance, but he was happy to get naked. He shucked his pants and boots in world-record time while she giggled like a little sex kitten. When he straightened up, she stopped laughing.

"Oh, Dusty, you are beautiful," she said on a long sigh. "Come here." She opened her arms for him.

"Not before I get you naked too," he said as he tackled her sneakers and then her holey jeans. "Wow, nice panties," he said when her black, lacy thong was revealed. "I think I want you to keep them on for a while."

He crawled into the ridiculously sumptuous bed, with the fluffy comforter and a bunch of throw pillows and velvet bed hangings. All that luxury paled in comparison to Amy wearing a black lace thong that he intended to take off slowly— like maybe with his teeth. And then maybe after he'd made her come at least once, he'd get what he wanted more than anything else in the world—to be inside her.

Chapter Twenty-One

Amy awakened to Dusty spooning her, his arms a warm cradle and his breathing deep and even. She settled back and closed her eyes. The sun hadn't come up yet; she'd enjoy her last few moments before they had to return to the real world. But as soon as she dozed off again, reality arrived in the form of a 5:00 a.m. wakeup call. Now the hard part started.

"We have to go," he said, and didn't even give her a chance to pull him back into bed. He headed for the sumptuous bathroom, where the sound of water running sparked all sorts of fun fantasies of shower sex. She let them fill her mind, but she didn't act on them.

Like Dusty, she had places to be, and work obligations. They had a corporate event at the manor, plus last-minute details for no less than three weekend weddings, one each on Friday, Saturday, and Sunday. Besides, Muffin needed attention even though Willow had assured her yesterday that the dog would be well cared for.

So she waited until Dusty finished in the bathroom and took her shower alone. Then they drove back to the hospital so he could pick up his truck. The drive took twenty minutes in traffic, and they said not one word the entire way.

But when she pulled the Z4 to the corner so Dusty could get out, she turned to him and said, "Don't think this was a one-time thing." She snagged his hand before he left the car. "I have to work today, but I'll come to your place as soon as I can. I also don't want you worrying about the funeral details, okay? Let Courtney and me handle them. For the record, I intend to get every member of the Episcopal Altar Guild to send casseroles."

"That'll be the day," he said.

"You think I can't make that happen?" she said in her best imitation of Aunt Pam's take-no-prisoners voice.

His mouth quirked at the corner, but maybe not in amusement. "If anyone could make it happen, you'd be the one. But seriously, I don't need casseroles."

"Sure you do."

He leaned in. "No, I don't. It's only me in my tiny house. And no one's going to stop by to give me condolences."

"You don't know that. Besides, I'll be stopping by."

His eyebrow arched, and she thought he might be about to say something. But instead he cupped the back of her head and drew her in for an erotic goodbye kiss.

Dusty's reputation as a Casanova was well deserved. He was incredible between the sheets, and Amy wanted a lot more of that. But she also wanted to take care of him because she'd fallen in love with him.

She almost said the words aloud when he broke the kiss

and opened the car's door. The words perched on the tip of her tongue, ready to take flight, but she shut her mouth and swallowed them back. Dusty didn't need the stress of her love right now. Maybe some other time, after the funeral, after the fallout from the fire died down. And certainly after she'd formally divorced her family and told them all to go to hell.

Or maybe never. Living in the moment seemed like a much better plan.

In any event, Amy had a lot of items on her to-do list. It turned out the Episcopal Altar Guild didn't think non–church members were entitled to their casseroles, even though Amy had been a member of their congregation her entire life and specifically asked for their Christian charity.

So Amy turned to Gracie Teague and Poppy Braden, both members of Grace Presbyterian, and by Monday afternoon the Presbyterians had come through in spades. So much so that Amy decided to leave the Episcopalians and join the Presbyterians as part of her family divorce.

She also took over the funeral details from Courtney the moment she arrived at work on Tuesday morning, not that Courtney had left all that much for her to do. She put the memorial service on the schedule for the Laurel Chapel on Thursday. There would be no graveside services because Dusty wanted his father's ashes scattered over the waters of Liberty Run. And everyone decided that an obituary was unnecessary.

Courtney, Willow, Grace, and Poppy sent e-mails and text messages to all of Dusty's friends. No need to let anyone else know where or when the memorial service would take place, not with some folks so upset about Ryan Pierce's injuries.

So living in the moment was easy. But even so, when Amy and Muffin arrived at Dusty's house on Tuesday evening bearing a huge shepherd's pie, she didn't know quite what to expect. Would he push her away or welcome her in?

He opened the door and greeted her with, "Oh, crap. Not another casserole. Did you actually make that?"

She shook her head. "Um, no. Antonin did, but it's shepherd's pie."

He chuckled, the sound like music. "Good. We can eat that right now because I'm not a big fan of tuna surprise. And my tiny refrigerator is already filled to overflowing."

She moved forward, but before she could cross the threshold, Dusty snagged her around the waist and pulled her up into one of his signature kisses. Muffin immediately sat down and gave a small woof of approval.

Amy stayed with Dusty on Tuesday and Wednesday nights. They made love. They held each other through the night. They settled into a mini-routine that grew more comfortable with each day.

Then on Thursday morning, Amy sat beside Dusty during his father's memorial service at Laurel Chapel, attended by about fifty people—members of the Eagle Hill Manor family, a few of Dusty's friends from the landscaping company where he'd worked before, and at least twenty members of the community, every single one of them a serious fly fisherman.

After the religious service, a small group of close friends accompanied Dusty on the walk down to Liberty

Run, where he scattered his father's ashes. The funeral was short and somber, and everyone, including Dusty, remained dry-eyed.

No one mourned Greg McNeil for long. By noon everyone, including Dusty, was back at work because of the killer weekend schedule followed by the *Vegas Girls* three-ringed circus on Wednesday. The decorations for that event would require an incredibly quick turnaround in the Carriage House.

Even with that much work on her plate, Amy needed to act on her divorce plans. So Friday, Amy drove up to the vineyard during lunch for what she had started thinking of as "the final confrontation." She found Daddy in his office on the ground floor of the gigantic house that he now lived in all by himself. The door was open, but she knocked on the doorframe and said, "You got a minute?"

Daddy gave her the patented Lyndon scowl. "Are you here to apologize for your rudeness on Easter Sunday and your behavior since?"

Amy would have laughed, except that laughing at Daddy would only annoy him further, and she'd come on a mission that would probably do a whole lot more than annoy him. So she said nothing as she crossed the deep-pile carpet and ensconced herself in the leather chair set in front of his desk.

Her heart beat ferociously, making her hands tremble as she reached into her purse and pulled out her platinum Amex card and her personal cell phone. She laid both on the table like offerings. "I'm not here to apologize," she said in a surprisingly steady voice. "I'm here to give back the phone and the Amex card."

Daddy straightened in his chair. "Amy, I told you I

didn't care about the goddamn credit card bills. I was wrong about that. I shouldn't have yelled at you about the bills. And I shouldn't have kicked you out of the house. I just thought that—"

"You thought I'd go running to Grady, right? But I didn't, and that should tell you something right there. And besides, you were right to yell at me about those credit card bills. I didn't realize how meaningless my life was until I had to sleep in my car for two nights. So you did me a favor. I know you don't see it that way right now, but I hope one day you will."

"Okay, I'll take the card, but not the phone. I have a good idea what your salary is, and you can't afford a cell phone, but you need one for safety."

"I'm fine. A cell phone comes with the job," she said, proudly showing her father the iPhone Willow had put in her hands the first day she'd started as an event planner.

"But—"

She held up her hand. "But nothing. Daddy, you're the one who said I needed to stand on my own two feet. What you didn't comprehend was that standing on my own means I can't marry Grady."

"Wait, no. It means no such thing. You can be independent and married to Grady. Honey, Grady is a great guy. The whole family approves of him."

"Yeah, Daddy, he is a nice guy. But I don't love him. And here's the important thing—I. Am. Not. Mom."

"What does Mom have to do with this?"

"Everyone in the family has always said I'm like her. And she stayed in a marriage that made her unhappy. She continued living with a man who cheated on her, and—"

"Wait. What?"

She folded her arms across her chest. This was a very awkward conversation. "Daddy, I know you were unfaithful to Mom."

"And you know this how?"

"Because when you and Mom argued, you shouted, and Mom always brought it up."

"It was a long time ago. Before you were born."

"Doesn't matter. It was an issue. And frankly, Mom should have left you long ago."

"You'd never have been born if she'd done that."

"Okay, I concede that point. But Mom stayed in a marriage that made her miserable because she didn't have the courage to face life on her own. So when you, and everyone in the family, compares me to Mom and then tries to marry me off to some rich guy I don't love, you ought to understand why I'm not happy about it."

Her voice wavered. "So I'm taking a break from the family. I'm doing what Jeff and Danny did," she said.

"What does that mean? Are you telling me you're moving to California? Tell me how running away makes any sense at all." His voice reeked of condescension.

What the hell? Did he think she was having a little temper tantrum that would pass like a summer thunderstorm? Well, he could think again.

"No, Daddy. As usual, you're not listening. I'm not running away. I'm not even leaving town. I have a job at Eagle Hill Manor that I like. A lot. But from now on, I won't be coming to dinners or holiday events at Charlotte's Grove or up at the winery. Not after what all of you did to me at Easter brunch this year. That was low and mean. Not just to me, but to Grady too."

"Amy, don't be ridiculous."

Damn, damn, damn. Always the same thing. She stood up and leaned on his desk. "Daddy, I'm telling you that I want a divorce," she said.

"You what? Amy, you can't divorce a family. Don't be silly."

Did he think that calling her names would change anything? Probably. Daddy loved her, but he didn't respect her intelligence. She bore some responsibility for that. Like Mom, she'd drifted through her life until recently.

"I'm not being silly. The fact is I love you, but we have irreconcilable differences."

"Good grief, Amy. What on earth are you talking about?"

"I'm talking about the fact that everyone in the family has taken to calling me names and challenging my intelligence. But here's the thing. Maybe I am a stupid ridiculous idiot, but I am also a free American woman. And that means I have the right to choose the person I love."

He glared at her for a long moment, his jaw flexing. "Amy, we're trying to protect you. I know you don't feel like a rich person right now, but one day you will be worth a great deal of money, and there are unscrupulous men who would—"

"Daddy, I get it."

Yeah, he definitely had the angry-daddy face going now, but this time she had no intention of running away from it. She could do this. She could hold her own with him. "I'm free to choose love over money if I want to."

His forehead lowered. "You think you can live without money? You think Dusty McNeil would be better for you than Grady Carson? Is that it?"

"Yes. I love Dusty."

Whoa, she'd said the words right out loud. Good thing she hadn't slipped up and said them to Dusty. If she ever did that, she had a feeling he might disappear faster than a package of Oreo cookies on Netflix night.

"Oh, for goodness' sake, Amy, you're being—"

"Stop. Don't say it. I don't want to hear it. Love is love, Daddy. And I've fallen in love with Dusty. He's the guy I want in my life. And if you'd give him a chance, you might change your mind about him. But I see now that you're never going to do that, so I have to make a choice. And I'm choosing Dusty instead of the family."

Chapter Twenty-Two————

Scattering Daddy's ashes didn't end Dusty's troubles. On Friday morning, his insurance company called to let him know that his liability coverage might be limited because the Jefferson County fire inspector had notified them of an arson investigation.

Since the building wasn't insured, the idea that someone had burned it down with a profit motive made no sense. Dusty carried an umbrella policy on the property, of course, in case someone injured themselves. And obviously, he and his insurance company were responsible for Officer Pierce's injuries. He'd already been in touch with Ryan's mother and offered to help with any and all medical bills. But if his insurance company refused to cover the claim, he'd be in deep shit all the way around. So he wasn't in the best frame of mind early Saturday morning when Jamie Lyndon darkened his door, wearing a take-no-prisoners expression on his face as he strolled into Dusty's small office, closing the door behind him.

"You're in a heap of trouble," Lyndon said, pointing out the obvious as he made himself comfortable in the chair in front of Dusty's desk.

"How so?"

"Chief LaRue is hopping mad at you. Paul can sometimes lose perspective on things when it comes to the guys on his force. He's determined to make someone pay for what happened to Ryan Pierce, and you're the one in his gun sights."

Dusty leaned forward in his chair and crossed his arms on the desk, assuming a pose of strength. "Mr. Lyndon, are you here to talk about the fire at the foundry building or the fact that Amy has been sleeping at my house the last few days? Because if you're trying to threaten me over the fire, it ain't working. I didn't set that fire, and I'm sure the investigation will show I had nothing to do with it. I've already been in touch with Ryan and his family about the medical bills."

Lyndon gave Dusty a feral smile. "The two issues are conflated."

"How so?"

"Because with the chief of police against you, living here in Shenandoah Falls is likely to become less and less attractive. Add Amy to that mix, and it's likely to become intolerable. The fact is, you need a fresh start in life. And I'm here to make that happen."

That was a surprise. Was the old guy coming around? "What are you suggesting?"

"I'm prepared to make a very generous offer for your land."

Lyndon pulled a yellow sticky note out of his breast pocket and passed it across the desk. Dusty picked it up and read the astronomical sum with a dollar sign in front of it.

"That's what I'm willing to offer you in cash. It's more than you'll ever get from the county. And after you pay off your mortgage, you'll still have plenty of funds to set up shop elsewhere."

Dusty locked gazes with the man. "And the quid pro quo?"

"You leave this town and never come back."

"Do I have to decide right now?"

Lyndon stood up. "No. But don't take too long to think about this. If you don't accept this offer in the next couple of days, I'll fund the county's effort to seize your property through eminent domain. So basically, you can do this the easy way or the hard way, but either way, the county gets your land."

Lyndon stood and strolled toward the door with the air of a man who had the means to buy whatever he wanted.

"Wait," Dusty said to his back. "I accept your offer."

Lyndon turned, the surprise evident on his face. Dusty took solace in that, and the fact that he'd just bested Jamie Lyndon, and the Big Man didn't even know it.

"I'm surprised," Lyndon said. "I expected more of a fight from you. I guess what folks say about you is true."

Dusty had a good idea what "folks" said about him. Dusty's reputation had been less than stellar for a long while, but his future in this town had been completely torched the minute Daddy burned down the foundry. "How quick can we make this happen?" Dusty asked.

"I'll check with my lawyers. I'm sure we can get the

papers signed and a check in your hands by Thursday or Friday of next week. After Danny's wedding."

"What do you need from me?"

"Not one thing. I already know everything there is to know about you."

Which was ironic, because he clearly did not.

⚜

Amy got through the small wedding on Friday without a hitch, but the wedding reception on Saturday got kind of rowdy and didn't wrap up until well after midnight. She was so exhausted Saturday night that she fell into Dusty's cozy bed up in his loft and didn't even think about making love.

Normally neither of them worked on Sundays, but this particular weekend they had a gigantic wedding and reception, complete with a flower-laden *chuppa* that had to be erected by the gazebo and two hundred wedding guests who had to be fed.

They both had to get up early on Sunday morning.

When the alarm sounded, Dusty batted it off and pulled Amy into his arms. "Morning sex would be nice," he said.

Amy buried her nose against his chest, drinking in the morning scent of him. Talk about an aphrodisiac.

He combed his hands through her hair and pulled her a little closer. "I need to tell you something," he whispered.

Her heart took flight. Was this the magic moment? She pulled back a little and looked deep into his heavy-lidded baby blues. The words of love she'd so wanted to say were right at the tip of her tongue.

She paused a moment before speaking her heart, and

good thing, too, because he pulled away and his gaze sobered.

Uh-oh. This wasn't the "I love you" talk. The momentary swell of emotion receded, leaving her hollow. "What is it?" she asked, her whisper almost strangled.

"The county fire marshal has opened an arson investigation. I found out about it on Friday, but I didn't want to worry you. Turns out my insurance company is sending their own investigator, and there's going to be an effort to tie me to the fire."

"But that makes no sense. Why would you burn the place down? It's not insured, is it?"

"No. But I do have liability coverage in case someone gets hurt. And that's what this is mostly about. Chief LaRue is ticked off, and he's blaming me because Daddy isn't here to blame. It's an old, old story."

"That's ridiculous."

"I know. I'll eventually be cleared of any wrongdoing. But that doesn't change the fact that I'm going to lose in the court of public opinion. That article in the *Winchester Daily* a few weeks ago makes that abundantly clear. Jefferson County wants to turn my land into a park, and everyone thinks I'm standing in the way."

"But the county doesn't have the money for the park."

"That's true now, but not for long."

"Dusty, you can't give up."

"Yes, I can. And here's the thing. Your father is giving me a second chance."

Alarm shivered up her spine. "What are you talking about?"

"He's offered to buy me out at a price that's significantly higher than what the county is likely to pay me. Quite frankly, he's willing to pay more than what the land is worth."

"How much more?"

"About twenty-five percent. I'd be a fool not to take the offer. So I did."

"What? But what about your business plan? What about your—"

He put his fingers across her mouth. "Hush. Your father's cash will allow me to invest someplace else."

She pulled his hand away. "But he's bullying you, trying to make you leave town because of me. I won't—"

"Hush. I know all that. But I've put one over on him, because you're going to come with me when I make the move to Montana."

"What?"

He pulled her closer, the touch heartbreaking. "Amy," he whispered in her ear, "I've got it all figured out. We'll go to Montana. I'll get a job as a fishing guide. We'll drive across country and explore the West together. It's all arranged. We'll go to closing on Thursday or Friday."

She pulled away from him and sat up in the bed. "I don't want to live in Montana."

"What?"

"You heard me. When did I ever say I wanted to move to Montana?"

"I thought you wanted to divorce your family. Montana is a—"

"I do want to divorce the family. But I don't want to run away from them. Did it ever occur to you that I might have something to say about what happened next? Or whether I might have some thoughts about where or if we should move? Why didn't you talk to me about this instead of taking Daddy's money? He's manipulating you, and I can't stand it."

"He didn't manipulate me. He made a big mistake trying to buy me out. He asked me to leave town and never come back, but he didn't stipulate that I couldn't take you with me."

Dammit. Dammit to hell and back again. Everyone—even Dusty—thought they could tell her what to do and where to go.

She pulled away from him. "I'm not going with you," she said, her voice wobbling.

"What?"

"I told you. I'm not going with you. I thought you were ready to stay and fight. I thought you believed in your cause."

"Amy, there's no way I can win. Don't you understand?"

"But you could."

He shook his head. "It's hopeless. I need to leave this place."

"And you think I'll just pull up stakes and go with you?"

Just then Muffin, who was required to sleep downstairs in the tiny house, started barking. The dog didn't like it when people got upset. No doubt she'd come from a broken home with a lot of drama.

Amy picked up her clothes from the floor where she'd dropped them the night before. "I gotta go," she said.

"Amy, come on. Don't be—"

"What? Ridiculous?"

He pressed his lips together, apparently wise enough not to answer that question.

"You're the one who's being ridiculous," she said, stepping into the dress she'd worn yesterday. She picked up her heels and headed down the steep stairs to the living room. He followed her, but she tried to ignore him. She didn't want to be sidetracked by all that gorgeous naked man.

She grabbed Muffin's leash, snapped it to the dog's collar, and headed for the door.

"Amy, please, let's talk about this," he said in a gruff voice.

When she got to the door, she turned around. He was amazingly handsome, standing there all nude and male and hot. But she could live without him, if living with him meant running away and letting him make all the decisions.

"Enjoy Daddy's money," she said. Then she peeled through the front door at a dead run and slammed the Z4 through its gears as she drove away. She almost broke a speed record covering the distance between Dusty's house and Jeff's cabin. When she got up the ridge, she ran a hot shower and cried for exactly ten minutes before pulling herself together. What had she expected anyway?

A lifetime love?

Ha! Not with the Casanova of Shenandoah Falls. Or Greg McNeil's emotionally scarred son. It had been a lovely affair, but it was over. And it annoyed her to no end that Daddy had been right about him.

Money meant more to him than love.

Chapter Twenty-Three —

Danny couldn't believe the transformation that had taken place in the Carriage House. He strolled through the French doors on Wednesday afternoon and literally goggled at the extravagant circus-themed decor. Hot pink and purple fabric streamers swathed the rafters and draped down the walls, creating the illusion of a circus tent. Pink, purple, and white lights twinkled below like fireflies on a summer's evening. Twenty tables dressed in purple and pink linens surrounded the dance floor, where an acrobatic rig had been set up, the steel structure hung with fabric to create the illusion of an open-sided Bedouin tent.

The room hummed with activity in advance of the reception, which would begin directly after the ceremony— in just a little more than an hour from now. The DJ and bartender were setting up. The camera crew was blocking out the best angles to capture the party for the *Vegas Girls* two-hour wedding special. Someone from the kitchen was fussing over a food station where ten different flavors of popcorn were available for the guests to enjoy. Other staff members were putting the finishing touches to the table centerpieces—gaudy feathered masquerade masks arranged like flowers in crystal vases.

Willow and her staff had done an amazing job transforming the Carriage House into a fantasy circus tent, but all that glitter and glam left him feeling empty. Not only had the expenses for this party come mostly out of his own trust fund, but all of it, right down to the popcorn, was nothing more than a ransom for control of his daughter's future.

"Danny? What are you doing here?"

He turned to find Amy, wearing a basic black dress and carrying a fistful of bright masquerade masks that sparkled in the subdued light as if each one had been hand-dipped in glitter. She didn't look very happy for him.

"I take it by your funereal attire that you're sending me a message."

Her mouth thinned. "I work here. The staff usually wears black or navy to events like this. We don't want to upstage any of the guests."

"But—"

"I've divorced the family. I'm sure you've heard the news. So tonight I'm here as Eagle Hill Manor event staff, and nothing more."

He shook his head. "You can't divorce your family."

"No? Isn't that what you did eight years ago? I've been watching the way the family treats you and Jeff, and the truth is, you guys get more respect than I do."

"Are you saying that I'm your role model? Because if that's so, I'd like to resign from that job. Amy, walking away from the family eight years ago may have been the worst mistake I ever made."

She leaned over the nearest table and put one of the masks into a crystal vase with clear marbles in it. She fussed a moment with the arrangement, draping feathers. "I'm not moving across the country. I'm just making a principled stand, right here in Shenandoah Falls. And besides, I think it's true what they say about absence making the heart grow fonder," she said. "If I stay away from family gatherings for a while, everyone will appreciate me when I return."

"That sounds more like a separation than a divorce."

She gave him a withering glance. "Did Aunt Pam send you here to talk sense to me? Because if she did, I'm not listening. My mind's made up. I'm divorcing all of you. And as for your wedding, don't expect me to be overjoyed about the choices you've made."

"You aren't going to do something stupid like stand up and start arguing when the minister gets to the part about speak now or forever hold your peace, are you?"

"If I did stand up and say something, it wouldn't be stupid."

Heat crawled up his face. "I'm sorry. That didn't come out the way I intended it. I just don't want anyone standing up at that part of the ceremony, okay? I'll make my mistakes, and you can make yours."

"Okay, but refusing Grady's proposal was not a mistake."

He shook his head. "No. I didn't say that. I'm not one of Grady's fans, to tell you the truth. I think you could do better."

"Really? You're the only one."

He chuckled. "Thanks, but I still think you need to have your head examined for getting involved with Dusty McNeil."

"Ah, I knew you would get around to that eventually. Well, you can stop worrying. Dusty and I have broken up."

"Oh?"

She turned and headed to the next table and started fiddling with the centerpiece there.

He followed after her. "So, what happened with Dusty?" he asked, knowing that he'd probably poked her right where it hurt.

"Daddy bought him out. Paid an exorbitant amount of money for his land. He's moving away. I gather that was one of the stipulations of the sale." She bit her lip and shook her head. By the slight tremor in her voice, Amy seemed close to tears.

"Shit. Do you love him?"

She nodded. "Yeah, I do. But clearly he doesn't love me. He didn't ask my opinion about selling the land or moving away. And even though he expected me to go with him, he never said he loved me or wanted to marry me. And you know what? I'm done having people tell me what to do and how to be. I'm done letting everyone run my life."

"Wait a sec. He asked you to go with him?"

She nodded.

"And you said no?"

"Yeah, I did."

"Amy, guys don't ask stuff like that unless they care."

She turned, a sheen of tears in her eyes. "You think?"

"I know."

"Well, he didn't say it. He merely informed me that he'd taken Daddy's money and was so pleased with himself because he planned to abscond with his daughter as well. To Montana. Can you imagine me living in Montana?"

He chuckled. "No, I can't."

"And that's the problem, because even though I'm ticked off at Daddy, I don't want to show him up."

"No? I thought you wanted to divorce him."

The corner of her mouth quirked. "Okay, so maybe I want a small separation until he comes to his senses and realizes that I'm not his baby girl anymore."

"Uh, Amy, I don't think he's ever going to come to that realization."

"That's depressing," she said on a long sigh.

"No, it's not depressing. It's just the truth. Honey, when a man has a daughter, it does a number on his head. Look around you. All this craziness is about Scarlett. And I gotta tell you, my view on Scarlett and boys is that she should be locked away in a tower and not be allowed out until she's at least thirty-five. Heaven help the boy who wants to take her to prom."

"I feel sorry for Scarlett."

"I love her more than life. And Uncle Jamie feels the same way about you too."

"Yeah, I guess. But little girls grow up, and daddies need to help them be independent. The truth is, until Daddy locked me out of the house, he hadn't done a good job of that. And I'm really ticked off that he used his economic power to send away the guy I think I've fallen for."

"I guess I can see that."

"So do Scarlett a favor, okay? You can love her with all your heart. You can marry her mother, even though it's a terrible mistake. But for God's sake, teach her to be independent. And when she's ready to leave the nest, don't hold her back."

Next week at this time, Dusty would be driving cross-country in his old pickup, on his way to an uncertain future in Montana. But right now he still served as the director of facilities at Eagle Hill Manor, responsible for today's event, which would be attended by a smattering of Hollywood B- and C-listers and a contingent of Washington, DC's elite.

The weather had decided not to cooperate with Mia the tyrant. The sun shone, but a big Canadian high had moved in overnight, sending temperatures plummeting into the low fifties, and a stiff breeze whipped down from the ridge. The wind seemed determined to knock over every flower arrangement set up for the outside wedding ceremony.

Dusty had recommended placing propane heaters at strategic points in order to keep the wedding guests from turning blue in the windchill. But Antonella had vetoed his suggestion because the tall heaters would obstruct camera views. So now the guests were filing in, huddling in their overcoats, their noses turning red in the gusts.

He tried not to care, but caring about guests at Eagle Hill Manor had become second nature to him, like an addiction he couldn't shake.

And speaking of addictions, Amy Lyndon ranked up there as well. He'd mistakenly thought that they had something really good going. And since she seemed hell-bent on defying her father, he'd naturally expected her to jump at the idea of blowing this one-horse town and heading out West. Her refusal had blindsided him worse than that sucker punch her brother had laid on him.

He pushed the sour thoughts from his mind just as the

Shenandoah Strings, the string quartet on contract with Eagle Hill Manor, struck up a classical piece that sounded vaguely familiar. The musicians sat in the gazebo with space heaters at their feet and several microphones strategically placed around them. Their music was piped through the state-of-the-art sound system that Willow had installed precisely for blustery days like this.

The music signaled the beginning of the wedding ceremony. It couldn't happen quick enough for Dusty.

Reverend Weston, also wearing a wireless mic, took his place in front of the gazebo. A moment later, Daniel and his brothers, dressed in ridiculous gray monkey suits, took their places. The camera crew panned the scene, and Pearl and Ivory made their appearance from behind the Portuguese laurels. They wore short, skintight purple dresses festooned with crystals that sparked in the late-afternoon sunlight. They carried bouquets of lilacs and white roses, but they treated the aisle as if it were a catwalk.

Once the showgirls took their places, the Shenandoah Strings struck up the traditional wedding march. Everyone rose, and Mia made her appearance. The reaction was immediate. Pam Lyndon's mouth turned down like an unhappy bulldog's, a number of wedding guests seated on the groom's side of the aisle gasped, and every heterosexual male in the audience ogled.

Dusty had no problem with see-through dresses. And this one, with its transparent bustier, would have been right at home on the Vegas Strip. He gave it high marks for displaying Mia's rack and maybe just a hint of one nipple. Clearly Amy had not applied duct tape to this woman. Her boobs were about ready to fall out.

No one was giving Mia away, so she came down the

aisle all by her lonesome and headed right toward her groom, whose face paled as she approached. Daniel Lyndon looked as if he were attending his own execution.

Dusty's work here was finished. He could go get a cup of coffee and warm up in the kitchen. He didn't have anything to do until the guests were shepherded into the Carriage House for the reception. Then he and his crew would have to take down the chairs and get them stored tonight because of the wind advisories.

He was just turning around when he spied Amy, standing to one side with Courtney. His heart lurched in his chest. She was beautiful today with her hair pulled back, exposing her long neck. Her slim dress clung to her subtle curves, displaying her in a classy way so unlike the women in the wedding party. He longed to cross the lawn, pull her into his arms, and...

What? Argue with her? Beg? Plead? Kiss her into submission?

He didn't know what. His chest clogged up with emotions that were confusing and new. It truly sucked to be dumped. He understood that now. Guess he'd learned his lesson.

He started to turn away when a disturbance caught the corner of his eye. Someone on the groom's side of the aisle in the third row stood up the moment the minister said those important words, "Speak now or forever hold your peace."

"Mia," the man said in a plaintive voice.

The bride glanced over her shoulder with a frown just as the man clumsily climbed over the people in his row and came to stand in the aisle. "I love you," he said, and Mia's frown melted into a tiny smile.

"What?" Dusty recognized the voice that came from behind the rows of folding chairs.

He whipped around in time to see Amy leave Courtney's side and come striding across the lawn. The Lyndon scowl rode her forehead, and she looked mad as hell. "Did you say you love *her*?" she asked again in a giant-sized voice, when she finally reached the aisle between the chairs.

The man in the middle turned. "Oh, Amy, hi. Uh, yeah, I do love her. I'm sorry. I guess I didn't know what love meant until I met Mia." The guy turned and took three steps toward the bride.

"Yeah, Grady, I guess not, because you've known her for what? Three days?" Amy said.

Grady? Holy shit. That guy with the bald spot on the back of his head was *the* Grady, the man Amy had dumped before she dumped Dusty. Good for her. Grady looked a little squirrelly. And besides, what kind of idiot stood up in the middle of a reality TV show taping expressing his undying love to a woman he didn't really know? Although now that Dusty thought of it, the *Vegas Girls* fans would probably eat this up like Thanksgiving gravy.

"Mia," Grady said as he reached the bride, "after what happened last Monday night, do you still want to go through with this?"

"What happened Monday night?" Daniel asked.

The bridesmaids gave each other guilty looks.

Pam Lyndon stood up in the front row. "Mia, you were in Washington on Monday at your bachelorette party. What could have possibly happened on Monday?"

The bridesmaids looked even guiltier.

"Mia, I can give you more than he can," Grady said,

jerking his head in Daniel's direction. "I'm way richer than he is and totally self-made. Every day I get a little more wealthy, while he's living off his granddaddy's money. And, baby, you already know how good I am in bed."

The audience gasped in unison, but Grady remained undeterred. "I've got tickets right here for the Seychelles, and I've booked one of the villas on North Island, the same place where the Duke and Duchess of Cambridge went on their honeymoon. Run away with me. Please."

Oh yeah, Dusty had recently tried that line, and it had failed. Maybe his mistake was offering Amy a road trip to Montana in an old pickup truck instead of buying her tickets to the Seychelles. On the other hand, Amy had told this asshole no. So maybe that wasn't it at all.

What the hell did Amy want from him anyway?

Mia turned toward Daniel. "You never offered me a honeymoon in the Seychelles."

Daniel had the good sense to keep his mouth zipped while Grady launched himself into that silence. "Mia, I adore you. I love you with all my heart. Let's be like Katharine Ross and Dustin Hoffman at the end of *The Graduate*."

Dusty had no idea what this referred to, but Mia clearly did, because her face lit up the way a bride's should; she got all dewy-eyed. She put her hand in Grady's and let him drag her down the aisle in the opposite direction.

Daniel finally sprang into action and chased after them. "Wait. What about Scarlett?" he asked.

Mia stopped, her expression thoroughly annoyed as she turned back toward Daniel. "Do you expect me to take the brat with me on a trip to the Seychelles?"

"For chrissake, Mia, we're filming this. Remember your image as a doting mother," Antonella said, marching right up to the bride and getting in her face. "You can't run off with someone other than Danny. It's in your contract."

"You can take my contract and your concern for my image and shove it," Mia said. "I'm done with this stupid show. I've been doing it for five years, and I'm no closer to a Hollywood contract than I was when I started. You want to exploit the fact that I started as a pole dancer. You've been licking your chops the whole time we've been in this Podunk town, working the angle about the tacky showgirl marrying the senator's nephew. And I'm tired of it." She turned toward Danny. "And I'm tired of your snobby family too."

Dusty could sure understand that point of view.

"Get out of my sight," Daniel said. "If you're willing to abandon Scarlett, then I have no use for you. I don't ever want to set eyes on you again." Daniel seemed surprisingly calm for a dude who'd been left at the altar.

Danny's words bounced off Mia. "Works for me," she said, then turned toward Grady with a cheesy smile.

Grady chose that moment to sweep the showgirl off her feet. But since Grady probably couldn't bench-press more than about a hundred pounds, and Mia was at least six feet tall, he managed not to appear either heroic or romantic as he toted her away.

Danny's emotions spun off in nineteen different directions as Grady hauled Mia down the path. He wanted to dance for joy, sigh in relief, hug his brothers, kiss his baby, and maybe find Roxy Kopp and do the same. But the shocked gazes of the wedding guests reminded him that jilted grooms weren't supposed to be happy.

Plus the cameras had zoomed in on his face, and he didn't want to give them any emotion at all. Not even shock. So he shut everything down and just stood there letting the quiet seep into him.

The quiet didn't last long though. Antonella got up into his face and started screaming, and when he didn't react, she turned and vented at the bridesmaids. At which point the cameramen turned off their video equipment. It was an unwritten rule that the show's producers were never to be shown on camera.

When the camera crew left the field, the bridesmaids followed, with Antonella in hot pursuit. That left him and the wedding guests.

Thank God for Uncle Mark, who stood up beside him and said, "Well, I guess the bar's open." And just like that the Eagle Hill staff, including Amy, jumped into the breach and shepherded the guests into the Carriage House, where the Bella Vista wine was sure to flow.

He let everyone move beyond him, standing still as the reality sank home. He was free. He had Mia on tape telling him she didn't give a crap about Scarlett.

He turned, pursuing Antonella across the lawn. "Wait," he called to her back.

She stopped just short of the French doors leading to the inn's library. "What do *you* want?" she asked as if she believed Danny had perpetrated this disaster.

"I need a copy of the video you just took," he said.

She shook her head. "I don't think so. We need to get Mia back and make her marry you."

"No. That's not going to happen." This statement came from Roxanne Kopp, who, unlike the rest of the guests, had remained behind. She came up on Danny's right and gave

Antonella a chilling look. "Mia made her choice, and that means Danny's offer of marriage is now null and void."

"Who are you?" Antonella raised her chin.

"I'm a lawyer, the daughter of a man who has argued cases before the Supreme Court. I would like to point out that Danny has a hundred and fifty witnesses who heard what Mia had to say about Scarlett, including several congressmen and a US senator. There is no way in hell he's letting Mia have custody of that baby. And if he wavers, I'm here to see that he doesn't do anything stupid again. No more sham weddings." She turned and glared at him.

He wasn't in the least offended. In fact, he met her glare with a smile, and just like that, her glare melted. "It's fine, Roxy," he said. "I have no intention of going through this again. Mia chose money instead of her child. And I'm thinking that I've got a family overflowing with lawyers. After abandoning Scarlett and calling her a brat in front of a lot of people, I think we could nail the custody case."

Roxy turned back toward Antonella. "And mark my word, we'll be subpoenaing the video within the hour. My father has already made the calls, and the papers are being drawn up as we speak. And don't think you can destroy the tape, because, as I said, there were a hundred and fifty witnesses, and you could be subpoenaed as well."

"Fine," Antonella said. "I'll send the relevant video clip to you via e-mail." She whirled and stomped off toward the manor house.

Danny turned toward Roxy. The cold had definitely affected certain parts of her anatomy, and her dark silk dress with the high neckline did nothing to hide her nipples or her incredible curves. She looked hotter than Mia, even though her dress covered her up.

"Is August really drawing up papers?"

She nodded. "Not Dad himself, but one of his associates. They should be e-mailed to us within the hour. If Antonella drags her feet, she's going to be surprised."

"So, what do you need from me?"

"Not one thing. It's being handled."

He smiled. "In that case, do you want to dance?"

"You feel like dancing?"

His laugh came from right out of his belly. "Hell yeah, Roxy, I feel like dancing, especially with you. In fact, dancing with you might be just the thing I need to recover from being left at the altar."

He took her by the hand. "Geez, you're freezing. I'm sorry. Antonella nixed the space heaters."

"Don't be sorry. About anything. I admire the way you were willing to sacrifice yourself for Scarlett. And I'm really glad that it didn't come to that. What do you plan to do next?" she asked as they hurried across the lawn to the shelter of the Carriage House.

"I don't know. I have a house in LA I need to sell."

"You're not going back there to live?" She stopped and looked up at him, her brown eyes full of concern and something else.

He shook his head. "I had to come back here to realize how much I missed the rain. I'm going to move back to Virginia."

"But what about your career?"

"My career is nowhere, Roxy. Career-wise, I'm a dud. But I do have an idea."

"Tell me."

"I'd like to make documentaries. You know, films that bring light to problems or change the way people look at issues and solutions. I've never had the desire to make blockbuster films. The money's good, but the price you have to pay is too high. I thought I wanted to make arty films, but it turns out no one ever watches those, and without an audience, I have to ask myself what I'm doing. So I've concluded that I'd rather have a smaller life and a bigger mission, you know?"

She nodded, a sheen of tears in her eyes. "I do. It's why I work for a nonprofit even though Dad had these grand ideas that I would become a litigator like him and Brandon. And...well, the truth is, I love kids. My job doesn't pay much, and fundraising can be so frustrating and difficult sometimes, but the money I raise means a lot to the parents of children with challenges."

"I already figured out that you loved kids, Roxy."

As if on cue, Mom turned up at Danny's elbow with Scarlett in her arms. The baby wore an outrageously expensive dress with frills and lace and embroidery. She sure looked like the prettiest girl in the room, except for maybe Roxanne.

"Are you okay?" Mom asked, her gaze flicking from him to Roxy and back again.

"I'm fine. I'm perfect. In fact, I think we should party until dawn." He reached out for his daughter, who came into his arms with a big hug and a kiss.

He glanced at Roxy. "About that dance. Would you mind if we made it a threesome?"

She grinned. "Absolutely not."

And with that, Danny and his daughter and Roxanne Kopp got out on the dance floor and kicked off the party.

Chapter Twenty-Four ———

The wedding guests took Uncle Mark up on his offer and were now getting buzzed on copious quantities of Bella Vista Vineyards wine while enjoying a parade of circus acts who juggled, ate fire, and performed acrobatics for them. Everyone wanted to dance at Danny's non-wedding. It became a huge frigging celebration the moment the *Vegas Girls* camera crew and cast left the scene.

But when Amy's brother Edward sought her out and asked if she was okay—as if she'd been the one left at the altar—she got right up in his face and said, "You should be thanking me. If I hadn't dumped Grady, Danny would be married to Mia now. I'm the hero of this story."

"Amy, everyone in the family realizes they made a mistake. We're all worried that you're not dancing."

"I'm not dancing because I'm working," she said.

"Oh, yeah, I forgot."

Right. "Tell everyone I'm fine," she said in a flat voice

before turning her back on him and hurrying through the door marked EMPLOYEES ONLY at the back of the banquet hall. She didn't have anything to do back here in the workroom. In fact, Courtney had told her to join the party some time ago. But Amy didn't feel like it.

Dusty would be gone in a few days, and she missed him already. She missed being in his arms. Being in his bed. Being by his side. They fit together so right that she'd been fooled into believing that he might be her true love.

Silly mistake.

She left the workroom via the back door and followed the footpath around to the Carriage House patio. The cold seeped through her dress, despite the propane heaters that had been brought out and scattered around the terrace. With the wind still whipping, none of the non-wedding guests wanted to brave the elements, so she stood there alone staring out at the gazebo. The west lawn was empty now. Dusty and his crew had broken down the setup a long time ago.

She'd watched them through the French doors, morbidly thinking that this would be her last glimpse of Dusty McNeil. Once, right before the final chair was loaded onto a trolley, he'd gazed up at the Carriage House, almost as if he'd known she'd been watching. Had he seen her by the French doors? Probably not, but her heart skipped a beat, and it took a lot of willpower not to open the door and rush into his arms.

She wished she could convince him to stay.

She wished she could convince herself to go.

But neither of those options seemed right. She couldn't go with him unless he loved her and understood that she wanted a partnership in which her thoughts, feelings, and ideas were valued. She let go of a giant sigh.

"That sounded practically mournful."

Amy recognized the voice. She turned to discover that her cousin Jeff had snuck up on her. He loomed over her, tall and thin, holding a glass of champagne. When it came to money, Jeff sat on top of the family heap, but you'd never guess that he had billions in the bank by his rumpled, off-the-rack suit or his long, shaggy hair and scruffy beard.

"Oh, hi, Jeff. Are you having fun?" she asked.

He gave her a pointed look that missed nothing. As a one-time investigative journalist, Jeff had a way of cutting through the bull. "Yeah," he said. "It's always a gas to hang out with Dad's family. The drama never fails to entertain."

"You know we love you, don't you?"

"Yeah, I know. But I can spend a maximum of three minutes in Aunt Pam's presence before I'm ready to explode."

She nodded. "I know the feeling."

"So, I wanted to talk to you about something."

She lifted her eyebrow. "Please do not ask me how I'm feeling about Grady Carson, okay? I was not the one left at the altar."

The corner of his mouth curled. "Have people really asked you that?"

"My brother. Aunt Julie. Uncle Charles." She sighed. "I don't know why everyone thought I loved Grady Carson. After all, I told him no in front of the whole family. Apparently everyone is hard of hearing."

"Rest easy. I'm not here to talk about Grady. I'm here to talk about Dusty. Willow told me that you and he have become...friends."

"Oh." Her mouth went dry.

"Yeah. Anyway, before you freak, I'm on his side. I was

ticked off by that hatchet piece Sally Hawkes wrote in the *Winchester Daily*. I understand why a majority of citizens would like to have a park instead of a burned-out building, but there's no reason to paint Dusty as a villain because he wants to keep his land. And no reason to go into his family's jaded past or their struggles with addiction. So when he gave me a copy of his business plan for his ecotourism resort, I saw a real opportunity."

"You have a copy of his business plan?"

"Yeah. We were supposed to meet, but the fire and his father's death got in the way. We haven't had a chance to reschedule. But I've been thinking about his plan, and I believe I've come up with a compromise that will make the Historical Society happy, while allowing Dusty to go forward with his lodge and fishing guide service. In fact, I'm willing to invest in Dusty's business, but I need your help with Aunt Pam. You're one of the few people in the family who can reason with her. The way I see it, Pam and her Historical Society ladies don't give a rat's ass about a big park. They just wanted to get rid of the derelict foundry building and grab the older blacksmith's forge for a living history exhibit.

"I've made a dozen or more phone calls trying to figure out where the bigger park proposal came from, and near as I can tell, Heather's opponent pushed the idea in the last election when David was thinking about running for Congress. The idea, apparently, was to pressure David, making him choose between his friend and the county. We all know he chose his friend and bowed out of the race, but the proposal remained on the docket, and the Historical Society kept breathing life into it every time it was about to die. The reality is that no one from the county wants another park to manage. So I think, in this case, we can split the baby in two."

Adrenaline surged through Amy until she remembered the deal Daddy had made with Dusty. "Jeff, you're too late," she said on a choked-up voice. "Dusty's sold out."

"What?"

"Daddy made him an offer he couldn't refuse. He took the money and agreed to leave town. Forever."

Dusty stood in his small office with its great big view of the Blue Ridge Mountains, packing his stuff in a cardboard box. For a man who had drastically downsized in order to live in a tiny house, he'd accumulated a shit ton of crap here at his home-away-from-home. Most of this stuff—a few posters, a couple of extra Eagle Hill Manor golf shirts, an old pair of muddy sneakers—would eventually end up in the trash. He'd decided not to haul much out to Montana, just some clothes and his fishing rods. He'd sell or give away the rest.

The fishing out West was supposed to be phenomenal. He'd waited his whole life for this trip, and he ought to be excited about it. But his chest felt tight with regret. His family had lived in Shenandoah Falls for generations. This should be his home, but the people here would never allow him to change. He'd been labeled and cataloged from the moment of his birth. What a bitch to discover that he didn't belong here in Jefferson County, in the place his ancestors had settled so long ago. All these years, he'd been spinning his wheels, wasting his time, hoping things would change.

But hoping didn't make it true. He should have written

up a business plan years ago, right after he'd bought Daddy out and way before the county got a bee up its butt about taking his land away. He should have had faith in himself a long time ago. He should have listened to Willow. He should have...

He should have done a lot of things differently. He had to lose everything he cared about to learn that lesson.

"You got a minute?"

He stiffened and turned. Willow stood inside the doorway, dressed to the nines for Daniel's wedding. "I was just packing up," he said. "I'm leaving in a couple of days."

She folded her arms. "Dusty, please. Don't do this."

"I can't win the fight with the county. We both know that. So it makes perfect sense to take Jamie Lyndon's money and run. It's time for moving on. I think maybe this day was inevitable."

"And what does Amy think about this?"

He barked a laugh. "I know you were worried about me breaking her heart, but..." His throat squeezed shut. Dammit, he'd become the weenie of the century.

Willow came all the way into the room and snagged him by the arm. "I may have told you to stay away from Amy, but I think that was a mistake. I'm trying to decide if you're running away from her or what."

"I'm not running away from her."

"No? Then tell me why you took money from her father."

"It's pretty simple. Jamie Lyndon offered me more money than the land was worth, and he made it clear that I either take his deal or he'd give the money to the county. And since a lack of funding has been the only thing stopping the county, I did the smart thing. I accepted the inevitable."

"Okay, but you don't have to move to Montana. That's running away, Dusty."

"It was the best option," he said.

"Jamie had a quid pro quo, didn't he? You had to leave town in order to get the money."

He nodded.

"Wow. I'm surprised. The Dusty McNeil I've known most of my life is a bigger fighter than that. Why give up now, right after you've come up with a wonderful business plan? What is it? Are you afraid of success?"

"That's just bullshit. People are afraid of failure, not success."

Willow shook her head. "No. You're wrong. When someone as smart and talented as you are decides to run away from a fight you could win, that's not fear of failure."

"You think I can win the fight? Against Jamie Lyndon?"

She gave him a nod. "I do, as a matter of fact."

"Why?"

"Because you thought you could blindside Jamie when you made that deal, didn't you?"

"What?"

"You asked Amy to go with you to Montana. You planned to take Jamie's money and his daughter too."

"Did Amy tell you that?"

Willow shook her head. "No. I figured it out with a little help from Juni. If you want to keep something a secret, it's best not to tell my sister about it over a beer at the Jaybird Café."

"Dammit, your sister has a talent for discovering everyone's secrets."

"I know. But here's the thing. I think your instincts were right about this."

He blinked. "You do?"

"Jamie thinks Amy is just going through a phase or something. But I don't think that's it."

"Yeah, well, you're wrong. Amy wanted a 'bad boy' experience, and when I asked her to come with me to Montana, she dumped me."

Willow closed her eyes and shook her head, her expression filled with disgust before she spoke again. "Do you remember what happened when David tried to finesse his relationship with me and his family?"

He blinked. "Uh, yeah, kind of. You guys broke up for a while. And everyone was miserable for a few weeks."

"Right. And do you remember how he got himself out of that particular hole?"

"Not really."

"Of course you don't." She rolled her eyes. "Dusty, think for a minute. What did Grady do today?"

"Uh, he successfully stole the bride. I'm thinking the tickets to the deserted isle did the trick. You think I should have—"

"Stop it. I want you to be serious and think about what happened. What did Grady say to Mia?"

"Uh, I believe he said something about the sex being good."

"Oh my God. You guys are all alike. You think with your dicks." She started pacing.

"I guess great sex isn't the answer, huh? For the record—"

She stopped moving and glared at him. "Don't say it. I don't want to know about your sex life. Come on, Dusty. What did Grady say to Mia? It was the first thing out of his mouth."

"I don't remember, and I don't see how playing twenty questions is helping. If you have some idea about how I can get Amy to reconsider, just tell me. Don't make me guess."

"I give up. If you can't figure it out on your own, then you don't deserve Amy." She turned and walked right through the door.

Why the hell did women have to be so damn confusing?

He collapsed into his chair, planted his head in his hands, and desperately tried to recall the entire Grady-Mia scene. It took him a moment and several run-throughs before he realized the mistake he'd made.

Willow was right. He was an idiot.

Amy dragged Jeff across the dance floor to the table where Aunt Pam, Uncle Mark, and Daddy were sitting. Daddy gave her a hopeful smile. "Hey, baby girl, want to dance?"

"No, Daddy. Jeff and I came over here because we have something we need to talk to you about. All of you."

Daddy glanced from Jeff to Amy and back again, his gaze sobering.

She took a big breath and started talking. "Jeff has a terrific idea he wants to outline for you. I think you'll all discover that this is a real opportunity for the Jefferson County Historical Society. But before he does that, I have something I want to say to all of you."

Aunt Pam leaned forward and patted Amy's hand. "Darlin', we know you've got to be upset about what happened today, and—"

"I'm not upset that Grady ran away with Mia. I never loved Grady. And it turns out that Grady never loved me either. I think he proved that today."

"Honey, I—"

"Daddy, this is not your time to talk. This is my time, okay? And I need for all of you to listen."

They nodded.

"Like I said, I don't love Grady Carson. I love Dusty McNeil." She put up her hand, palm out to stop the rush of disapproval. "Don't," she said. "I know you disapprove. And that hurts, a lot. Because I love you all. You're my family, and I'd like to think that you'd be interested in making me happy.

"But, Daddy, I don't know if I can forgive you for what you've done. Instead of talking to me about Dusty, you decided to buy him off. But it wasn't a fair transaction—not when you had the power to force the issue by giving the county the money they needed to move forward with their eminent domain case. And you thought you were so clever, offering him that money in order to prove your point. But here's the thing. Dusty asked me to run away with him to Montana."

Oh boy, that did the trick. She'd finally shocked them all into listening.

"You can't," Pam said. "We'd never see you again."

"Where is he?" Daddy pushed up from the table. "I'll kill him."

Uncle Mark, always the calm voice in the family, yanked his younger brother back down. "There will be no killings," he said dryly, before turning his senatorial gaze on Amy. "So does this mean goodbye? Or has Jeff come up with an idea that will keep you here?"

"I'm not leaving," Amy said. "I told Dusty I didn't want to run away with him under those circumstances."

"But you said you loved him." Pam's voice sounded confused.

"I do love him. But I'm not ready to follow him to Montana."

Pam nodded. "Thank God. There's nothing in Montana."

"I beg to differ. The fishing in Montana is exceptional," Uncle Mark said with a humorous gleam in his eye. Was Uncle Mark on her side? Amy couldn't believe it.

She squared her shoulders and continued. "I don't think Dusty should have to run away from his home. His people have been living here for as long as we have—longer maybe. His ancestors built the blacksmith forge that you want to turn into a museum.

"And that's the irony of this situation. Don't any of you remember that this town used to be called Liberty Forge way before it became Shenandoah Falls? There wouldn't even be a town here if it weren't for the McNeils. And there are plenty of McNeils buried alongside the Lyndons up at the old cemetery.

"Dusty belongs here same as you and me. Making him leave is wrong and cruel."

Mark nodded when she'd finished her speech. Daddy and Pam looked on with stony expressions.

"So, Daddy," Amy continued, looking him square in the eye, "when you forced him to sell out, you put me in the position of having to walk away from my family or to fight for the man I love. I know you thought you were protecting me, but wrapping me up in Bubble Wrap and forcing me to choose between you and Dusty isn't the right approach." She ran out of words and glanced at Jeff, who stepped in.

"I didn't know any of this until a few minutes ago," Jeff said. "Dusty came to me a few weeks ago with a plan that I think will make everyone here happy. And I'm prepared to pay for it."

He went on to outline his idea of dividing Dusty's land, giving part of it to the county for a park so the Historical Society could restore the old forge to working condition. The rest of the land would remain in Dusty's hands with zoning covenants that would limit the development to an environmentally friendly eco-resort with a lodge, a fishing guide service, and canoe and kayak facilities for float trips on the Shenandoah, all of which would be managed privately.

"The county and the Historical Society are winners," Jeff concluded, "because the cost of managing a smaller park won't strain the county's already limited resources. And by privatizing the activities on the adjacent land, the county saves money, keeps a valuable member of our community here, and creates jobs—more jobs and better-paying jobs than a park would create."

"I like the way you think, Jeff," Uncle Mark said. "Have you ever considered running for the county council?"

Jeff shook his head. "No, thanks. I'm not interested in politics. I'm interested in solving problems."

Uncle Mark turned toward his wife. "Will the Historical Society be happy with this compromise?"

She glanced at Jeff and then Amy and nodded her head. "Yes, I think so."

"Jamie?"

A muscle twitched in Daddy's cheek. "I still want to murder Dusty McNeil."

Uncle Mark's gaze narrowed. "I don't blame you. But

that's not the question at hand. The question is whether you are capable of compromising. Jeff's plan may be the only way to keep Amy from eloping with Dusty McNeil. And unless I misheard him, Jeff's plan will also save you a lot of cash, since he's the one who'll be paying for it."

Daddy glowered at Jeff and then Amy, but he said nothing.

"Looks like everyone's having a real nice time," Uncle Mark said in a happy voice as he cast his gaze over the dance floor where couples slow danced to the romantic music the DJ had started playing. "Including Roxy and Daniel." He gave Aunt Pam little a wink, and Pam smiled.

Whoa. What was up with that? Did Pam and Mark get the whole Danny-Roxy thing? Maybe she'd underestimated them.

But she hadn't underestimated Daddy, who still glowered at her. She was trying to come up with something that would take his frown away, when someone shouted, "Amy Lyndon, I love you."

The music played on, but everyone on the dance floor stopped moving. Amy stood up and turned toward the French doors, where Dusty McNeil stood like a Norse god, dressed in khakis and a golf shirt.

"Did you hear me? I love you. And if you don't want to go to Montana, we can go somewhere else. Just so long as there's fishing nearby."

The tears Amy had been holding back for days sprang to her eyes, making it hard to actually see as he started walking toward her. And in that moment, she no longer cared whether her father approved or not.

Holy crap. Dusty McNeil loved her! He'd said the words right out loud.

Amy dashed the tears from her eyes and took off across the ballroom in his direction. They came together on the dance floor, where the party guests stepped aside to give them room.

"I love you," he said, this time in a much more intimate voice. "I screwed up before. I put the cart before the horse. I was so focused on one-upping your daddy that I forgot the most important thing. I don't want to live without you, Amy. You've changed me. Made me a better man. I can live anywhere because, wherever you are, that's where my home is." He brushed a tear from her cheek with his rough thumb. "Don't cry. I hate the idea that I made you cry."

She threw her arms around his neck. "We don't have to go anywhere. Jeff is going to invest in your plan, and he's come up with an idea that will satisfy the Historical Society. You're going to be that famous fishing guide you've always wanted to be."

He blinked down at her, a strange expression on his face. "But do you love me?"

"Oh, uh, sorry. I guess I goofed up too. Of course I love you. You changed me by teaching me self-reliance. That snipe hunt was the best thing that ever happened to me."

And then, to everyone's surprise, Dusty McNeil, the Casanova of Shenandoah Falls, got down on his knee, took her hand in his, and in a loud voice, he said, "Amy, I love you more than life. Will you marry me?" His baby blues sparkled in the candlelight.

He didn't have a ring. And she suspected that when he did put a ring on her finger, it would be modest—something he could afford—not the umpteen-carat Cartier rock that Grady had tried to give her.

But it didn't matter.

"Yes," she said. "Yes, I'll marry you."

He scrambled up and kissed her like she was the bride, right there in the middle of the dance floor. And then the DJ said something over the PA system that Amy missed because kissing Dusty always blew her mind. But a moment later, the sound system came back to life with the romantic Anne Murray song "Could I Have This Dance for the Rest of My Life."

And Dusty danced with Amy at Danny's wedding that never was.

Epilogue

Amy peeped through the crack in the Laurel Chapel's door. The meadow just beyond the churchyard was dotted with purple *Lupinus perennis*, white *Gypsophila elegans*, and yellow *Chrysanthemum maximum*, otherwise known as wild lupine, baby's breath, and Shasta daisies.

Whichever name Amy used, the wildflowers put on a heart-stopping show—the perfect backdrop for an outside wedding. Reverend Weston stood right in front of an arched trellis festooned with dozens of pink roses with Dusty right beside him, the sunlight turning his hair to gold. David stood beside the groom, and his sister, Heather, had just taken her place as the maid of honor. A small group of people—mostly family and friends—stood waiting for the bride to show her face.

A flute and harp duet struck up "Jesu, Joy of Man's Desiring," and Courtney said, "It's showtime."

Amy stepped back from the door and turned toward

Daddy, dressed in his dark pinstripe. "Are you ready to give me away?"

"No." He scowled at her.

She rose up on tiptoes to kiss his cheek. A sheen sparkled in his eyes behind the glare. "Don't cry, okay?"

"I'll try not to," he said in a gruff voice, and then dashed a tear from his cheek. "I wish your mother had lived to see this. She would be so happy that you decided to wear her dress."

Amy didn't believe that for a minute. Mom would probably have insisted on buying some overpriced and over-the-top dress because Mom, bless her heart, had lived a shallow, dependent life.

Maybe Amy had invited bad luck by wearing Mom's dress, but Amy had fallen in love with it the moment she saw it. Plus, since she and Mom were both little, the dress fit her without any alterations, saving lots of money. And all of her extra money, after paying for the reception, was earmarked for development of Shenandoah River Guides, the business Dusty had just incorporated.

Amy had learned that money couldn't buy happiness or love, which was why this wedding had a shoestring budget. She made the best of her employee discount and the beautiful setting out here in the meadow. In fact, she couldn't think of a more perfect place to marry Dusty McNeil, small-town boy, fisherman, and horticulturalist. A guy like that needed to be married outside, with nature all around him, in a simple ceremony without a lot of drama or expense. Dusty was a straightforward, kind man who lived in a tiny house, just large enough for two people and a dog. He didn't do frills or extravagance. And Amy loved him for that.

She took her father's arm. "Let's do this thing."

Courtney opened the chapel's door, and Daddy helped her down the stairs and into the meadow. It was a short walk to her groom, who watched her with hungry blue eyes that made her whole body flush. She couldn't wait until they were back in each other's arms.

The minister pulled her from her naughty thoughts and asked the question "Who gives this woman?"

And Daddy, bless his heart, said, "I do."

Laurie Wilson is devastated when she's left at the altar—until best man Andrew Lyndon comes up with a plan to help her win back her fiancé. But the plan soon falls apart when Laurie realizes that Andrew really is her best man...

A preview of *Here Comes the Bride* follows.

Chapter 1———————————————

If Laurie Wilson could have controlled the weather for her wedding, she would have. She had controlled, planned, organized, and directed every other aspect of her special day. So when it rained for a solid seven days before the ceremony, Laurie exhausted herself with worry.

She could have saved herself the angst because, when August twenty-sixth finally arrived, it dawned cloudless with an endlessly azure sky more like September than late summer. And in true silver-lining fashion, the rain had ended the deep August drought, leaving the asters, woodbine, and rudbeckia that grew in the meadow beside Laurel Chapel in full, glorious bloom.

The day was as perfect as her dream.

So was her wedding dress.

She stood in the tiny room at the back of the chapel staring into a full-length mirror. The stunning reflection revealed the woman who was about to become Mrs. Brandon

Kopp. Alençon lace dripped from her gown's bodice while the Swarovski crystals along the sweetheart neckline sent colorful sparks of light up the walls and ceiling. Laurie pressed her hands down into the yards of netting in the skirt, feeling giddy.

"You look gorgeous, princess," Dad said from behind her, a tremor in his voice.

For the first time in her life, Dad's pet name actually fit. The A-line ball gown was princess-worthy, and her thick, unruly tresses had been braided into a crown that now bristled with baby's breath like a living tiara.

She turned around to find Dad with his hands jammed in the pockets of his dark gray suit, his dahlia boutonniere slightly askew. She stepped up to him and fixed the flower. "There," she said, the butterflies flitting around in her core.

He captured her hand and gave it a little kiss. "I can't believe my little princess is getting married," he said, a sheen in his eyes. "But I heartily approve of your groom."

"I do too," she said with grin. "And I'm happy the planning is finally over. I thought Mom and I would come to blows a few times over the last few months."

The door opened, and Laurie's bridesmaids invaded in a swirl of burgundy chiffon and laughter. Madison Atwood, Emma Raynerson, and Mindy Westbrook were dear friends from college, and Brandon's sister, Roxanne, was the maid of honor.

"Courtney sent us to let you know that Brandon and the groomsmen are about to take their positions. It's only a few more minutes," Roxy said. "And I just wanted to tell you before the wedding toasts start that I'm so happy you're going to be my sister-in-law. Brandon couldn't have chosen any better."

A wave of joy percolated through Laurie. "Thank you so much." She gave Roxy a fierce hug. "Not just for saying that, but for holding my hand the last few months. All of you have been terrific, really. I know I can get a little OCD about things, and you all have been so supportive, especially when Mom started throwing her weight around."

A tearful and slightly giggly group hug ensued, but it didn't last long because Courtney Wallace, the main event coordinator for Eagle Hill Manor, opened the door and said, "It's showtime, ladies...and gent." The strains of Bach's "Air"—played on organ and violin—floated in from the sanctuary. A little flutter of excitement gnawed at Laurie's insides as her friends left the room, lined up in the chapel's small vestibule, and one by one made their walk down the aisle.

She took Dad's arm and looked up at him. He smiled and winked. "I love you, princess," he said.

"I love you too," she murmured as the music changed from the Bach to Pachelbel's Canon in D. She'd had a huge argument with Mom about this music choice. Mom wanted the traditional "Bridal Chorus" from Wagner's opera *Lohengrin*. But Laurie was a bit of an opera buff, and in her estimation, the wedding in *Lohengrin* wasn't one she wanted to emulate. That wedding was never consummated, and the poor bride ends up dead at the end of the opera. So no "Bridal Chorus" for her. She regarded it as bad luck.

Without the opening fanfare of "Here Comes the Bride" to signal her arrival, the wedding guests didn't rise to their feet very quickly. But they did eventually get the message that the bride had arrived. She gripped Dad's arm and looked ahead to where Brandon waited, dressed in a dark gray suit with his curly dark hair falling over his forehead.

He aimed his big blue eyes at her, and her heart beat a little faster.

They'd known each other for ten years, since freshman year at George Washington University. They had hooked up a time or two in college but not seriously until five years ago. Brandon was the love of a lifetime. The only man she'd ever slept with. Her heart swelled in her chest as she arrived at the altar without tripping on the train of her dress. Thank God. She could check that worry off her list of possible disasters.

She looked up into Brandon's eyes. She'd imagined this moment thousands of time. His eyes would sparkle, maybe with unshed tears of joy. His mouth would curl at the corner and expose his adorable dimple. He'd wink...

Wait. She'd never imagined him frowning at her. What? Did he hate her dress? Was it too princessy? She knew it; she should have gone with the mermaid dress even though Mom hated it. Crap. The moment was spoiled forever.

The minister interrupted her inner rant. "Dearly beloved, we have come together in the presence of God to witness and bless the joining together of—"

"Wait," Brandon said.

"What?" The minister laid his finger down to mark his place in the *Book of Common Prayer*. Then he looked up at Brandon over the rims of his half-glasses.

The bodice of Laurie's dress chose that moment to become a tourniquet, shutting off her air supply.

"What on earth are you doing?" Brandon's father said from somewhere in the first pew on the groom's side.

Brandon ignored his dad. He kept staring at Laurie with panic in his eyes. "Uh, Laurie, um..."

"How dare you!" This came from Mom in the pew on

the opposite side. Like Brandon, Laurie tried to ignore her mother while simultaneously trying to breathe.

"I can't," Brandon said.

"You can't or you don't want to?" Roxy asked. "Because, baby bro, there is a big difference."

"I... Well, neither of those, actually."

"What?" Laurie finally managed to push out the word and suck in a gulp of air.

Brandon took her by the hand, and the touch sent ice up her arm. She wanted to pull away from him, but she was frozen in place. "Look, Laurie, you're more or less the only girl I ever dated."

"So?" someone asked. Laurie wasn't sure, but maybe it was Andrew Lyndon, the best man.

"I just don't think either of us is ready for this. I mean, we don't have enough experience."

"What?" That was definitely Mom's voice. "You're twenty-eight years old, for goodness' sake. You're not a couple of teenagers."

"Is there someone else?" She could only whisper the words as the foundations of her world crumbled.

His eyes widened. "No, never. I swear, Laurie, I have never cheated on you. But I think we need a break. I think we just got on the wedding carousel and..." He stabbed a hand through his hair. "Shit," he said under his breath as he turned away.

"If there's no one else, then—"

"I just want a break, okay? Like six months. We can see other people, and after that time we can decide. You know, like a trial separation."

"For crap sake, how can you have a separation if you're not even married?" Mom asked.

"Susan, sit down and stay out of it. Let them discuss it," Laurie heard her father say in his best Solomon-the-wise judge voice. She glanced at him, still standing there waiting to give her away. His face had gone pale and grave. He turned toward Brandon. "What is it you want, son?"

"I just need time. You know, to make sure this isn't a mistake." And then he gave Laurie a sweet, sad smile and said, "And you need time too, Laurie. I think it would be good if you saw other people. Really. And then we could decide."

"Are you crazy? I love you. I don't want to see other people."

He shook his head. "I'm really sorry. I know you spent a lot of time and money planning all this." He took a step back and then turned and strode down the aisle and out of the chapel. His father, who was still standing, climbed over a couple of wedding guests and hit the aisle at a dead run. Laurie hoped the old guy didn't give himself a heart attack chasing after his son.

Roxy must have had the same thought, because she dropped her bouquet and tore after Mr. Kopp, saying, "Daddy, don't kill yourself. He's not worth it."

Dad glanced at Mom and snarled something obscene while the wedding guests went ominously silent, except for Mom, who collapsed in the front pew, openly weeping and maybe even wailing a little.

Someone grabbed Laurie by the hand. "Come on. Let's get you out of here."

She looked up. Andrew Lyndon, the best man. Funny how he'd stayed and Roxy had gone. He tugged her forward, and she followed down the aisle like a confused puppy. Behind her, the bridesmaids and the groomsmen followed in a disorderly retreat, and all Laurie could think about was that the musicians were supposed to play Mendelssohn's "Wedding March" during the recessional.

Andrew marched out of the chapel and down the path to the inn, his little sister, Amy, running ahead of him, clearing the way. Behind him, the remaining bridesmaids and groomsmen, including his brother, Edward, and cousins Matthew and Jason, followed like a formally clad flash mob.

They hurried across the lawn, into the inn, up the sweeping staircase, and arrived at the Churchill Suite, Eagle Hill Manor's signature guest room and sitting room on the second floor. Amy, who worked as an assistant wedding planner at the inn, opened the door with her passkey.

"C'mon, boys, let's go get some of the wine from the bar in the reception hall," Amy said, snagging Andrew's brother and cousins, who were also members of the wedding party. She looked up at Andrew and winked. "We'll be back. In the meantime, you hold down the fort."

His brothers, cousins, and sister escaped, leaving Andrew to guide the distraught bride into the room, which was cluttered with suitcases packed and ready for a five-day honeymoon in Bermuda.

He came to a stop on the Persian rug. Now what?

In his professional life, he'd mediated complicated disputes between litigants, but this situation had Humpty Dumpty written all over it. No one was going to put this back together.

He turned and allowed himself to look Laurie in the face

for the first time. Her big, hazel eyes stared back oddly vacant. She might have been a wax statue, the way she stood stiff and unmoving without real expression. A beautiful wax statue, with her golden hair braided with flowers.

What kind of idiot walks away from a woman like this?

Before he could act, Madison, Emma, and Mindy closed ranks around Laurie and guided her to one of the wing chairs in the sitting room. She sank down into it, her big skirt billowing up around her.

"I think we should find Brandon's Camaro and mess it up," Emma said.

"Screw that. I want to kill him, not his car," said Mindy.

"Can I castrate him first?" Madison asked.

"But I love him," Laurie said in a watery voice as the first tear escaped the corner of her right eye.

"Oh, baby, don't cry for that SOB," Madison said, then hurried into the bathroom, returning a moment later with a big wad of tissues that she pressed into Laurie's hand. Laurie accepted the tissues but did nothing to stanch the slow drip of tears. That controlled release of emotion wrenched Andrew's heart more than sobs could have. She ought to be disconsolate. She ought to be angry.

His fury boiled down in the pit of his stomach. He hadn't felt rage like this since last spring when he'd gone after Amy's husband in the mistaken belief that Dusty was taking advantage of his sister. He'd been dead wrong about Dusty, his new brother-in-law. And Dusty, a man with a very slow fuse, had taught Andrew that letting his emotions carry him away had not been the answer.

And yet a little piece of him wanted to strangle Brandon. How could he do something so outrageously hurtful? He felt an all-consuming compassion for Laurie. He knew what being dumped felt like. Val had walked out on him two years ago without any kind of warning. And he still hadn't gotten over it.

The door banged opened, and in walked Matt and Jason with several bottles of champagne and a big bucket of ice. Amy trailed behind with a tray filled with champagne flutes.

"We lost Edward, but we nabbed some of the champagne that was reserved for the wedding toast. We figured, since it was already paid for, we—"

"Shut up, Matt," Andrew said, rolling his eyes toward Laurie. "Just pour it. Don't explain, okay?"

The champagne was opened, and a glass pressed into Laurie's hand.

"Here's to castrating and then murdering Brandon, but only after we destroy his car," Mindy said, raising her glass.

The bridesmaids chorused, "Here, here."

Jason and Matt looked uncomfortable. Laurie just sat there.

"Uh, I don't really feel like killing or castrating Brandon, and if you mess up his Camaro, he's going to be really pissed," Matt said, ever the socially insensitive one.

Everyone looked at him as if he'd just farted in church. But Matt held his ground. "Look, you guys, Brandon is a friend. He's more than a friend, really, since we all grew up with him and Roxy. I love Brandon like he's another cousin or something, you know? And I'm just saying that he should be praised for walking away if he wasn't three hundred percent sure."

"Get the hell out of here." Mindy got right up into Matt's face and almost pushed him out of the room. Thank

God she'd done it; otherwise Andrew might have had to take care of putting Matt in his place, and that would have created a huge rift in the family.

"I think I'll go too," Jason said, leaving his untouched champagne glass on a side table.

"Uh-oh," Amy said, looking up at Andrew. "This is going to get messy, isn't it? Like a divorce. You should know that we didn't exactly lose Edward. He said Laurie had enough support and someone should be thinking about Brandon."

Amy was right in spades. For Andrew, negotiating those fissures and cracks would be doubly difficult because he was an associate at Wilson Kavanaugh, the law firm where Laurie's father was a partner. In fact, Laurie had helped Andrew get his job with the prestigious firm. Their dispute-settlement practice was nationally known and respected. It was, in a word, Andrew's dream job, and he'd spent the last few years busting his balls trying to make partner.

He downed his champagne and stepped across the room, sinking into the ottoman beside Laurie's chair. "Laurie," he said gently.

She looked up at him, her face marred by tear tracks. He wanted to pull her into his arms and tell her to weep and sob and yell, even though he knew from experience that none of those things would change the situation. But crying in public was probably not Laurie's thing. It wasn't his thing either. Like her, he tended to hold things inside.

"What would fix this situation for you?" he asked.

"I love him," she whispered, her voice so tight it sounded brittle.

"So you'd be okay if he changed his mind and we started over? You still want to marry him?"

She nodded, biting her lower lip. "I certainly don't want to kill or maim him." She glanced at Madison. "Or mess up his car."

"Let me go talk to him, okay?"

"You can't be serious." Emma downed the last drop of her champagne and glared at him. "He left her at the altar. That's like the worst humiliation a woman can suffer. It's like he—"

"Shut up," Laurie said, her voice surprisingly strong. "I'd take him back," she said.

"Okay. Let me see what I can do."

He got up and headed toward the door, but Emma followed him.

"You aren't seriously thinking about talking Brandon into going forward with the ceremony, are you?"

"Why not?"

She rolled her eyes. "Because he left her at the altar. That means, *de facto*, that he's a dickwad, and Laurie deserves better than that."

"Maybe he just had a moment of—"

"No. He walked away from her. You want her to grovel and ask him to come back? Really?"

"It's not about what I want, Emma. It's about what Laurie wants and needs, and what Brandon wants and needs. The object is to find a win-win situation for both of them."

"You're unbelievable. Laurie is not capable of judging what she wants right now." Emma's fists landed on her hips.

"And you are?"

Emma shook her head. "No. But I think Laurie loves the idea of Brandon. I think she's been overlooking a lot of problems with the real Brandon."

Andrew let out a long breath. "Look, she asked me to talk to him, okay? I'm the best man, and it seems to me that it's kind of my job to see if I can fix this situation."

Emma folded her arms across her chest. "Knock yourself out. But you aren't going to change Brandon's mind. My guess is that he's been cheating on Laurie." She turned and ducked back into the Churchill Suite.

Was there someone else? Andrew didn't think so. But, hell, he'd been surprised that day when he'd come home from work and found Val all packed and ready to run off to her lover.

Laurie looked down at the champagne flute, studying the way the late-afternoon sun sparkled on the bubbles and her two-carat, pavé-set Tiffany engagement ring. She remembered the day Brandon had put that ring on her finger. It was at her birthday party, two years ago. She hadn't thought too much about the fact that members of their close group of friends each brought a balloon to the party with a single letter on it. But it all became clear when Brandon suggested a group picture with the balloons. And suddenly the balloons spelled out "Laurie, Will You Marry Me?"

Brandon had gotten down on his knee and presented the ring in its beautiful robin's-egg-blue Tiffany box. She'd loved the ring from the first moment she'd laid eyes on it. It was classic and maybe a tiny bit old-fashioned.

And now she would have to give it back.

Something broke inside her heart, and the tears she'd been trying not to shed welled up like a fountain. How could a man who'd organized such a romantic proposal walk away from a wedding?

She slipped the ring from her finger. "Someone needs to give this back," she managed to choke out.

"Aw, honey," Mindy said. "You are not giving that back. You're going to sell it on eBay and pocket the ten grand. You'll need it to fix up that house Brandon talked you into buying. Now, drink your champagne. It'll take the edge off."

She did as she was told, and just as soon as she'd drained the flute, Madison refilled it. "I just don't get it," Laurie said through her tears.

"Neither do we," Emma said. "But the important thing is that a man who leaves his bride at the altar is a jerk."

Laurie shook her head. No. Brandon was a great guy. The problem wasn't Brandon. It was her.

She sniffled back her tears and downed another glass of champagne. Yes, definitely. She was the problem. She'd been a fool to think that they had a special relationship that could weather her problems in the bedroom. She needed to accept the fact that she was a dud when it came to sex. She was uptight and OCD and had trouble turning her brain off. Who wanted to be chained to a wife like that?

She downed another glass of champagne.

"So, girls, you know we really can't kill him or castrate him. But the Camaro... We could really mess it up."

"Maybe we could find a bottle of spray paint and write the words, 'Left the bride at the altar' across his back window," Madison said.

"You're an amateur," Mindy said. "I vote that we go to Lowe's and buy a pickax and turn the Camaro into Swiss cheese."

"That would be too obvious," Emma said. "We should just put sugar in the gas tank."

The girls continued to discuss ways of destroying Brandon's beloved car while they sipped several more glasses of champagne.

Meanwhile, Laurie obsessed over all the things she'd done wrong. It was amazing that Brandon hadn't found someone else. Assuming he'd told her the truth. But it didn't matter, because as soon as he started playing the field, he'd lose interest in her. She bored him in the bedroom, and that's why he wanted her to date other guys. Maybe he thought she needed the experience. Like the opposite of slut-shaming or something. But sleeping around would be like cheating on him.

Except it wouldn't be cheating. Not now.

The truth exploded on her like a stinger missile, and suddenly all the champagne she'd been sipping didn't want to stay down. She didn't make it all the way to the bathroom before she hurled it up.

Well, that was it. Her beautiful seven-thousand-dollar wedding dress was utterly ruined. Even if Andrew could talk Brandon into marrying her, Laurie now had nothing to wear.

About the Author

Hope Ramsay is a *USA Today* bestselling author of heart-warming contemporary romances. Her books have won critical acclaim and publishing awards. She is married to a good ol' Georgia boy who resembles every single one of her Southern heroes. She has two grown children, a couple of demanding lap cats, and a cockapoo puppy to keep her busy. She lives in Virginia where, when she's not writing, she's knitting or playing her forty-year-old Martin guitar. If you'd like to receive information about upcoming releases or book signings, you can join Hope's mailing list at http://www.hoperamsay.com/mailing-list/.

You can learn more at:
   HopeRamsay.com
   Twitter @HopeRamsay
   Facebook.com/Hope.Ramsay

Fall in Love with Forever Romance

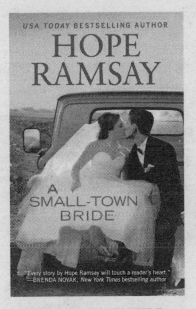

A SMALL-TOWN BRIDE
By Hope Ramsay

Amy Lyndon is tired of being "the poor little rich girl" of Shenandoah Falls. In her prominent family, she's the *ordinary* one—no Ivy League education and no powerful career. But when her father tries to marry her off, she finally has to stand up for herself, despite the consequences. Cut off from the family fortune, her first challenge is to find a job. And she's vowed to never rely on another man ever again, no matter how hot or how handsome.

Fall in Love with Forever Romance

HOLDING FIRE
By April Hunt

Alpha Security operative Trey Hanson is ready to settle down. When he meets a gorgeous blonde in a bar, and the connection between them is off the charts, he thinks he's finally found the one. But after their night together ends in a hail of gunfire and she disappears in the chaos, Trey's reasons for tracking her down are personal... until he learns she's his next assignment. Fans of Rebecca Zanetti and Julie Ann Walker will love the newest romantic suspense novel from April Hunt!

THE HIGHLAND DUKE
By Amy Jarecki

Fans of *Outlander* will love this sweeping Scottish epic from award-winning author Amy Jarecki. When Akira Ayres finds a brawny Scot with a musket ball in his thigh, the healer will do whatever it takes to save his life... even fleeing with him across the Highlands. Geordie knows if Akira discovers his true identity, both their lives will be jeopardized. The only way to protect the lass is to keep her by his side. But the longer he's with her, the harder it becomes to imagine letting her go...

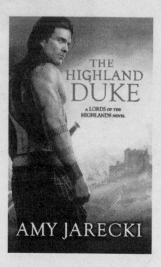

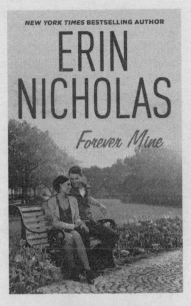

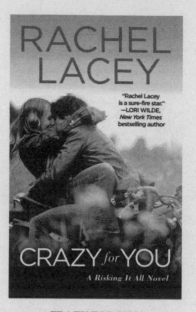

"Rachel Lacey is a sure-fire star."
—LORI WILDE, *New York Times* bestselling author

CRAZY FOR YOU
By Rachel Lacey

Emma Rush can't remember a time when she didn't have a thing for Ryan Blake. The small town's resident bad boy is just so freakin' hot—with tattoos, a motorcycle, and enough rough-around-the-edges sexiness to melt all her self-control. Now that Emma's over being a "good girl," she needs a little help being naughty...and Ryan is the perfect place to start.